MW00790121

THE GARDEN
OF TALES

Celebrating
30 Years of Publishing
in India

Praise for *The Garden of Tales*

A whirlpool – that is what I would call Vijaydan Detha's stories, for I was just pulled into them and completely absorbed. Vividly imagined, beautifully narrated, highly entertaining, these stories are magic spread across words and pages.

— HANSDA SOWVENDRA SHEKHAR

Oral and written literary traditions converge in Detha's stories, challenging our assumptions about modernity and morality. These translations are essential reading.

— ARUNAVA SINHA

THE GARDEN OF TALES

The Best *of*
VIJAYDAN DETHA

Translated from the Rajasthani by
VISHES KOTHARI

HARPERPERENNIAL
An Imprint of HarperCollins *Publishers*

First published in English in India by Harper Perennial 2023
An imprint of HarperCollins *Publishers*
4th Floor, Tower A, Building No. 10, Phase II, DLF Cyber City,
Gurugram, Haryana – 122002
www.harpercollins.co.in

2 4 6 8 10 9 7 5 3 1

Copyright for the original Rajasthani © Mahendra Dan Detha 2023
English translation © Vishes Kothari 2023

P-ISBN: 978-93-9440-744-2
E-ISBN: 978-93-9440-752-7

This is a work of fiction and all characters and incidents described in this book
are the product of the author's imagination. Any resemblance to actual persons,
living or dead, is entirely coincidental.

Vijaydan Detha asserts the moral right
to be identified as the author of this work.

All rights reserved. No part of this publication may be reproduced,
stored in a retrieval system, or transmitted, in any form or by any
means, electronic, mechanical, photocopying, recording or otherwise,
without the prior permission of the publishers.

Typeset in 11.5/15.7 Adobe Caslon Pro at
Manipal Technologies Limited, Manipal

Printed and bound at
Thomson Press (India) Ltd

To my parents

Contents

A Note from the Translator

I HAVE NOW SPENT FIVE years in Vijaydan Detha's world, and my time in it has been full of whimsy, déjà vu and delight. This world lies at the intersection of two worlds: that of folk stories and songs which sustains entirely in the intangible, that is, the voices, minds and memories of people; and that of written Rajasthani literature.

This exercise in translation is to allow readers who cannot read the original texts, glimpses of this world. Which glimpses would be the most representative? How is this world, *sustained entirely in the intangible*, to be translated? How is this world, *sustained entirely in the oral traditions of Rajasthan*, to be translated? These are the questions that have constantly been on my mind throughout this process of translation.

The folk traditions of Rajasthan are incredibly diverse. Komal Kothari, the folklorist, drew connections between the sheer amount of movement required to lead a semi-sedentary, semi-migratory lifestyle, and the corresponding richness of oral traditions and memory. Historian Tanuja Kothiyal draws connections between this pastoral and mercantile way of life and the political and ecological realities of this land as a frontier which remained a site of contestation and confluence between many powers and empires.

Sure enough, our traditions of storytelling are incredibly diverse. We have love ballads, religious stories, origin myths, fables for children, didactic tales, stories narrated at gatherings for entertainment. Many of these 'folk tales' also appear in older handwritten manuscripts – some in the form of the traditional 'baat' prose literature, while others appear in the collections of stories used by monks in their sermons. Even though the 'storylines' might be traditional, it is Detha who cast them into the form of the modern short story. I have tried to include the best examples of each of these types. Of course, there are those stories that instantly identify themselves as classics – 'Aasmaan Jogi', 'The Creed of Crows', 'The Truthful Thief' – not much thought was needed to include these in the collection.

Bijji – as Detha is fondly known – had a deep sense of anguish about the deprecated status of Rajasthani in modern India. Kept out of the 8th Schedule of the Constitution, the language has not been afforded any right to official existence, despite having its own very developed literary traditions and Sabadkos (dictionary), and despite continuing to be the language spoken throughout much of Rajasthan. Bijji regarded Anton Chekhov, Sarat Chandra Chatterjee and Rabindranath Tagore, all of whom wrote in their mother tongues, as his gurus. Like his gurus, he decided that he would also write in his mother tongue – a radical choice for his time.

I share Bijji's belief in the right of the people of Rajasthan to have their officially recognized language, and the act of translation thus also became an act of assertion. I felt it my duty to communicate in translation the unique quirks and cadences of the language, its sounds and rhythms, its developed poetics which influenced prose writing in the language over hundreds of years, the manners of speech, the flora and fauna and its food cultures. Rajasthani has suffered greatly from the constant conflation with Hindi – this is something I have consciously avoided.

What was even more radical about Detha, perhaps, was his choice to look to folklore for his literary inspiration. Many in the Rajasthani and Hindi literary fraternity questioned whether Bijji could even be considered a writer or an author, and instead thought 'folklorist' or 'archivist' might be more appropriate epithets. Bijji has, of course, emerged victorious in this debate and is without doubt one of the most, if not *the* most, important writer of Rajasthani prose in the twentieth century.

Here, it is impossible to ignore the fact that Bijji belonged to the Charan caste – a caste of bards, primarily patronized by the royal courts and feudal lords. Bijji was conscious of his literary inheritance – his own grandfather was a well-known poet. He rebelled against the traditions of his caste – both, of writing chaste 'high' poetry in the esoteric Dingal register, and of writing about his caste's traditional patrons. Instead, he made the common man, and more so, the common woman his sources of inspiration.

Bijji's works are regarded as epochal not only because he chose the lore of the common folk of Rajasthan as his literary inspiration, but also because of how effortlessly his prose is able to convey the orality of these tales. I have tried to preserve this effortlessness in translation. In trying to bring readers as close as possible to the original voice of the stories, I have used some tools. The prose is peppered with Rajasthani words from the original and, where needed, footnotes have been added to allow the reader to see their meaning without having to turn to a glossary. Caste and kinship names, food and flora are some instances where the original Rajasthani words have been used.

Of course, not all is rosy in these worlds. Social realities shape these worlds of whimsy, and often I'd hit a familiar block of what to do with something that is casteist, racist or sexist in these stories. The call that we took was that the worlds need to be presented in translation as they are – fantastic and yet problematic – and we decided against any sanitization.

My own point of entry into Bijji's world has been from the world of oral literature. I have been immersed in this world from a time when I did not know the meanings of these words. This world is set in timescales that are immediate and yet eternal, and in spaces that are limited to the village and the lake just outside but at the same time cosmic. And these worlds have their own internal logic. The stones, trees, animals, wind, rain, gods and goddesses are all active participants. The landscapes are alive with stories, and it is the story which is used to make sense of the world all around.

I have translated this world with an intuition that has been guided by intimacy, fondness and assertion. I hope these stories can help readers make sense of this world I share with Bijji, and perhaps, of their own worlds.

~

My gratitude to Dalpat Rajpurohit and Joyeeta Dey for their assistance. My agent, Kanishka Gupta of Writer's Side. Rinita Banerjee and Rahul Soni at HarperCollins for their meticulousness, patience and dedication. And special mention must be made of Mahendra Detha for giving me permission to translate these stories.

– Vishes Kothari

New Birth

I HAD TO GO FROM Bilara to Devli for some work. I knew Raseed bhai, the driver of the Haripur–Raipur bus, well. As was my nature, I checked with him several times and requested him repeatedly, 'Raseed bhai, I will go to the hospital and return in no time. If I do get slightly late, then you must hold the departure of the bus. I need to reach Devli today itself, don't you...'

Raseed bhai smiled and said, 'Why do you have to give such a long explanation? This bus is like your own.'

As luck would have it, I got rather late at the hospital. I ran towards the station holding the edge of my dhoti in my hand, but when I reached, there was no sign of the bus there. What a mess! More than Raseed bhai, I felt annoyed at myself. Poor man! How long could he have waited? But then, there was no way I could have come any earlier from the hospital either.

The next day, when Raseed bhai saw me in Devli in a car, he enquired in surprise, 'Vabha,[1] how come you are here? Did you hire another taxi and reach Devli?'

'No,' I replied, 'I hired a bicycle. By the time I got to Haras ra Deval, it had started to pour. I reached late in the evening and with quite a bit of difficulty.'

'You went through a lot of trouble then, vabha,' said Raseed bhai. 'Had I known you would run late, I would have driven the bus to the hospital itself. I waited for quite a while. But in the end, when it looked like it would rain, I had to leave. I thought perhaps you had changed your mind. Were it not for the fear of rain, I could have waited for another half an hour.'

I said, 'Missing the bus yesterday bore great fruit. It would have been a disaster had I been able to board! I have come to the bus to say you did well to leave without me.'

Raseed bhai understood why I said what I did. As soon he heard the praise, pat came the reply, 'Why, did some great story fall into your hands on the way?'

I smiled and said, 'Yes, that is exactly what happened, Raseed bhai. What can I say? An invaluable pearl fell into my hands yesterday!'

Raseed bhai said, 'You must read it to me once it is written. Sometimes, a small mistake can lead to a lot of things. Now I do not regret leaving you behind.' Then,

---

1   Vabha: A respectful term to address someone who is like an elder brother.

teasing me, he said, 'When it does eventually appear in *Vani*, do acknowledge that you came upon this story because Raseed bhai left you behind.'

I teased him back, 'Hope you won't leave me behind again just so that I can find more stories!' Raseed bhai laughed loudly.

Yesterday, I had been very annoyed at having missed the bus. But annoyed or not, I had to reach Devli. So I went straight to the bicycle-wala's shop. There, I hired a new bicycle and began pedalling to Devli, while asking for directions. There were rainclouds up above, and it looked like it could begin raining any moment.

I had just passed Haras ra Deval when it started. It was a drizzle at first, but then it began to pour. I continued to cycle even as it poured. By the time I covered another mile and a half or so, the water was up to my knees. Then I got off and pulled the cycle along. Somehow, I managed to cover another mile. When it became harder to move against the flow of the water with the bicycle beside me, I decided to rest for a bit at a pyau[2] just by the road. I left the bicycle against a pillar there and wrung my clothes, flicked the water from my head, and then took off my slippers and went into the veranda. Seven or eight people were gathered there.

---

2   Pyau: Usually a charitable public drinking-water utility. Here it refers to a traveller's rest house.

One of them looked at me and said, 'You have come at just the right time. You can leave once the rain stops. Until then, listen to this story. There isn't another storyteller like this baba in all the nearby villages. The story was just about to begin when you arrived.'

Joining the group assembled on the veranda, I said, 'I myself am a connoisseur of tales. Go on, let the story take flight.'

Raising his eyes, the baba looked at me. He had a comely white beard, a white turban on his head, and an angrakha, also white. A golden necklace hung round his neck.

'Vabha, have you eaten rotis or not?' he asked. 'We just ate.'

'I have eaten, baba,' I said. 'But what is this question you ask me in the middle of the story?'

Stroking his beard, the baba said, 'This story is such that, after hearing it, one does not feel like eating rotis any more. If you haven't eaten anything, do not hesitate. I have enough food.'

'Ni baba,' I replied. 'I am stuffed. Please favour us with the story now.'

'Then sit tight and listen carefully,' he said, and then began:

'Seeing this pyau, I am reminded of another pyau, and a kumbhar[3] who lived in it. My mother told me this story

---

3   Kumbhar: Potter, or a man from the potter caste. Female: Kumbhari.

when I was a child. You must have thought that this baba
has been like this since birth! But no, even I spent nine
months in my mother's womb. When I came out, I cried, I
crawled, learnt to stand, and then learnt to talk with a lisp.
This white hair came about as time has passed. How fond
I was of stories as a child! Where are those stories now?
Every day, I eat rotis and feel full, but I never feel like I am
full after a story. When I was little, even the stars in the
sky longed for a story! I still have a childlike fascination for
them. God knows why I have this utter faith in my heart
that if someone were to tell a story even after I die, I will
come back to life.

'So may Ramji bless us all, there was a kumbhar. They
were a family of just three – husband, wife, and the third,
their son. This story begins when the kumbhar's son turned
ten. One day, the rich seth[4] of that village came in person
to the kumbhar's home. The kumbhar, leaving his potters'
wheel, went to greet him. The seth said, "Brother, there is
a problem. But you can solve it if you want. A child has
been born in my household after fifty years. You simple folk
will not understand the extent of this happiness. To mark
the joyous occasion of the birth of a son, I want to have a
large pyau constructed. Many get a pyau made inside the
village – nothing great about that. I want to have a pyau
and a rest house constructed at the intersection where the
four khejda trees stand."

---

4   Seth: A merchant or rich man. Female: Sethani.

'The kumbhar thought about it and then said, "There is no village near that intersection. The nearest village is at least three miles away. There will not be much use for this pyau in that deserted expanse."

'The seth said, "This is exactly the problem. You people do not have any sense at all! If one feels thirsty in a village, water can be found in every home. But one finds out the true value of water when out on the road. The approaches to twenty villages pass through that intersection. A spot more perfect for a pyau cannot be found for hundreds of miles! If you take on the responsibility of this pyau, I will be at peace. Fate only meant for me to arrange this money, but if we cannot find a capable man to look after it, the money will be of no use. You are well known and respected in this region. The work of the pyau is especially suited to you. I will pay a good wage. The task is much better than the bother of baking clay. Profitable and charitable. I will get a room made for you right next to the rest house. You will have to stay there twenty-four hours a day, all twelve months. You might as well assume that you were born there. Think of that pyau as your home and your village. No traveller should pass by thirsty or unrefreshed. Take whatever wage you want; it will be wrong of me to haggle over that. But there should be no shirking in carrying out the tasks I speak of."

'The kumbhar said, "Something must have crossed your mind to make you come here. Now if I refuse you, it won't reflect well on you or on me. Get the foundations for the pyau and the rest house laid at an auspicious hour. There will never be any shortcomings in my work."

'Pleased, the seth left the kumbhar's. He then had an astrologer consult his charts and fix a propitious hour to lay the foundations for the pyau and the rest house. The seth had no shortage of money. Within a few days, all three structures, including the room for the kumbhar's family, were completed. The very next day, after the inauguration, the kumbhar moved in with his family.

'Sweet rainwater stored in the reservoir was kept separately, and water from the well was kept separately. The kumbhar would ask after travellers and serve them. In the summers, he would keep water in large earthen matkis. Cold and refreshing. Travellers would halt there for the night without fear. The kumbhar's name came to be known in every village, more widely than even the seth's. No traveller could stop singing his praises once they had drunk the cool water of the pyau or heard the pleasing voice of the kumbhar.

'Yes, one more thing: the kumbhar would keep the storehouse stocked with fodder and dry wood. He would sort them with his own hands. He would provide firewood to travellers who wanted to make their own rotis, even before they asked for it. At night, no matter how deep a slumber the kumbhar might have been in, never would a guest have to call him a second time.

'The kumbhar's son was also very decent, clever, understanding and obedient. Handsome. Eyes like little bowls, a round, fair face, a sharp nose, shapely teeth, a long neck, and a sweet voice. The travellers were extremely fond of him.

'One day, as fate would have it, a seth stopped at the pyau while on his way to foreign shores. With him was his sethani and their two sons. By the time they reached the pyau, the sethani had fallen ill. Upon the kumbhar's persuasion, they changed their minds about going further. He saw the sethani's eyes and said, "She has been hit by the hot desert wind. I will not let you go before she recovers fully."

'The kumbhar asked his son to tend to the sethani. With a wet towel, the son wiped the sethani's head and made her drink amlano[5] two or three times. After two days, the sethani regained her health. Even then, the kumbhar urged them to stay on. The seth was immensely pleased with the kumbhar's good-natured son. Even those born from one's own belly can hardly provide such care. How wonderful would it be if such a worthy child were to accompany them to distant lands! The seth relayed his thought to the kumbhar. At first, the kumbhar refused point-blank and said, "He is my only son. My heart does not wish to send him to such faraway places. If he stays with you, he will earn very well, but how can I push my only son away for the sake of procuring wealth? In the morning

---

5   Amlano: A sweet-sour drink made with tamarind and consumed in the summer months to guard against heatstroke.

and at evening, we eat whatever dry, crusty scraps we have, after which we drink cool water and feel as if we are the rulers of heaven. If the body can survive without the soul, I can survive without my son. His mother will collapse if she were to even hear of this. You are too gracious, and it is very embarrassing to refuse, but…'"

The baba continued: 'Sons cannot understand this pain of parents. Just speaking of a separation made the kumbhar's eyes well up. His throat choked. He could not continue any further.

'When the seth saw the state the kumbhar was in, he interrupted, "I understand this pain of yours only too well. But I suggested this for your son's well-being. If he goes abroad, he will become a man. Here, he will remain useless. A diamond attains its true value when it is dug out of the earth. I will keep aside a share in my business for him. Today, you sit in this pyau built by the seth and draw a wage; then you will go building pyaus in village after village. Before long, you will be building grand havelis! You foolish man, if you toil in the mud, then mud is all you will end up with. Do baniyas wear some special crown? If you people get into doing business, then wealth will grow in your homes too. If you want to keep this watermelon buried in the mud, that is your wish. In the end, it is only you who can think about what you will gain and what you will lose. What's the use in me carrying on with this empty chatter?"'

It was rather humid in the pyau's veranda. Unfastening the strings of his angrakha, the baba said, 'My dears, it is the whiplash of wealth which is the worst. The biggest and strongest of men cannot endure its force, then how could that poor kumbhar, who dug earth, stand in the way of such a flogging? All his life he had embraced mud. How could the greed for gold have glimmered in his heart? But the seth's words gave him a glimpse of this sparkle, and he was blinded. A kumbhar – and an actual mansion! Ni, ni, was this even possible? But what if it did come to pass? What more could one ask for? The kumbhar felt as if someone's invisible hands were undoing the tangled mass of nerves in his head.

'He said hesitantly, "Seth, I will somehow manage to bear parting from my son. I am a man, after all. But his mother's heart is as soft as the flesh of a pumpkin. I will think of some way to convince her. It is a mother's heart, it will not be easy."

'The seth did indeed want to take the kumbhar's son with him to foreign shores. There were two reasons for that: one, because he had looked after the sethani so diligently when she was ill; and two, because the seth had read the omens and was convinced that the boy would bring good fortune. Thick earlobes, a broad forehead, slightly large teeth with small gaps in between them, and a small mole on the right side of his face, just under his right eye. It was likely that the seth would make great profits by keeping the boy with him.

'Earlier, the seth had taken along a baaman's[6] son with him to distant lands in the same way. He had made profits worth thousands in his business, never made losses. But the boy died an untimely death from bone fever; otherwise, the seth would have been a crorepati by now. So, keeping in mind his own financial gain, he wanted to keep a share for the kumbhar's son in his business.

'He said to the kumbhar, "The two of you discuss this carefully between yourselves. Never again in your life will you find anyone who gives you such decent advice. If you had the intelligence to think about what you could turn to your advantage and what you might make a loss on, why would you be suffering this fate?"

'The nerves in the kumbhar's head had straightened out quite a bit. When he broached the subject with his wife, she retorted sharply, "You have come to convince me? Put your hand on your heart first and ask yourself how you could even think of sending our only child abroad. What do we need wealth for? We sit here in this pyau in the service of travellers, take the name of God morning and evening, get rotis to eat on time, people sing your praises, and the seth has trusted you and spent so much on building the rest house, the pyau, the rooms, the reservoir and the well … And here you are, dreaming dreams of becoming a seth yourself! Let the wealth in the world remain with the world, no point getting into these needless calculations."

---

6   Baaman: Rajasthani word for Brahmin. Female: Baamani.

'His effort to sway his wife had badly misfired, the kumbhar thought. Rubbing his teeth with a neem twig he said, "If you don't approve of it, then we shall refuse the seth. I only brought the topic up to find out what was in your heart. Whether we send our son away or not, that is another matter altogether. First, let us at least discuss it properly at home."

"'Why ask the way to a village to which we don't have to go?" said the kumbhari. "There is no need to take any advice on this and no need to think about it. We have been born into the bodies of kumbhars, and we must hand them back when the time comes. If seths and baniyas were immortal, it would have been another matter. We have come into this world empty-handed and crying, and will leave empty-handed with our families crying after us. I do not understand why you let your heart wander in this lust for money."

'The kumbhar nervously licked his lips and said, "Do you think I am so foolish as to let my heart wander in vain? I am giving the matter so much thought only for your sake. If you do not agree, there is no way I will. But first, answer this question. Don't you want to see the son you have brought into this world become a big man? If a trunk full of gold jewellery glitters on your body, will you be bitter about it?"

'The kumbhari made a face. "Don't you utter such absurdities! We don't have even a speck of gold today and you speak of trunks full of gold! Will this ever happen even in our dreams? How big a man can a son born into the house of kumbhars become? He can craft pots with finesse – that is as far as he can get. Then why do you wrack your brains over that which is out of our control? Nothing will change, and on top of that, your greed will only bring grief."

'This time, the kumbhar retorted forcefully, "This is the thing! If we don't take bites from the plate that has been served to us, will the rotis eat themselves? Even after taking a bite, we have to chew the food. Tell me – if we don't make pots, or if we don't work at the pyau, will our stomachs fill themselves? We will get the fruit our toil deserves. If we dig the ground, our feet will get nothing but dirt on them. Why don't you at least ask the seth? Twenty years ago, he left for distant shores with nothing. Today, his wealth is in lakhs. He did not have even a roof over his head then. Today, he is ready to keep a share in his business for our son. He will take our son with him, and our son will live with him too. He will regard our son as one of his own children. If you still cannot see sense in this, then I have no problem. You think I'd let the seth take our son against our wishes!"

"'Why get annoyed with the seth needlessly?" said the kumbhari. "He never said he would take our son away against our wishes."

'That said, she began to bite the nails on her fingers. She felt as if some invisible hand was grinding the nerves in her head with a pumice stone. She said, "I am a mere woman. What do I know? You do as you see fit."'

The baba looked at me and smiled. Then, after clearing his throat a couple of times, he said, 'This is how devious maya deceives. If one could recognize her subtle trickery, would there be the need to weep? The most powerful kings do not stand a chance in the face of this deception, then what were the kumbhar and kumbhari who kneaded mud for a living? They could not but be blinded when dazzled by the glitter of gold.

'The husband and wife cried and cried when they saw the face of their son as he departed with the seth. Sobbing, the kumbhari said, "Seth, my heart won't give in today. Stay one more day, I beg you with folded hands. A mother's heart – it changes from moment to moment. To toughen it so is beyond my power."

'Smiling, the seth said, "I have no problem. I will leave tomorrow if that is what you want. But you must be thinking the sun will not rise tomorrow! Just like today, you will have to bear the pain of separation tomorrow too. But I will not wait after tomorrow. You decide what you would like to do."

'"Ni, seth," said the kumbhari, "by no means am I going to stop you tomorrow. I want your mercy just for this one day."

'After this, the kumbhari clasped her son tightly to her chest the entire day. At night, she made him sleep beside her. While he fell asleep, she stayed awake all night, gazing at his face. The hours passed by as if in an instant. The sun was, of course, going to appear at its appointed time.'

I glanced at the baba's eyes. Tears had welled up in them as he narrated the parting of the mother and son. In a choked voice, he said, 'Each time I have related this story, I have never been able to describe the pain of their separation. Please understand without being told. These are not matters that need words.

'The kumbhar and kumbhari's hearts were still not at peace. So they went with the seth for a few miles to see their son off. The two of them walked barefoot by the cart, while the others were seated in it. The seth had to send them back against their wishes. "My dears, will you walk with us all the way to the distant lands we're heading to?"

'When they saw their son, sitting in the cart, leave them behind, they stopped where they were, looked at each other and wept. Had their son died, they would have blamed it on their own fate and borne it somehow, but this parting was turning out to be even more unbearable. For some time, they stared at the clouds of dust kicked up by the departing cart. Then, as they were walking back, they began to console each other. Why spoil our son's life for our sake? If he grows up and comes to own incalculable wealth, then we should be happy about it. May God make him live a thousand years, and may his fame spread through the length and breadth of the land. And we? We will survive praying for his well-being.

'"Everything else will be fine," said the kumbhari, "but now we are stuck with what we agreed on with the seth – that he won't send our son back for sixteen years.

Every moment feels like an eternity. When will sixteen years end?"

'To cheer her up, the kumbhar joked, "Sixteen years will end when we are sixteen years older! You have started to think about it from today itself. This will make passing the days even harder."

'The kumbhari wiped her eyes and said, "There will be a golden sunrise the day I see my son's face again, when I hear of his fame in the world with my own ears. I agreed to bear this misery only to witness that day. May the seth's words come true. My suffering will end when I see my son become a great man. Only if I tear my heart out and show it to you will you be able to see the torment inside me."

'For the next ten or fifteen days, the husband and wife were nearly driven out of their minds by their sorrow. The kumbhari would take her son's name and weep through the night. She would sit up with a start and imagine seeing the cart on which her son had left home.

'One day, she told her husband, "Would we have sent our son away to such distant lands to earn a fortune if we had plenty? We had to bless our own child and send him away only because of our thirst for wealth. I sometimes think that if people in this world did not crave for more wealth, it would bring about such peace. Every man needs just enough to fulfil their basic needs, but any more than that is a frightful thing. I think the more wealth a man comes to possess, the lesser is his worth."

'The kumbhar said, "If I find some buried treasure, I will go and fetch my son back. We sent him away for the sake of a life of ease and abundance. Is God just another name for wealth or what?"

'The kumbhari said, "How wonderful it would be if, instead of the water we draw from this well, four or five buckets full of gold were to emerge from it! Then I would not let anyone's son leave home to earn.'

'The kumbhar and kumbhari would sit together every single day and imagine the impossible. One day, past midnight, the kumbhari woke her husband up and began whispering into his ear: "Every day we dream of finding buried treasure, imagine buckets full of molten gold. But Lichmi[7] walks to us on her own every day. Yet we have never paid any heed to that. The seth and sethani who sleep in the rest house – how much wealth they have! The sethani is yellow with gold, yellow! It's as if she's a golden doll!"

'"This crossed my mind too," said the kumbhar, "but I did not say it out loud to you out of fear."

'The kumbhari said, "I do not fear any more! What are you waiting for, then?"'

The baba continued dispassionately: 'And from that day onwards, the two of them didn't think twice or hesitate. Whichever traveller they suspected was carrying a lot of wealth, they'd bury them then and there. Having a good name and fame are important – so never did anyone suspect the kumbhar. As more and more gold began to pile up in their store, the kumbhar became more and more honey-tongued, and fussed over the travellers even more.

---

7   Lichmi: Lakshmi, the goddess of wealth.

'Whenever conversations about those who had disappeared would start at the rest house, the kumbhar would join in, expressing shock and surprise. He would, in fact, outdo the others in it.

'One day, the kumbhari said conceitedly, "We sent our son away for such a trivial matter. And here, we have amassed enough wealth to fill chests and trunks. This is the eighth year since our son left home. I say, you should call him back. We can build our mansions with this wealth. I am hardly of an age to wear jewellery, but after another eight years, there is no way it will suit me."

'"Don't even think of such a thing,' said the kumbhar. 'We will have to somehow wait out another eight years. If people get even an inkling of what we have done, we will be killed before our time."

'The kumbhari understood right away. A new thought struck her. "Then, let us send for our beendni.[8] She will help us with our chores too. She's a grown-up girl, it would be best if she stays with us."

'Admonishing her again, the kumbhar said, "You do not have the slightest brains! If even a whisper of this falls on a fifth ear, then only others will enjoy this wealth. If you can help it, then don't even dream of such things! If you spill our secret even in your dreams, it will be the death of us. We will send for our beendni only once our son returns.

---

8   Beendni: Wife. Also used for daughter-in-law. Beend: Husband.

We will send him to his in-laws' accompanied by the beat of drums and much merriment. There are not too many years left now. We have lived out half the suffering. He himself will have earned much and come back with a vast amount of wealth. Ours will blend into his. No one will ever have any cause to doubt us. A year after his return, I will lay the foundations for the haveli. I will build four pyaus such as this one. When our beendni wears two chests full of gold jewellery and sits in the jharokha, then this birth of ours will be successful."

The kumbhari said, "We will build a separate mansion for ourselves. And I am warning you, I won't wear less jewellery than our beendni. If you grumble later, I won't listen to anything you say."

'And in this manner, as they weaved dreams of trunks of gold jewellery and two three-storeyed mansions facing each other, sixteen years passed by. The kumbhar and kumbhari could barely contain their joy. Now their son would return any day. The kumbhar merrily chirped, "How long did it take for sixteen years to go by? If I had listened to you that day, how would we have passed all this time? It is as if our very lives have changed. And we are free from having to knead clay! In our caste, nobody would ever have been as wealthy as us, and nobody will ever be!"

"'I have let you have your way once," said the kumbhari. "But listen to this carefully, with both your ears open: this time, I will not let my son go away even if I have to die. We have gathered enough wealth for him here. Remember that innocent boy? My heart still burns for him, even in my dreams. I tried so hard to stop you, but you would not listen. His face resembled our son's so much, it was like he was actually our son's younger brother."

"What is past is past," replied the kumbhar. "If I had listened to you that day, then all our past sins would have been exposed. The cauldron of our misdeeds would have lain shattered. I do nothing without careful consideration."

That very evening, a lakhpati seth came to the kumbhar and kumbhari's pyau to spend the night at the rest house. He had with him a cart full of diamonds and pearls. When the kumbhar and kumbhari's eyes fell on the seth's necklace, their brains went into a tizzy. Despite being so rich, the seth had not an ounce of arrogance in him. He chatted a lot with the two of them about their families. He asked, "Baba, have you no son?"

"Seth," the kumbhar said proudly, "take that back! My lone son is equal to one hundred. More handsome than even the sun. It would be unbecoming of you to stand beside him. Please do not mind, he is twice, no, he is four times more beautiful than you are!"

The seth laughed. "Where is he? Let me see him at least. Are you hiding him from the evil eye?"

"He has gone to distant lands to earn a fortune like you," the kumbhar replied. "He is about to return now. We look forward to seeing him every day as the sun rises."

"How did you persuade your hearts to let you send your only son away for sixteen years?" asked the seth.

'"Don't ask how we did that," said the kumbhari. "We would have to tear our hearts out and show you, or you would have to bear parting from your own son to know how."

'The seth was enjoying the banter and seemed to be in no hurry to go to sleep, but the kumbhar and kumbhari were distracted. Finally, they made their way to their room for the night. As he was leaving, the kumbhar enquired, "Seth, it is very cold. Should I get you more blankets?"

'"No," said the seth, "I have enough."

'That said, he set off for the rest house. After about two hours or so, the kumbhar reached the rest house and called out softly. "Seth," he said, "are you being able to sleep all right in this new place?"

'There was no response from the seth. He was snoring peacefully. Which was exactly what the kumbhar wanted. With one swish of his sword, he chopped the slumbering seth's head off! The seth could not even utter a sound. Quickly, he tied up the body in a bundle with the sheets and buried it along with the seth's cart. Then, he buried the urns full of diamonds and pearls. Lastly, he hid the sword away.

'Then he told the kumbhari, "Light the lamp and check the rest house carefully lest a drop of blood was left behind. I did not let any fall on the way. Never has fortune smiled on us as it has today. We can buy the whole world if we like!"'

By now, I was certain that I had never seen a storyteller who could match the baba. All of us sat astounded, latching on to every word that left his mouth. The baba continued:

'When even Bhagvaan Ram was beguiled by the golden deer and could not resist the temptation to chase it, then how could that clay-kneading kumbhar not be ensnared in the maya of power and wealth?

'Just like darkness disappears the moment the sun rises, the events of that night vanished completely from the kumbhar and kumbhari's minds. They forgot what deeds their hands had carried out the night before. At dawn, they had breakfast, and then sat chatting.

'The kumbhari said, "My right eye has been twitching since yesterday. Our son is definitely going to come home today. If you say so, we can sit on the mound of fodder up front and keep an eye out. My eye never portends wrongly. I told you about it yesterday too, but you did not take me seriously."

'The kumbhar said, "Your eye might or might not twitch, but my heart says that he must be heading here. He should definitely be home before evening."

'The kumbhar and kumbhari were sitting and chattering away in this manner when they saw a woman on the road heading towards them. As she came closer, they recognized her – she was their own son's wife. They both ran out to greet her and asked, "Beendni, how come you are here all of a sudden?"

'The beendni was beside herself with joy. Her smile beaming through her veil, she said, "If you give me five mohurs, only then will I tell you the good news!"

'The kumbhari looked at her husband and said, "There! Did I not tell you?"

'The kumbhar clapped his hands. "My heart knew it even before your eyes did," he said.

'After that, both of them came up to the beendni and said, "Silly girl, why did you ask for only five mohurs? Even a thousand would fall short! It's all right that in your greed for a reward you have hidden your husband and come first. But now let us see his face quickly! We cannot bear to wait another instant!"

'The beendni giggled. "But you have been seeing his face since last evening! Have you still not had your fill? He told me that he would reveal the secret as soon as he woke up in the morning. Has he not told you yet?"

'The kumbhar stammered, "What secret? Beendni, please tell me clearly, don't speak in riddles! Why, he has not even come here!"

'Then the beendni laughed and said, "He came last evening, but you did not recognize him. It was he who arrived with the cart full of diamonds and pearls!"

'The kumbhar and kumbhari's legs went numb. The earth slipped away from under their feet. Both of them screamed, "What did you say? But that was a seth, and he went on his way with only an hour left for daybreak."

'The beendni would not stop laughing. "He is still teasing you!" she said. "He will be back soon enough. He came to me late in the day yesterday. Rested for a while. He had brought along urns full of diamonds and pearls but would not give me any. I begged him so much for a pearl to string in my nose ring, but he would not part with even one. He said I could have all the urns after he had handed them to you, but that without the permission of his parents he could not give even a single pearl away. He has such respect for you, and you could not even recognize him? I did ask him if I should run ahead and give you the good news. But he stopped me and said, 'Let me see if they can recognize me after sixteen years or not. I will not tell them that I am their son all night. I will pose as a seth. I will tell them at dawn and they will be beside themselves with joy and surprise.'"'

If us listeners could barely breathe, then who knows what the kumbhar and kumbhari must have felt upon hearing this...

'The beendni continued, "I recognized him the moment I saw him. And you were not able to do so after staying with him a whole night? I cannot imagine how he could have kept up the ruse for so long..."

'The two were listening to the beendni's words like wooden dolls. It was as though their feet were glued to the ground.'

The heart of the baba who was narrating the story was also aflutter. Pausing awhile, he said, 'How can this ignorant man describe the thoughts that were running in their minds at that moment? Had they said something, I would have expressed it too. But the kumbhar uttered not a sound after listening to the beendni. After a while, Ram knows what possessed the kumbhar, but he suddenly left and came back with a naked sword and chopped the beendni's head off in one stroke. Then he cut his wife's throat, and afterwards, his own.

'While the kumbhari's and beendni's heads were severed in one clean sweep, the kumbhar's own was cut only halfway through. He died after a couple of hours, but not a sound escaped him during that time.'

As he ran his hands over his white beard, the baba said: 'All of you must be thinking of the kumbhar and kumbhari's deaths. But I think they were reborn. Yes, I do regret the beendni's death. But what use in being pained now? Poor thing came running to give good news and died for it. She did not even find out why she was murdered by her father-in-law.'

Then, smiling, the baba said, 'It is a godforsaken habit of mine, that whenever I speak of death, I cannot help laughing. Perhaps the tears inside me have dried up. Now my only prayer to all of you is that, in exactly the same way as this story reached your ears from this mouth, each of you must make it reach the ears of others from yours. Only then will my soul be free of its bondage...'

Aasmaan Jogi

THERE WAS A SETH. HE had seven sons and one daughter. She was the youngest of them all, about to turn sixteen. She was beautiful, good-natured, and full of desirable qualities. Patient, virtuous and talented. The women the seven brothers were married to were beautiful too. The wives were affectionate towards their only sister-in-law. The daughter was the light of her parents' eyes, and for her brothers, a ruby among pearls, the ring on their fingers, the kajal in their eyes!

The Teej of Saavan[9] is especially celebrated by young girls and married women. They set out in their finery, competing with the verdant and beautiful earth. 'I am the best, look at me,' the earth says. 'We are better, look at us,' the women exclaim! There, the lightning in the skies, and here, the women on earth. There, the cuckoos, frogs and

---

9   Teej of Saavan: The third day of the lunar month of Saavan.

peacocks calling out. And here, the nectar-like sweetness of the women's songs. There, the birds, and here the women! There, flocks of parrots, and here, groups of women. In every cloud, flashes of lightning. On every swing, women revelling.

The vibrant month of Saavan had arrived following Aasaadh. In the lush green gardens of the village, swings were strung upon neem trees and a carnival was underway. It was as if, with these swings, the earth itself heaved up and the very sky stooped down. On each swing sat two women, swaying back and forth. The colours of Inderlok[10] seemed drab compared to this revelry. And the seth's seven daughters-in-law and his daughter – what to say of them! Their beauty outshone the beauty of apcharas[11] from heaven, and so did their finery. On the swings, they looked like butterflies that had, by some enchantment, assumed the form of women!

As they swung, something strange occurred. The daughter and the youngest daughter-in-law were sharing the same swing. Like a rainbow that would keep forming and being wiped out. The swing rose so high that the women touched the branches of the neem tree and came down. But how come the swing returned empty this time? This had never happened before. Were they hiding

---

10 Inderlok: The abode of Inder (Indra), the king of gods.

11 Apchara: Apsara – a celestial nymph / fairy / supernatural being in mythology.

themselves among the branches? The neem tree was remarkably large and leafy, so dense that even the sun's rays could not pass through it. Surely, they were playing a prank.

Two other daughters-in-law came to sit on the same swing and began sweeping back and forth. And again, the swing returned empty. In this way, all eight women were gone! The picnicking women panicked. Amidst this commotion, the seth's seven sons arrived at the garden. They climbed the tree and checked every branch. But they could not find even a trace of their missing wives and sister. Even death does not play such a trick – when life takes leave, at least the body is left behind. Had death changed its ways? All eight women had vanished at once!

The family grieved every day. Soon, their tears dried up, and somehow, they took a hold of themselves. What else could they even do? And along with the daughter and the daughters-in-law of the mansion, its peace and well-being also disappeared.

Half a mile away from the village was a large lake. Its embankments were dotted with tall trees all around. Among them was a banyan tree, alone as large as twenty. One day, the seth's youngest son was slowly trudging towards the lake for a bath. About ten steps ahead of him was a group of paniharis, women out to fetch water. They were dressed in beautiful clothes, and had colourful idhanis[12] with tassels

---

12 Idhani: Circular rests on which pots of water are balanced
    on the head.

and trinkets on their heads to balance their pots on. The pots were delightful to look at too. As the son heard the pleasing sounds of their trinkets, he got lost in his thoughts. He too had a wife once, and six sisters-in-law. And he had a sister who was one in a million. Even their shadows would outshine all this beauty in front of him. But of what use were such dreams now?

Just then, a curious muttering from the mouth of a kumbhari fell on his ears. 'Look ladies, what has befallen this seth's mansion! That fit-for-setting-on-fire Aasmaan Jogi captured all eight women from the swings and vanished. Not a sound did anyone hear. That monster has thousands of women. And despite that, has he had his fill? All day he roams the skies in his vimaan.[13] And at night, he has the pleasure he desires. Savours the new tastes of the bodies of new women! But the bastard still does not seem to be satisfied! Why must almighty God think twice before finishing off such a villain? Such anger I feel, but what can a mere woman do? And the seth's seven sons are sissies too. Ram knows how they are just sitting quietly.'

Every pore of the son's body had turned into an ear. He listened intently to everything that was being said. However, he remained silent. He sensed that to ask the kumbhari in front of everyone else would be a bad idea. Who knew if she would even answer him or not? Somehow, he kept the words jostling in his mouth on a leash.

---

13 Vimaan: A flying vehicle.

He forgot about bathing altogether, and quietly went and sat atop a large rock. Lifting the pots filled with water on to their heads, all the paniharis left the lake. The kumbhari, though, stayed back. She raised a pot to her head and entered a hollow in the huge banyan tree and then came out with a second empty pot. While the kumbhari was straining the water and filling the pot, the son approached her. As soon as he was within earshot, he said, 'Dear woman, I heard everything you said about the Aasmaan Jogi. We seven sons are not sissies at all. What could we have done if we did not possess this knowledge?'

The kumbhari looked at the seth's youngest son while straining water into the pot and said, 'Even after finding out the truth, no one can do much! The Aasmaan Jogi dwells in the skies. We, who dwell on the earth, cannot fight him. And even death does not hold sway over him. Leave aside one, even a thousand people are no match for him. Immensely powerful. Incredibly evil. I see countless imprisoned women weep every day, and my heart wells up, but what's the use of crying? It is easier to push a mountain than bend a single strand of hair on this Aasmaan Jogi's head! On top of this, you will lose your life trying.'

'But what is there in living like this?' asked the son. 'No danger worse than death can come one's way, can it?'

As she raised the pot on to her head, the kumbhari said, 'If you have made up your mind to die, then there is nothing to fear. I was waiting for just such a person to come along. I will keep nothing from you. But don't you speak about this in front of anyone else. Do not speak about it to your parents and brothers either. The Aasmaan Jogi will vanish without a trace. What limits for he who dwells in the skies! If he changes his home, or suspects me and casts me out, then even God won't be able to help us! We must plan everything carefully.'

After having made the son swear to secrecy, the kumbhari revealed that she filled pots for the Aasmaan Jogi. A pot of water for each new woman he took captive. She was filling eight pots for the seth's daughters-in-law and daughter. Each new woman might have just a single pot, but the water would never finish, not even if she were to keep it upside down all day.

As soon as all the pots were placed in the hollow of the banyan tree, the Aasmaan Jogi's vimaan would arrive. It was visible to no one. The Aasmaan Jogi had seven such vimaans, and he kept changing them. He had given the kumbhari a parrot feather. By blowing on the feather seven times, an empty vimaan would come flying down on its own. If the son touched his eyes thrice with that feather, he too would be able to see the vimaan.

As soon as the pots were ready, the vimaan would fly out of the hollow to the Aasmaan Jogi's dwelling on its own. On the other side of the mountain and high up in the sky was the Aasmaan Jogi's nine-storeyed Badal Mahal – his Cloud Palace! Inside, lightning glimmered and stars sparkled. The pillars were made of flowers. The floor of saffron, encrusted with diamonds and pearls. The

ceilings of kumkum, decorated with rubies. The outermost
gateway of the Badal Mahal was made of a hundred
maunds of gold. It would open as soon as it was touched
with the parrot feather. And throughout the entire palace
were thousands of golden beds, on which lay thousands of
weeping beauties. The more tears the Aasmaan Jogi saw,
the happier he became. He found weeping women all the
more beautiful. As soon as the tears left their eyes, they
turned into pearls. The eyes of the women from the seth's
household had been pouring forth like the very clouds of
Saavan. And the Aasmaan Jogi, when he saw their streams
of tears, was so glad he could not stop laughing.

The Aasmaan Jogi glowed, as if the very glimmer of
lightning had been cast in the mould of his body. Against
his teeth, even the foam of milk appeared dull. His body,
so tender, it seemed as if it were made from the essence of
flowers. Pink nails. A heaving ocean of intoxication in his
eyes. Even the beauty of Kamdev,[14] the kumbhari reckoned,
would surely seem commonplace against the Aasmaan
Jogi's. The Jogi was attracted to the beauty of women like a
bee to flowers. It was as though he was born to feed on the
nectar of their bodies. Born, and that too, without death.

These blisters had been festering in the kumbhari's
heart for a long time. Today, after having confided fully
in the seth's son, she felt relieved. As soon as eight pots
were filled up, she blew seven times on the parrot feather.

---

14 Kamdev: The Hindu god of love and desire.

The vimaan landed in some time. The kumbhari kept the pots inside it. Then, once the two of them had seated themselves inside the vimaan, it took flight. After crossing the mountain, the vimaan flew at a great height. As soon as one lined one's eyes with kajal from Sesnaag's[15] fangs, they would begin to see the Aasmaan Jogi's Badal Mahal clearly. Everything was as the kumbhari had described. The Aasmaan Jogi had set out in search of new women. No sooner had the outermost golden gate opened, than the kumbhari and the seth's son headed straight to his wife, his sister and sisters-in-law. Their eyes had turned blood-red from crying. They were overjoyed to see him and enquired about everyone at home, spoke to him of their suffering. Now their births would be meaningful only if they could see the trees of their village and their sunlit courtyard again. But hurry! The villain would be back any moment. Even the son's life would be in danger if the Jogi returned. They sat in the vimaan without further delay and flew towards their home. Soon, they were near the lake outside the village. They stopped the vimaan at the hollow in the banyan tree and alighted promptly.

They were just about to get off the vimaan at the edge of the lake when the Aasmaan Jogi's vimaan passed overhead. He recognized the eight women instantly and descended to earth at once. As soon as they saw him, the

---

15 Sesnaag: Sheshnaag – the multi-headed, primordial king of all snakes in Hindu mythology.

women froze. He got all of them to sit inside the vimaan again. And then, he chanted a spell and turned the seth's youngest son into a statue made of white stone!

To the women, the Aasmaan Jogi's laughter felt like the hissing of a snake. Even as he laughed, he said, 'Why did you stop crying? Cry as much as you want! It's twice the gain for me. The tears turn to pearls, and I find the weeping faces of women all the more beautiful. I warned you! Yet you fled with this man. What greater pleasures lie here than in my palace in the clouds, that you long for them all day? I have thought and thought, but I still cannot fathom it.'

'The day you come to understand it, you will find your palace in the clouds to be more disgusting than a dump!' said the seth's daughter. 'To live for another's pleasure, according to another's wishes, is itself the greatest grief. Your fulfilment is different, our fulfilment is different. We are powerless in the face of your power. But powerlessness does not remain powerlessness forever. And power, too, is not constant. If we did not hold this belief firm, the spring of tears within us would have dried up a long time ago. Now, it will not do to be scared or meek. We will have to tell you what we truly feel. Today, as I sit in this vimaan again, I realize for the first time that being afraid of hardship worsens it, and facing hardship destroys it. From this day on, I fear no pain.'

'For me, if you are scared or if you are not scared, it is all the same,' the Aasmaan Jogi said. 'In the face of my pleasure, I neither see another's pain, nor hear it. I am immersed in my own delight. I have power, so why not exert it? Leave aside humans, even God cannot do anything when confronted with my power! I will be the lord of this universe the day I so wish! But there is much pleasure to relish yet. And what greater pleasure is there than the pleasure derived from a woman's body? Women possess beauty only for me to take pleasure in; their youth brims only for me to draw pleasure from.'

'If what you say were true, then no other human would have been born into this world,' replied the seth's daughter. 'But they are born in spite of you, and their happiness too is despite—'

'But only if I believe it!' the Jogi broke in. 'Even in my dreams, I do not believe that there exists anyone but me in this world! And if there does, that they desire anything other than that which gratifies me!'

He suddenly poked his face out of the vimaan and peered down. Bored, he said, 'Look, lean out and look once at least. Like the sun, I too look down from above! Who is a match for me? All of the world is under my feet! If women had even a shred of brains, why would they love anyone else? This palace in the clouds – with pillars of flowers, a floor of saffron encrusted with diamonds and pearls, ceilings of kumkum decorated with rubies, golden beds, golden doors – I don't know what other pleasures they pine for? And what paeans must I sing of my own beauty? You can see for yourself. Tell me, is there a face that equals mine? Pigs and women have the same nature.

You can keep thirty-two delicacies in front of them, but they will partake of only one. I grew tired of this and had to change my nature. As pigs can be taught, so can women. If I had waited for them to smile and make love, I would have suffered all my life! Now, I like weeping, wailing, morose and suffering women. You would not change, so I have. How can one cover all the thorns on the earth with carpets? Better to cover one's feet, so one can be safe from the thorns. If we don't walk barefoot, the thorns won't prick us.'

The seth's daughter retorted sharply, 'But why do you not like it when others cover their feet? This is the biggest flaw in you – you spread thorns yourself, and get others to bare their feet. Why this injustice?'

'Because I can!' replied the Aasmaan Jogi. 'As long as God can get away with it, even God won't back down. This is the foremost law of nature. How can the powerless compel others to do their bidding? If a rabbit had the strength of a lion, would it let other animals go free without killing them? If a pigeon had the power and daring of a hawk, would it go about meekly pecking grain? The wailing of a pigeon or a rabbit won't change the ways of justice. Justice demands equal standing and equal power, which nature will not accept. And who can go against nature, pray? An ant and an elephant, a lamb and a wolf, a rat and a cat, an insect and a snake, a deer and a lion – they cannot be weighed on the same scales of justice. Sermons on justice, unity, brotherhood and equality have not changed the ways of nature, nor will they ever.'

This time, the seth's youngest daughter-in-law spoke up. 'What rises must sink, what is born must die, what grows must crumble, the sun and the moon get eclipsed – this, too, is the way of nature. At dawn, there are shadows here; in the evening, there—'

Restive, the Aasmaan Jogi interrupted her, 'I have heard this rote nonsense a lot; I have been told this numerous times. You can keep churning out this rubbish until your tongue tires of it, but nothing will happen with all this empty talk. Does the sun not rise from the fear of setting? Is no one born from the fear of dying? And does no one flourish from the fear of withering? Every day, the sun goes down, and rises again when it must. Time is unpredictable, but countless creatures are born every instant. Leaves are shed and new shoots sprout. Birth and death are in their separate places. To speak of both in the same breath is the biggest folly. This foolishness infuriates me. Does the sun blacken in fear of setting as soon as it rises? If nature begins to work as silly humans say, then forget about the light of the day...!'

The seth's daughter was feeling rather bold. 'It is not only the sun that one must rely on for light,' she said. 'In the darkness of night, one gets by with only an earthen lamp.'

The Aasmaan Jogi said, 'This is the biggest illusion women have – that because they have a head at the end of their necks, they also have brains! I think women and brains are sworn enemies. You must be feeling proud, thinking you have said something very clever. But there can be no greater misconception than this. This is man's biggest mistake – he thinks he is above nature! Pokes his nose into nature's workings. Why must he meddle and light a lamp and burn away the darkness like this? The splendour of the dark is no less than that of light. If nature has made darkness fall, then why clamour to light it up? Each is where they are supposed to be. By burning the darkness away, man can never find happiness. Nature may allow man to mould her for his own interests, but if he thinks she can be conquered, she will blow him to smithereens. When a mare is in heat, she does not think who this stallion is, who that stallion is! When a cow is in heat, she does not distinguish between bulls. All this fuss is made only by humans: this is my woman, that is your woman! This is your bed and that is my bed! To look here and there is immoral ... But all this hollow morality does not last long. Unseen by man, nature dances her dance. And man is under the illusion that what he cannot see, does not exist. Husband and wife, brother and sister, brother-in-law and sister-in-law, father and daughter, mother and son – are all relations for humans, nature does not care for them at all. The foremost quality of the eyes is their light. The shame in them is just an illusion humans possess. The same as shutting one's eyes to imagine darkness. What use are brains that cannot be taught? The rituals of marriage are not enough to stop the mischief of nature. Believe me, I am the true face of nature! I reign over the skies and the earth. I am the Aasmaan Jogi. Accept me with open arms. Your beauty has roused every pore of my skin! Don't darken my Badal Mahal with the smoke of your wedding fires. Laugh and smile and illuminate my bed so that this birth of mine is worthwhile. Making love to a crying woman does not satiate my heart any more. Your beauty drives me insane! You should also surrender all your senses to my beauty – this is nature's demand. Anticipation and excitement are what's apt for the time of love, not tears! Your tears now sting my heart. The way the clouds are the greatest patrons of the earth, there is no greater patron of women than the Aasmaan Jogi! Just as you can't compare a well to the clouds, how can your men bear comparison to me?'

The seth's eldest daughter-in-law said, 'Who can rely on the clouds? They may pour or they may not pour. They may be sullen and parch the roots, or they may pour and spoil the roots. But the well is measured – a constant companion.'

'But don't clouds pour on the well too?' the Aasmaan Jogi teased them. 'A bit of rainwater mixed with the water from a well only makes the roots stronger!'

This time, the seth's daughter said, 'There will be no end to all this sparring. No one's head can be put on another's. Your thoughts are yours, our morals are ours. Just like your thoughts cannot be changed in a day, our morals cannot be altered easily. We ask for only six months. After

that, we will do as you command. Who knows the ways of
nature better than you? Then you must know that animals
don't get together every day. Among some animals, males
live with the females and still abstain for up to a year. It
is not the way of nature to make love every day. You have
sung such paeans about nature, so I remind you this. If even
then you don't accept this, what can we do in the face of
Your Majesty's power?'

The Aasmaan Jogi was somewhat pleased to hear this.
Laughing aloud he said, 'I used to think women don't
have brains, but what you said is quite clever. Indeed, who
knows more about nature than me? I am the very avatar of
nature. The animals who practise abstinence, abstain. And
the animals who get together ten times a day, get together
ten times a day! But man is different from everyone else.
There are so many things he feels no shame doing, but
he sure does feel shame in showing it. Anyway, forget all
this. If I abstain, it is my wish; if I do not, that too is my
wish. There is no dearth of women either in my palace in
the clouds or in this world. And neither has my power
dried up. You can have your six months! For the first time,
this Aasmaan Jogi has had mercy on someone. When the
time comes, do not forget this favour. Women are not as
innocent as they seem.'

The vimaan stopped at the entrance to the Badal
Mahal. Just then, the kumbhari was setting foot inside a
vimaan to return to earth and her eyes fell on the Aasmaan
Jogi. Damn! The accursed Jogi had brought back all eight

women. This murderer must not have left the son alive. How horrible all this had turned out to be!

As soon as he saw the kumbhari, the Aasmaan Jogi thundered, 'This is all your doing! No one else knows the secret of entering the palace other than you! Tell me, why did you betray me?'

If she got scared, the situation would worsen, the kumbhari thought. Fearlessly, she said, 'If you want to get rid of me, do so. Why look for false excuses? If you cannot afford me, relieve me from tomorrow itself. I will be just fine – it will be me and my clay.'

The Aasmaan Jogi said, 'You forget what I can afford. You can take back a pot of diamonds and pearls from here every single day if you so wish. I trust you immensely. I have known you for years. But then, how did they find out this secret?'

Pulling a long face, the kumbhari said, 'How would I know? Is there any dearth of silly bitches here! Someone must have written out a note and thrown it down. But now, I do not wish to serve at a place where I am not trusted.'

Such a trustworthy and good woman would not be found again. They could not manage even a day without her. The Aasmaan Jogi calmed down at once and said, 'You are the special mistress of this Badal Mahal. Whoever said you are a servant here!'

The kumbhari turned her face away and retorted sharply, 'I do not want this special treatment. My hands and legs are still working. Neither is there a limit to the clay in this world, nor have I forgotten how to mould it. You keep your pearls and diamonds to yourself.'

The Aasmaan Jogi had to indulge her a lot before she agreed. He was still somewhat suspicious, but he kept that to himself. He looked at the kumbhari's sulking face. Ram knows why sullen faces are so pleasing. But he had to ensure that he was not betrayed again. He thought to himself: 'I romance new women every day in front of the kumbhari, make love to them. How can she possibly digest this? She must be burning and squirming with jealousy.' A woman overlooked in such a way could betray him, but one who shared his bed would not betray him so easily. Why had he not regarded her closely all this time? She was no less beautiful. She was getting on in years, yes – but age, too, brings with it its own distinct flavour.

What had come to pass was unexpected, but the kumbhari did not protest at all. This man could not be deceived easily if one did not make love to him. How could she see hundreds of thousands of women suffer every day? Something would have to be done to enable their escape! The scoundrel had cast a pall on all happiness in the seth's house. Let's see when the chance for revenge presents itself, she thought. Entwining her gaze with that of the Aasmaan Jogi, she said, 'Who can pass over Your Majesty's wish! But when so many beautiful women are at hand, how is it that my turn has come today? Do tell me this much first…'

The Aasmaan Jogi said, 'If I wanted you to burn with rage, I would have said that too much dessert leaves one craving for something spicy and savoury. But that is not true. How many women possess a body as lean and firm as yours? I am bored of soft and fair. Too much neatness and pleasant scents are not always appealing.'

The kumbhari lowered her head and said, 'I have been seeing scores of women in your Badal Mahal and wanted to ask you for days if the flavour of every woman is different. Can't one survive on one woman for all of one's life?'

The Aasmaan Jogi replied: 'I can speak only for myself. I too was caught in this illusion once. The thirst for new women does not die, but the taste of all women is one. Before getting into bed, it surely feels as if this time the taste will be different; but once one is in bed, it is all the same. In bed, neither does beauty matter, nor colour. These differences are only in the eyes. Beauty means nothing beyond one's sight. Would you believe me if I said that now I am just living out old habits? The force of habit is no less than the force of nature. Sometimes I feel I must chop women up into pieces and eat their fried meat to silence the craving of my heart! Living women just do not have much to offer! But in a while, again, there is that same thirst that will not be quelled. The more I drink the water of beauty, the more this thirst flares up. Let me see how the water from the kumbhari's pots quenches my thirst!'

The charkha of the Aasmaan Jogi's habit and thirst kept spinning. The lovemaking in the palace in the clouds did not abate. Neither did the screams of suffering in the seth's household. Every time, the kumbhari would reveal the secret and one of the seven brothers would rush to the Badal Mahal, take all eight women and return to earth in the vimaan. But each time, the Aasmaan Jogi would catch them as they would be on the verge of alighting at the edge of the lake. He would then mutter an incantation and the son would turn into a statue made of white stone. After that, the Jogi would take the seven daughters-in-law of the seth's household and his daughter, and return to the Badal Mahal.

In this way, there came to be seven statues by the edge of the lake. Having defeated them so thoroughly, the Aasmaan Jogi's pride doubled. How could a man live by himself and for himself? How could delight spring in the heart of one who caused others grief, if the latter did not suffer and wail? For so many years, no one knew how these beautiful women had disappeared, where they had gone. If they were alive or dead. The Aasmaan Jogi, too, had not been able to find out how the families of these women had mourned after them. So, his own pleasure had grown fatigued. How can pleasure multiply without despair?

But this time, the seth's sons had followed their sister and their wives, trying to rescue them frantically, and the Aasmaan Jogi had seized the women and brought them back – this made his fervour and pleasure boundless. The more difficult it is to come by something, the more precious it is. If diamonds and pearls were found like pebbles on the wayside, who would ask after them? The only thing that is strewn under the feet are dust and stones. He would know his own potency when weighed against the impotence of others. After the first time, he was annoyed with neither the kumbhari nor the seth's daughter and the daughters-in-law. If women took him into their arms as soon as they saw him, then why would he follow them? Now he was able to truly relish his Badal Mahal, his vimaan, his power. If someone accepts defeat without fighting, then the very rapture of victory dries up. These months of waiting were more pleasurable for the Aasmaan Jogi than intimacy with any woman had been. After three months had passed, he began counting each day. If he had not been bound by the promise of waiting for six months, he would never have known this pleasure. If, as soon as one wishes for something it lands up in one's hands, then where is the limit to this sorrow? The hardship in attaining something is the source of the truest pleasure.

From his vimaan, he would see the old and shrunken seth and sethani come to the banks of the lake every evening. They would gather pots of water and wash the statues, and light incense sticks and lamps. They would chant prayers and be wracked with sobs. They would hug the statues of their dead sons. Witnessing this, the Aasmaan Jogi would be delighted; he would take great pride in his clout. He would circle the lake on his vimaan. He saw the world, but the world could not see him! He would be visible only in his palace in the clouds.

When the kumbhari would see this spectacle as she filled the pots with water at the banks of the lake, her heart would begin to explode. What consolation did these lifeless statues offer the seth and sethani? What contentment could these figures, in place of their real sons, give the parents? Could lighting incense sticks ever make the statues speak out? Were their parents' tears capable of melting their hearts? The sons were now statues by the banks of the lake, and the daughters-in-law and the daughter were prisoners in the Badal Mahal. Alongside thousands of other imprisoned women. Ram knew when they would be free? Without this freedom, happiness would never return to the earth. And how long could the human race survive without this happiness? How would it survive when its beauty and youth were entrapped in the palace in the clouds? When would this beauty be able to escape the confines of those golden doors to freedom, and how? In this freedom now lay the foremost pleasure of man.

That kumbhari had only one son. He was sixteen years old, handsome, well built and fair. An innocent boy, with narrow eyes. Every time he laughed, his teeth glimmered like lightning. The kumbhari had not gotten him married out of fear: what if the Aasmaan Jogi took his wife away? How ghastly would that be! When did that devil listen to anyone's pleas?

One day, as she left for the lake to fill the pots, her son began to insist that he, too, would like to accompany her. When he just would not listen to her, she had to take him along. At the edge of the lake, the boy saw the seth and sethani lighting incense sticks near the statues and sobbing, and he asked his mother what it was all about. At first, the kumbhari tried to avoid answering the question. But when he would not let it go, she had to tell him everything about the statues: how the Aasmaan Jogi had captured the seth's seven daughters-in-law and daughter from the swings and taken them away to his Badal Mahal; and when the sons tried to rescue them, this is what befell them. Since when had she been filling water for the Aasmaan Jogi? How did she help the seth's sons seven times, albeit unsuccessfully? Now, how would these women attain their freedom?

As she continued to fill the pots, the kumbhari said in a choked voice, 'Beta,[16] it was from this fear that I have still not had you married.'

'That you did not marry me off yet does not bother me. But you kept the secret of this Aasmaan Jogi from me for so long – that was not a good thing to do!'

Then, even as she filled the pots with water, the kumbhari told her son everything about the palace in the clouds. Told him about all the women there, including the seth's daughters-in-law and daughter, described to him their beauty individually. She praised the seth's daughter much for how clever she was. The son heard everything carefully and devised a plan.

As the kumbhari entered the hollow in the banyan tree, her son reminded her once again, 'Pass my message on to the seth's daughter. Let's see how well you do everything.

---

16 Beta: Son. Beti: Daughter.

This Aasmaan Jogi will meet his end at my hands. Let's find out how quickly you get the answer to the question I have asked. There will be nothing to worry about after this. I am waiting for you right here.'

Though the kumbhari did not have any confidence in her son at all, she still passed his message on to the seth's daughter. The daughter heard everything carefully. The kumbhari consoled her and asked her to be hopeful, not that she herself had any faith in what she was saying. But even the seth's daughter thought this was merely the reckless daring of a child and did not count on him. What would this all-powerful Jogi care for that tender child? Five months had gone by. How long would it take for another month to pass? When Ram himself had not protected them, who else could? But then, what was the harm in honouring the wish of a child? She would ask the Aasmaan Jogi what the kumbhari's son had wanted when she got the chance and send him the response. If this could make a child happy, then why would she refuse? Her own life was fated to be devoid of happiness – this much was certain.

The kumbhari and the seth's daughter were engaged in friendly chatter when, suddenly, the outermost door of the palace opened. How come the Aasmaan Jogi had returned so early? As soon as he came in, he went and lay down in his rangmahal.[17] His rangmahal was made of water! A bed made of water and sheets made of water. Yet, nothing

---

17 Rangmahal: Pleasure pavilion / private chambers.

would get wet! Such was the manner in which everything was forged from the sparkle and essence of water.

For a few days now, the Aasmaan Jogi had grown addicted to wine. He beckoned to the kumbhari, so she followed him with a golden pitcher of nectar and a pearl-encrusted bowl in her hands. She indulged him, and he gulped down two bowls of wine. As soon as he did, a slight intoxication overtook him. As he drank from the third bowl, he said, 'Tell her, kumbhari, tell that foolish seth's daughter plainly. Five months have somehow passed. I won't lie, the pleasure of waiting has been immense. But after being engulfed by such a fire, there must surely be rain! Now I cannot wait for another thirty days.'

The kumbhari concocted a story. She said, 'But if you break this enchantment of the seth's daughter, she will turn blind! If Your Majesty has relished the pleasure of waiting for five months, then why not for another month?'

'As you wish,' said the Jogi. 'Who knows what is good for me better than you?'

After this, the seth's daughter entered the Aasmaan Jogi's chamber herself and sat beside the kumbhari. The kumbhari handed her the bowl of wine and left, giving some excuse. The Aasmaan Jogi's words had begun to slur somewhat. He said, 'I told the kumbhari to convince you. She said that you are working up an enchantment. If you break it a month earlier, your eyes will burst. But these spells and enchantments of the earth don't work in this Badal Mahal. Trust me, you are in no danger. Now

I cannot wait for another thirty days. If your eyes burst, I will get you a thousand new eyes. I am a god after all! You still do not know the full extent of my might. This Badal Mahal hangs in the sky like the sun and the moon! Is this any small feat? Even death cannot reach my palace in the clouds!'

But the seth's daughter was not to be persuaded. She said, 'If you are as powerful as God, then make the days shorter. Why make them shorter – make thirty days pass in an hour!'

Creases appeared on the Aasmaan Jogi's forehead. As he sipped the wine, he said hesitantly, 'To be honest, I cannot make the days grow shorter. It is only here that my power doesn't reach.'

'Why only here?' asked the seth's daughter. 'There are many things that are beyond your reach. But you are not aware of them. You are blinded by your miracles. Savour the pleasure of waiting for another thirty days. Then everything will happen as Your Majesty wishes.'

The Aasmaan Jogi said, 'Yes, this too is no small pleasure. But listen to something astonishing – the intoxication of this drink is no match for the intoxication of your beauty! The effect of a drink wears off as soon as I see you. There is no telling if it is wine or water.'

But these words were also spoken in the intoxication of drink. The Aasmaan Jogi's eyes were now the colour of vermilion. His speech slurred. The vivid colour of his face had drained away. To test the Jogi's words, the seth's daughter made him drink three-four more bowls of wine. The Aasmaan Jogi began to say, 'Today, for the first time, I will tell you a secret of the heart. From now on, I will no longer bring any woman of the earth to this Badal Mahal. Those who are here will remain. Turning them out will make this palace empty. You too will have someone to talk to. But now I am sick of the earth's women! This time I will take my vimaan out in search of the apcharas of Inderlok, or the fairies of the moon. A pot may be full of gold, but if it's already open, it gives no pleasure. Prising the lid open has its own pleasure! If the kumbhari and you had said yes, it would have spoilt the pleasure. I ask you every hour so that you can refuse! The satisfaction in daring to get something beyond one's reach is something else altogether. If you are with me, then the company of Inderlok's apcharas or the fairies of the moon would be no great thing.'

This time, the seth's daughter made him drink the wine with her own hands. 'Really, your desires know no bounds!' she said. 'But Ram knows why my heart is not at rest. God forbid, but if something happens to you, then what days will befall this Badal Mahal! How will all these women live out their suffering in this abandoned palace? We have already lost our families. But if this comes to pass, what will be my lot? The mere thought makes every fibre of my being tremble.'

Now the Aasmaan Jogi had begun to lose control of his hands. Consolingly, he said, 'Why not just say that you are scared that I will die? Do not worry about it even in your dreams. No one can kill me. My death is in my control! Besides, why would I die of my own wish? Trust me, even death will have to die if it kills me. Rid your heart of this fear, silly! No one can kill the Aasmaan Jogi!'

The seth's daughter said, 'My fear remains despite your comforting words. Now, if there is some secret I do not know about, then that is your business! I have only you to lean on in this world now...'

The Aasmaan Jogi said, 'Silly, what secrets from you? For the first time, I will tell you a thing no one else knows. Then even you will start believing that I am immortal!

And then, the Aasmaan Jogi revealed to the seth's daughter the secret of his death. Slurring and stumbling over his words, he said, 'Across the seven seas is a temple. Surrounded on all sides by only the water of the ocean. At each of the four doors to the temple sit two lions, hungry and roaring. And deep beneath the temple is a chamber in which lies a golden cage. In the cage is a parrot. And in the parrot is my life. Now do you believe me? Can death reach there, pray? Everywhere in the ocean are crocodiles under my spell. They will gobble up death in a single gulp! If by some cunning it does reach the temple, the ravenous lions will tear it apart in a second. I say it loud and clear: Let death try and even go there, then death itself will be wiped off the face of this earth! But if the entire world becomes immortal, then what will set me apart? This is why I don't let death know this secret. Tell me, now is your heart at ease?'

The seth's daughter smiled insincerely, and said, 'How can it not after hearing such a thing?'

The intoxication of the wine was now beyond control. How much wine could he drink after all? At last, he passed out on his bed, and the seth's daughter came out of the Aasmaan Jogi's rangmahal. She told the kumbhari the entire secret. The kumbhari did not wait for a second after that. She sat in the vimaan and returned to the banyan tree. Her son was still sitting there. She recounted to him the secret of the Aasmaan Jogi's death. But she could not have even dreamt that, after hearing everything, he would be all set to cross the seven seas and get his hands on that parrot. Had she known, she would never have told him about it. How could she push her only son into the very jaws of death? How she raised him to be an adult, only she knew or God knew! Her heart wept for the suffering women in the Badal Mahal, but how could a mother set her son on the path of death? Patting his head, she said in a shaky voice, 'Beta, when a two-year-old sees a snake, it rushes to grab it. When the snake bares its fangs, the child smiles. But this is the child being ignorant. Your excitement to get this parrot is like the ignorance of the child! You know not the danger in what you insist on doing; I do.'

The son smiled and said, 'Does death not arrive when lying in a mother's lap? If it stopped because mothers forbade it, then no son would ever die. If it was in a mother's hands, would she let the son who suckles at her breast meet his end? If upon your bidding, I were not to go to get that parrot beyond the seven seas, will you be able to keep me alive forever? Death alone knows whether the fortune of seeing the rising sun at dawn tomorrow will be mine or not! If you do, tell me! Then I will never contest what you say.'

The kumbhari was quite taken aback on hearing these words coming out of her son's mouth. This son, to whom she had given birth, had surpassed her in wisdom. He who thinks this is ignorance is himself ignorant! Spitting to ward off the evil eye, she said affectionately, 'My darling son, I never knew you were so clever. Listening to all you have said, I feel as if I was not the one who gave birth to you; instead, it was you who gave birth to me. Now I will be at ease only once I see you off.'

Once the mother was ready, what could delay the departure? The kumbhari put jaggery in her son's mouth, stroked his head, and gave him her blessings. And even as the mother watched, the son left. Pearls of happiness began to glimmer in the mother's eyes.

The son set out as if in the dream of a deep slumber. Soon, he reached the shore of the sea. He stopped by the shade of a coconut tree and was just about to open his bag of food when he sighted a golden fish – Sonal Maachli – wriggling in the fine scorching sand and put her back into the water. As soon as he did so, she felt the life force return to her. She began dancing in the water. The kumbhari's son was delighted. He had seven sweet puris with him tied in a cloth. He fed her all seven, bit by bit. The fish would gulp each piece as she danced and gleamed in the water. Then, as he dusted the cloth clean, he said like a child, 'You gobbled up all seven puris! My golden fish, what do I feed you now?'

'I do not need anything more,' replied the Sonal Maachli. 'But did you get these puris just for me?'

The son told it as it was. 'No, I had gotten them for myself,' he said. 'But seeing you dance, I could not help feeding you the puris. Hunger does not bother me much.'

Then the Sonal Maachli poked her mouth out of the water and said, 'Brother mine, today you saved my life. You fed me sweet puris and went hungry yourself. I am the Queen of Fishes. If you are ever in trouble, then take my name!'

The son's brains worked at the opportune time. 'When else would there be trouble?' he said. 'It is because there is trouble that I have come to this seashore!'

After this, the son told the Sonal Maachli everything about the Badal Mahal, the Aasmaan Jogi and the parrot. The fish said, 'This will be child's play for me. Get on my back. I will take you to the shore of the temple right away. No creature of the ocean can even touch you. Once we reach the temple, I will think of a way to deal with the lions.'

The son sat on the back of the Sonal Maachli promptly. The fish charged ahead, tearing through the water. She moved faster than even the wind. When they were far out into the ocean, the boy gazed around him and up at the sky. The ocean was a wonder of creation! On the ground, one's gaze got entangled here and there – uphill, downhill, trees, dunes, mountains, huts and mansions. But here, there was nothing. Not a speck of dust, not a pebble, not a stone. There would be no opportunity to skim any stone, or pick the small fruits of neem and khejdi, or play on the trees. Neither would anyone fall, nor would they break their hands or legs. And if one did not break any limb, why would their parents be annoyed? There was the clear blue sky above, and all around, clear blue water. Water and more water. No end in sight to this water! How did such a huge quantity of water gather? No matter how dark it got, there was no chance of bumping into anything at all!

Just then, a massive storm assailed them with a deafening howl. Screaming hoo-hoo! Monstrous, fearsome! As if the wind was charging into battle. A storm fierce enough to shatter mountains. The Sonal Maachli said, 'There is no need to be scared at all. This storm will pass as it has come. Hold on to me with both your hands.'

The son did exactly as he was told. It looked like this storm would blow the very ocean away. Waves the size of mountains came crashing down. But they kept moving forward through them, rising high and ducking down, as if on a swing.

A while later, the storm passed. It felt as if, all of a sudden, thousands and thousands of dhol-nagaras had stopped being beaten. Their field of vision grew wider by the second. How far the eyes could see! And there was not even a sign of bushes or barbs. One could run barefoot without a worry – there was not a thorn to be pricked by, neither a stone to get scraped against.

The sun began to set rapidly. After burning for so long, it seemed to have made up its mind to descend. Soon, its edge was immersed in water. Would this ball of fire be extinguished? Once a perfect circle of fiery pink, it was now just a half-circle! There, it had drowned! It had drowned! Now one knew that this sun took a dip in this ocean every evening. And that is why, when it rose at dawn, it was nice and cool.

The dark of night spread across the sky swiftly. The ocean too began to darken. The stars that had been playing hide-and-seek all day were now beginning to appear sprinkled across the sky. Like the flames of a fire become larger when one blows on it, slowly the moonbeams assumed a larger glow. The silver moonshine of the ocean seemed infinite. How cool the touch of the ocean had made it! Is it the moonshine that drenches the ocean, or the ocean that drenches the moonshine? And this freshly bathed moonshine began to ride the waves. Its touch made the dark water glisten!

The son's heart was abloom with flowers. In these three days and three nights he had lived a lifetime of a thousand years! His heart's desires would have remained unfulfilled if he had died without witnessing this sight. What a strange and other-worldly place this temple was in…!

The Sonal Maachli had hatched a plan to lay her hands on the cage as soon as she reached the temple. It was midnight when they arrived. The full moon in the night sky was drawing the ocean in waves. The hungry lions had grown weary and fallen asleep. Who would walk into the fangs of death? The ocean kept rising until it began to touch the doorway to the temple. The Sonal Maachli took the son into the temple without leaving the water. There, he took down the cage that was suspended from a ring. The lions awoke with a start as soon as they heard the parrot call, and began to roar so ferociously that even death would have trembled at hearing them. But they did not dare jump into the water. Even lions do not like death.

Here, the parrot's cage left the temple, and there in the Badal Mahal, the Aasmaan Jogi began to feel extremely uneasy. He leapt out of his bed with a start. The kumbhari was standing nearby and fanning him. The Aasmaan Jogi's heart quivered. He touched his head and said, 'Kumbhari, what is this all of a sudden? My life force writhes and flutters!'

The kumbhari said, 'It is a mortal body. Something must not be right. I will press your head; you will feel at ease in an instant. Is the heart aflutter for the seth's daughter? I will get her if you so command. I understand this unease. But only three more days to go. Then all this pining will cease!'

Shaking his head, he said, 'No, kumbhari, this unease is not that! It is something else. Has someone deceived me?' The Aasmaan Jogi's voice was laced with fear.

Feigning surprise, the kumbhari said, 'What is it that I hear you say today! Deception, and with you? Cheating? If even God is powerless in front of you, then what are poor humans?'

The seth's daughter received the kumbhari's summons. Only three more days remained now. Ram knows with what unknown hope she had asked for six months' time. Now even those six months were about to end. Her feet felt burdened, as if with the weight of a mountain. She dragged herself to the Aasmaan Jogi's chambers, and came in to stand quietly by the kumbhari. In her company, she felt the comfort of a mother.

What the kumbhari said turned out to be true. The Aasmaan Jogi's heart calmed upon seeing the seth's daughter. In some time, all his trepidation vanished. Smiling, he said, 'The two of you do not leave this chamber and go anywhere for three days. Ram knows why my heart is not at peace with other women now.'

It was now the last night of darkness before the six months would end. For the Aasmaan Jogi, it would be a golden sunrise. And for the seth's daughter, a dawn of darkness. There was no escape from this Badal Mahal even in death. The Aasmaan Jogi would sprinkle a few drops of nectar on her and bring her back to life. There was no peace while living, there would be no peace in death. What grief could be bigger than this? Who could bear the dark veil of this nightfall? And this night would surely give way to dawn. The shameless Aasmaan Jogi would feel no shyness in the light of the sun. At dawn, he would do what he had wished to all along.

With only an hour left before dawn, sleep deserted the Aasmaan Jogi. But he did not open his eyes. What if, upon seeing her, he lost all control? Now, only a few more moments were left to go. With the sunrise, a new dawn would light up his life.

The kumbhari and the seth's daughter did not sleep a wink all night. They had remained seated, looking at each other's faces in silence. Conversing without exchanging words. At the end of this pitch darkness, they could see an ocean of sorrow. There had been no news from the kumbhari's son.

Suddenly, the Aasmaan Jogi stood up and let out a blood-curdling scream! The agony in the scream sounded as though a thousand lions were roaring in the grip of death. Its echo made the Badal Mahal tremble. The Jogi ran frantically, dazed.

'Kumbhari,' he cried out, 'I have been betrayed! But even as I die, I am not going to leave this murderer alive. Where is my vimaan? You come with me too!'

Then, catching hold of both the women's arms, he dragged them out of the palace in the clouds and jumped into the vimaan, still not letting go of them. The vimaan began to fly. The pleasant, cool glow that precedes dawn had spread across the earth.

It seemed as if every pore of the Aasmaan Jogi's body was being scalded with embers. He said, 'Today this sun will rest only after it incinerates the universe! The earth will burn, and the sun will look at the flames with his fiery eyes and laugh!'

As he alighted at the bank of the lake, the Aasmaan Jogi looked at the seth's daughter and said, 'I trusted you so much! But the race of women is not worthy of trust! It was my biggest mistake. Now, I will have to suffer!'

Among the seven statues made of stone stood a young boy, smiling. In his hands was a golden cage, and inside the golden cage, the Aasmaan Jogi's death in the form of a parrot! He was about to open the cage and take the parrot out when the Aasmaan Jogi darted like a gust of wind. He shouted, 'Leave it, boy! Leave the parrot! I can finish you off even as I die. All right, I gift you my Badal Mahal ... Now you leave this parrot be.'

Breathing fire, the Aasmaan Jogi was just about to reach the son, when the latter broke both the parrot's legs and threw them away! That very instant, the Jogi too lost his legs and tumbled off the bank of the lake. He tried very hard to climb back up, but kept crashing down each time. The Aasmaan Jogi's legless body was now soaked in blood.

Just then, the kumbhari shouted from where she was, 'Beta, even God has not been able to put a stop to this Aasmaan Jogi's power! Don't you waste time. Twist the parrot's neck and be done with it!'

Smiling, the son said, 'He has relished the taste of pleasure all his life. Now let him savour pain for a while. One cannot truly know pleasure without experiencing pain.'

The legless Aasmaan Jogi screamed and wailed no end, but the kumbhari's son would not leave the parrot. Covered in blood, he kept writhing on the ground.

Meanwhile, the seth's daughter took out a tiny bottle of nectar that she had brought with her. No sooner had she sprinkled it on the statues than all her seven brothers sprang to life! Yawning and stretching they said, 'How deeply we slept!'

The kumbhari spat, 'May such sleep never befall even your enemies!'

When their eyes fell on the bloodied Aasmaan Jogi, they recalled the events of the past. Upon seeing his sister, the youngest brother asked, 'Where are your seven sisters-in-law?'

'Be patient,' said the kumbhari. 'They will appear in front of you right now!' She took out the parrot feather from inside her blouse and blew on it seven times.

They waited a while and craned their necks but could not see any vimaan coming. But to their great surprise, the Badal Mahal had sunk much further down. Seeing this, the kumbhari told her son, 'Delay no more, beta. Without the Aasmaan Jogi's death, the Badal Mahal will not descend to the earth!'

The son twisted the parrot's neck hard. There was a loud boom, as if of a thousand thunders! And no sooner had the Aasmaan Jogi died than the Badal Mahal landed on earth. Its golden gates opened, and at once, all the women were free! As soon as the women left, the palace collapsed, and on earth there sprouted saffron and other radiant flowers! Heaps of diamonds, pearls and rubies appeared!

When the old seth and sethani arrived at the edge of the lake to light incense sticks, they were flabbergasted at what they saw! Their prayers had not been in vain. Amidst that horde of countless women, the faces of their seven daughters-in-law, their daughter, and their sons had begun to glow! What was this more glorious Teej that had arrived much earlier than the Teej of Saavan?

The seth's daughter was married off to the kumbhari's son amid great pomp and merriment, to the jubilant beats of drums and nagaras. The numerous women who had been released danced the ghoomar, and how! They sang wedding songs too!

As soon as they heard the news, the families of the once-missing women came running. The kumbhari gave each of the women diamonds and pearls as gifts, and bade them farewell as if they were her own daughters.

Following the Aasmaan Jogi's demise, an aak tree grew at the spot where his body had fallen, and a large dhatura bush grew at the spot where his head had fallen!

That day, by some stroke of luck, I too was there. I witnessed all this with my own eyes. Those who believe this to be true will be happy like the kumbhari's son! They'll have the wedding of their dreams, with pomp and splendour! And those who don't, will grow here and there as aak and dhatura trees after they die!

Power

The many tastes of stories and tales,
Some, like sand, subtle and fine,
Others, bigger than God divine,
Some, like droplets, swift and fluid,
Others, like the ocean, slow and languid,
Some that flow like a breeze so fine
Others totter like a man after wine…

THIS STORY IS AS ANCIENT as the night sky sprinkled with stars, when, at the crossroads of a certain time, there lived a Kaji[18] who had the special favour of the Paatsa.[19] Husband to seven wives. But as fate would have it, the Kaji was unable to father children. Even then, such was the Kaji's

---

18   Kaji: Qazi – a magistrate or judge.

19   Paatsa: Badshah – a king or monarch.

thinking that, instead of finding any sort of fault in himself, he could only find fault in his wives!

When, even after three years of his seventh wedding, the Kaji was unable to extend his line, his elder brother's son petitioned the Paatsa for the position of Kaji – but in vain. The Kaji had the special favour of the Paatsa. He had the Paatsa's blessings. The Paatsa told the nephew in no uncertain terms that he could succeed his uncle only when the latter turned a hundred, not earlier. And no one could do or say much once the Paatsa had spoken. The nephew returned home, morose.

When the Kaji found out what had passed, he was very cross with his nephew. The sting of this anger was so sharp that he stopped speaking to him altogether, even banned him from coming to his mansion. And once the Kaji turned his back on his nephew, everyone in the entire neighbourhood turned their backs on him too. Not even a bird would fly past his doorstep.

In place of the children he couldn't have, the Kaji brought home a dog to shower his affection on. The animal was very bright. In just a few days, she became so dear to the Kaji that he could not bear to be away from her for even a second. The dog had a shiny jet-black coat of hair, as soft as velvet, a bushy tail, drooping ears, a long and fluffy mane on the head, a sweet and pleasing bark.

The people from the neighbourhood emulated the Kaji and began to shower the dog with great affection. And as they competed with one another to show who loved the dog the most, the clever people's affection only grew. The Kaji would look on as they inundated her with kisses, petted her and bathed her, got her ghewar, malpuas and gulgulas made of ghee and sugar, in neat bundles. They would feed her with their own hands with such fondness! Seeing such warmth being demonstrated by everyone, the Kaji could hardly contain the delight in his heart.

Once, an extremely astute gentleman suggested that the dog be given a suitable name. The Kaji readily agreed. And in no time at all, a crowd congregated at his mansion. Everyone was eager to suggest a name. So a stream of names began to make its way to the Kaji's ears: Kalsoom, Jebun, Kuseeda, Khatoon, Phatoon, Raseedaan, Allaraan, Jetoon, Jubedaan, Fatma, Mariam, Majeedaan. Caressing his waist-length beard, the Kaji said, 'No, don't suggest such names. Us humans are named according to our caste, but it's better if cattle and dogs aren't bound by it. What do you think?'

'It will be as you say,' the gathered people said. 'Our minds can agree to nothing that you don't agree to. But you are the one who will have to name her.'

Furrows appeared on the Kaji's forehead. He continued to caress his beard and said, 'Think of some colour, a plant, or maybe some bird...' And then, all of a sudden, a name emerged from the Kaji's own lips. 'Koel, Koel!' he exclaimed. 'I think Koel is the perfect name!' as that is how we write it in Rajasthani. it is a name after all.

Everyone who had gathered at the Kaji's mansion agreed in unison and exclaimed that such a good name would not have occurred to either Khuda or Ram himself! If one were to compare a koel to their dear dog and her sweet voice, the bird would lose seven times over.

In just a few days, hearing everyone call her Koel, the dog too understood that it was her name. But what was immensely surprising was that no one could tell where the koel birds that lived in the gardens and parks of that neighbourhood vanished, one after the other! Meanwhile, sweetness filled the mouths of those who took the dog's name. Perhaps even the gods turned envious of the good fortune of the Kaji's dog!

In those days, kajis were feared even more than thakars[20] and lords. Religion and God were, of course, important in their own ways, but everyone was frightened of the Kaji. And owing to this dread, small and big, young and old, none dared forget the name Koel.

But cursed Death, she can neither be convinced by devotion nor be pleased by flattery; neither does she care for one's honour, nor does she fear anyone. She embraced Koel in the guise of rabies. And finally, after three days of immense suffering, even as she looked at her owner with eyes full of pain, she left for the shelter of Ram. The Kaji looked on helplessly as his darling Koel's body became lifeless and cold.

---

20 Thakar: Thakur, feudal lord. Female: Thakarani.

As soon as those surrounding the Kaji and his dead pet saw his eyes moisten, they began to wail and howl relentlessly. There took place such a contest of bawling and beating of chests and heads that your eyes would scarcely believe it! Deep within every single one was just this wish – that the Kaji would take especial note of their grief. In that race, everyone's throats became sore and the tears streaming from their eyes would not abate. Seeing people weep in this manner, the Kaji's own tears stopped flowing.

Now, the question was: How was Koel's lifeless body to be honoured? Cremated, buried, or surrendered to the water or the air?

Initially, a burial was suggested. But the Kaji's grieving heart could not accept this. He shook his head and said in a choked voice, 'No, I'm not going to bury my Koel in this dirty mud! She'll be covered with mould. Her body will rot.'

After this, neither would he agree to have Koel cremated with sandalwood, ghee and coconuts, nor would he consent to surrender her to the air or immerse her in water. In the same choked voice, he said that if she were burnt, there would be no trace left of his beloved Koel. Leaving her out in the open would mean crows, vultures and stray dogs would tear her apart. And leaving her in water would make her bloat up. The Kaji would rather die than abandon his Koel to such a terrible fate!

How, then, could the last rites for the lifeless Koel be performed?

After a while, a fresh idea occurred to the Kaji: she should be embalmed with the utmost care and placed in a golden cage to be hung from a branch of a banyan tree, so that travellers passing by the tree could benefit from the opportunity to see the blessed Koel!

Having shared his plan, the Kaji looked at the throng that had gathered around him and asked, 'What do you say?'

'Absolutely! Whatever you think is fit!' they replied promptly, restless as they were to come to a decision about what to do with the dog's body. 'But now we must begin performing her rites. It will reflect well on us only if her rites are performed as befits her great qualities! Where will one even get to see such a sacred being?'

Thereon, the inhabitants of the Kaji's neighbourhood, clever and competent as they were, got everything done in no time at all. No one needed any explanations. Each one of those eager people got for Koel the jewels they could and piled them up in front of the Kaji willingly. While the jeweller melted the gold and built a cage, deft craftsmen stuffed the dog and filled her with preservatives and chemicals. The Kaji looked on teary-eyed while all the preparations were carried out swiftly. A gold chain was suspended from a ring, also made of gold, to hang the cage from the banyan tree. Even after seven births, the virtues of such well-meaning and devoted people could not be forgotten. Tears began to pour down from the Kaji's eyes. If the Kaji cried so, how could the people hold back? From every pair of eyes, there flowed so many tears that twenty eyes would not be enough to hold them! When the cage was finally raised on to shoulders and was about to be taken from the Kaji's mansion, the throng gathered there wailed and bawled.

Four pallbearers, a golden cage balanced on their heads, walked ahead, with a crestfallen Kaji following them. And behind him was the throng. The Kaji barely noticed when the pallbearers changed. Then, the strangest of rumours was heard – that the tears from everyone's eyes had pooled to form a small stream! And there were as many rumours as there were mouths. Why, people even said that half a dozen innocent children had drowned in that stream!

Once the cage was hung from a branch of the banyan tree, the Kaji begged the people to get a hold on themselves, and it was only then that their eyes finally had some respite. After accompanying the Kaji to the threshold of his mansion, they returned to their homes.

The next day, even before the sun had risen, a horde of people flocked to the Kaji's house to condole with him. They feared that if they didn't, they would fall out of favour. The infinite and unseen dread of power is not without reason.

They would not stop singing Koel's praises. One said how, once when he was eating rotis, Koel had joined him and partaken of the same. And despite that, he had not found it filthy. 'Let a man even try to be as clean as her!' he said.

While the Kaji was delighted to hear this, everyone else was perplexed, not knowing what to say. No one wanted to be left behind. Shortly afterwards, another man concocted a fresh tale and began: 'I don't want to flatter even God...'

The Kaji broke in, 'I get angry even hearing the word flattery!'

The man continued: 'But one has to speak the truth after all! Everyone in the neighbourhood knows that I had a boil on my lower lip. I tried to have it treated, took medicines, but nothing helped. One day, it was a stroke of good luck that Koel licked my lip with her soft and moist tongue. By the third day, it was as if the boil had never even existed!'

Hearing this, the man who had Koel eat with him felt like someone had slapped him. Before he could come up with another tale, the others rushed to sing such praises of Koel that he never got a chance. Blisters on the soles of someone's feet healed at once when Koel licked them. A bald spot on someone's head was completely covered in new hair when Koel drooled over it. Another had ringworm disappear from his face after a full seventeen years when he smeared it with the gunk from Koel's eyes. The touch of Koel's tail had instantly rid yet another of a migraine, and now he could not recall how his head used to hurt even if he tried. Koel's licks had cured one of eczema and yet another of leprosy. The pain in someone's eye had vanished upon applying kajal mixed with Koel's saliva on it. The rashes on someone's hand had gone away altogether after he had bandaged that portion with Koel's shit. Such were the remedies that those gathered to grieve with the Kaji began to vouch for, that even Dhantar Vaid[21] would not have been able to think them up!

The Kaji, despite being her owner, had not expected Koel to have such virtues. Hearing about them helped his grief recede considerably. Running his hand over his curly beard, he said, 'I've racked my brain and grown tired of doing so, but I can't understand one thing: if you all are in such a piteous state after Koel has departed, what catastrophe will befall you when I'm gone? The very thought makes my heart wish I never die!'

All around him sat people who were sad and spoke nothing but the truth. Promptly, they said, 'If it's not what your heart desires, then why should you die? There are enough of us sitting right here to die! As long as we are around, how can we let it be your turn? Just hearing of you dying makes us want to stop living. Don't you let such terrible thoughts come to you, even in your dreams! We will stop breathing before it is time for you to embrace death. If you pass away, the sun itself will freeze and fall out of the sky. And once the sun has fallen, there will be no moisture and there will be no rain. And without rain, what grain, what fodder and what cattle? The whole world will perish

---

21 Dhantar Vaid: Dhanvantari, the god of medicine and the father of Ayurveda.

in suffering and torment! No, we cannot do without you for even a second. Being our master, how can you even think such evil things?'

Softening, the Kaji said, 'If this is what you want, I will never let such thoughts enter my mind! I was only wondering what you all thought.'

Amidst such conversations, the forty days of mourning for Koel came to an end. The Kaji's nephew did not visit the mansion even once during this time. People gossiped. The Kaji was incensed. He did not want to even see the face of such a good-for-nothing nephew! If he were to come near his house even by mistake, the Kaji would have him dragged away. There is a limit to even spitefulness after all!

Does death have ears? Even Vemata[22] would not know the answer to this question. But as fate would have it, the very next year, on the very day Koel had died, the Kaji too passed away while he was cleaning his teeth. But what was most surprising, given the Kaji's stature, was that no chaos broke out in the neighbourhood following his demise. Forget the sun and the moon, not even a green leaf on any of the trees in the settlement seemed to grieve his passing. But what was so unexpected about this? It was bound to happen sooner or later. Without much effort, the same thoughts began to form in the mind of every individual in the neighbourhood. Man is not like insects or animals, is he? Neither does he have horns on his head nor a tail on his

---

22 Vemata: The goddess who writes our fates.

back. He is a being of unmatched intelligence. The rituals of humans are similar. Their homes are similar. The way they speak is similar. And the way they think and feel is similar.

Even he who is the most foolish knows fully well that, once dead, neither does a raja come alive nor a paatsa! Then what is a mere kaji? The dead can neither be pleased nor displeased. They can neither bless nor condemn. And without being able to do these, one is worse than even a stone. A stone can at least be used to build something. When thrown at someone, it works as a weapon, does the job of cracking open one's head. Then what match is a dead man's body for a stone?

It is man's intelligence that he only bows to the rising sun. Respects power. Fears the ruler more than even death.

The new kaji was everything to the people now. The master of their peace and their pain. Power itself knew better than to deny his wishes! Neither country nor faith come before self-interest – to be mindful of this is the foremost virtue of a clever man.

What harm could it possibly cause if one person didn't attend the Kaji's burial? There wasn't a paucity of people in the neighbourhood. Without needing any guru to guide them, everyone instantly thought the same things. Respect for the dog followed from respect for the Kaji. People fear a dog because they fear its owner. Koel's golden cage had fulfilled their wishes before; why would it not now? Why, does even the sun glimmer like gold? How pleased would the new Kaji be to lay his hands on this invaluable cage! As this thought flashed through their minds, everyone dashed to the banyan tree. In no time at all, there was a gathering of people as numerous as the countless leaves on the tree. At once the cage was lowered, and the dog's body taken out and thrown away. The cage was thoroughly washed and polished. Meanwhile, the dog's skin was trampled underfoot by the spirited throng. The preservatives and stuffing mingled with the dust, became indistinguishable from it.

Without anyone leading them or telling them anything, the crowd's feet, accustomed to their ways for ages, turned towards the new kaji's home on their own. The mind, whose job it is to think, did not have to think at all.

The new kaji was lost in thought over some quandary, when, suddenly, hearing a commotion, he stepped outside. As soon as his eyes fell upon that gleaming golden cage, he was stupefied, but recovered in an instant. The nectar-like chants of 'khamma ghani, khamma ghani' began to swirl in his ears. How wrong he had been to ever doubt or be annoyed with such devoted and clever people! Not a single person turned their face towards the forlorn mansion of the dead Kaji. No one even asked after the well-being of those mourners who had indulged in the drama of wailing. How could such a sincere lot utter any falsehoods, pray tell?

It is the misfortune of the dead Kaji that, as soon as I started to write about his burial, my pen ran out of ink! But I have full faith in the intelligence of my virtuous readers...

In the Donkey's Skin[23]

I tell a story true –
Krishna's Radha bloomed
Krishna threw a stone
Which struck Radha's bone
Radha wouldn't speak
The peacock let out a shriek
A potter tumbled to the floor
His pots shattered to bits
The broken shards hurt an ox
The ox cast a curse
Out came a Soni's[24] hearse
It trampled on a snake

---

23 Author's note: *I heard this story from Bansilal, the Rav
(genealogist) of the Bawarias. Bansilal had heard it from his
predecessors, owing to his ancestral occupation.*

24 Soni: Caste that, traditionally, works as goldsmiths.

The snake bit a Mali[25]
The Mali turned blue –
I tell a story true

SO MAY RAMJI BLESS US all with good days, that aeons and aeons before all men and before all beasts, Lord Inder drank wine from glasses encrusted with pearls in Inderlok and found pleasure in the dance of apcharas. All the gods loved song and dance! Through the day, they romanced apcharas to the sound of music. No worries, no thought. There was no fourth thing to do after love, music and song. The children of the gods learnt the art of love in their mother's wombs!

One day, Lord Inder and his son were watching the dance at court. Inder was intoxicated with his drink and his son was drunk on his youth. Inder suddenly noticed his son's eyes. Kamdev danced in them! The son heeded nothing around him.

Inder scolded him sternly, 'If you dare come into these soirées in my presence, then you will see what I do! Get lost this very instant!'

The son ignored his father's words and continued to stare at the apchara lasciviously. When his father reprimanded him again, he asked, 'My crime?'

Lord Inder said, 'You make love to this apchara right in front of my eyes and then ask me shamelessly what your crime is?'

---

25 Mali: Caste that, traditionally, works as florists and gardeners.

Calmly, the son said, 'In our Inderlok, one can love anyone. Coming in the way of love is surely a crime! If this is something lowly and shameful, why don't you change your ways?'

Every pore of Inder's body was aflame with rage. He dragged his son out of the court and shouted, 'Don't you dare set foot here again! Let this be a lesson!'

The son, however, learnt nothing. The following day, when that apchara did not turn up at court even after quite some time had passed, Inder enquired after her. Then he was told that she was with his son in the gardens, making love. It was only yesterday that he had warned his son, and today this! That apchara too had not obeyed him. But if he cursed the apchara, he would certainly regret it. It was his son who was the root of this trouble.

Lord Inder headed to the gardens himself. What he had been told was indeed true. But how difficult it was to bear the truth! He kicked his son and cursed him – for twelve years, he would have to suffer life in a donkey's skin! Such a stubborn scoundrel deserved to be in the mortal realms. There could be no space for him in the realms of the gods.

No sooner had the curse been cast than the son breathed his last. How can one love a corpse? The apchara who had been cavorting with the son, now cast his body aside and began to make love to his father. Such are the ways of love in the realm of the gods!

And there, the son was reborn in the womb of a donkey in a kumbhar's barn in the town of Patan. That kumbhar was the head of a big family, and the chief of five hundred villages. A large household. The choicest of animals. Several donkeys. It was a life of comfort and plenty for the old man. His sons were all earning well. He himself went around involving himself in the village politics.

The male donkeys were kept in one shed, the females in another. The old man took special care of such things. Unless the animals were in heat, they were never left together. Yet, two months later, the kumbhar noticed that one of his best female donkeys was pregnant. How was this possible? He asked his sons and grandsons, but no one knew a thing.

The donkey's stomach kept swelling day after day. The old man kept wondering and the days kept passing. Every night, he would sleep in the barn. And in this way, eleven months passed.

One day, the old man was snoring in his sleep when, just after midnight, a strange voice reached his ears. 'Prajapat[26] baba, are you asleep or awake?' it said. It was not before the words had been repeated twice or thrice that the old man sat up startled, looking here and there. There was no one in sight. Again came the voice: 'Prajapat baba, are you asleep or awake?'

26　Prajapat: Used as a term of respect for someone from the Kumbhar caste.

The kumbhar was now ten short of a hundred years. Never had he had such an experience. Nothing to be seen, but a voice that could be clearly heard. Once again, 'Prajapat baba, are you asleep or awake?'

Gathering his wits about him, the old man said, 'I am awake. How can this worried man sleep? But who are you? A ghost? A spirit? Show yourself.'

The voice replied, 'No. I am neither a ghost, nor am I a spirit. I speak from the womb of your favourite donkey.'

Now, the old man's astonishment knew no bounds. 'The donkey who has conceived you does not speak,' he said. 'Then how did you, conceived in her womb, learn to talk? Tell me!'

From the donkey's stomach, the voice said, 'Baba, you may be the leader of your clan. But it is best that you stay out of my business. You need to deliver a message to Rajaji. Do so immediately. I will be born the day after tomorrow, on the night before the full moon.'

The old man thought: what if meddling made matters worse? So he agreed to deliver to the king whatever the message was. However, when he finally heard the message, he began to tremble. He was nearly out of his skin with fear and shock. On hearing such a message, the king would have his entire clan crushed alive in the oil mills. There would cease to be even any memory of them. The message the being in the donkey's stomach had asked the old man to convey to the king was that he must have his youngest daughter married to the donkey's offspring at sundown the day after. Otherwise, he would destroy the town of Patan! This ancient town would fall silent! The Raja and Rani would die like dogs afflicted by leprosy!

Such a message to be conveyed to the king! What was this sorcery that had taken root in the donkey's womb, only God knew. If the old man refused, he did not know what tragedy would befall him; but if he did deliver the message, it would certainly be the end of his family. He was stuck between the jaws of a lion. Why did he even say yes before listening to the message? What could he do now? For a while, he just sat in silence. And then, he decided that he would take his entire family and leave the village quietly. Let the donkey handle things on her own.

But whispers of the kumbhar's plan to leave the village began to make the rounds. And as soon as they heard about it, the whole clan gathered at the old man's door. When they asked him the reason for wanting to flee, he tried to avoid giving them an answer. What could he even say? If the truth emerged from his lips, his reputation would be destroyed in this ripe old age. And he had been an honest man all his life; he could not bring himself to lie. Seeing his silence, the clan members became all the more convinced that something was up, or he would not be planning to go away. So they would also leave with him. But why wouldn't he say what was wrong?

Out of a community of a hundred kumbhar households, twenty-seven decided to leave with the old man. When the remaining ones found out about this, they reported the matter to the king. They were all leaving the village together and they would not say why.

The Raja left his court and rode to the old man's place with his diwan.[27] Once he got there, no one could take a step further without first explaining the reason for their departure. The rest of the people simply said that they were following their leader. They would know why if the old man had told them why!

When the Raja asked the old kumbhar, he just stood there. He would neither speak nor move. When the Raja implored him, he said that he would stay on only if the king made a promise.

The Raja knew the old kumbhar well, so he gave his word. The old man told him that the Raja, the Rani, the rajkanwaris,[28] and all the members of the royal court would have to spend that night in his barn. Only if they did so, would they find out why he was leaving.

The Raja had made a promise, so of course he had to keep it. The barn was given a royal makeover without the king saying anything. The king's bed was put there. The donkeys were all tied to one side as per the old man's instructions.

Everyone lay awake, gossiping late into the night. At midnight, from the pregnant donkey's belly was heard the same magic voice: 'Kumbhar baba, are you asleep?'

---

27 Diwan: Minister.

28 Rajkanwari: Princess. Rajkanwar: Prince.

'How can sleep come to this sufferer?' replied the old man.

Then he turned to the Raja with folded hands and said, 'My lord, please listen carefully now. You will know the reason behind my grief.'

Everyone, including the king, was all ears. The voice spoke again, 'Kumbhar baba, did you deliver my message to the Rajaji or not?'

Then the old man said, 'In this old age, I forget everything. My memory has deserted me. Who are you and what are you? Please explain once again.'

'I speak from the womb of your donkey,' came the voice, and everyone could hear what was being said clearly. 'I will be born tomorrow, on the night before the full moon. Tell your Rajaji in no uncertain terms that he must have his youngest daughter married to your donkey's offspring. Else, I will destroy the town of Patan! This ancient town will fall silent! Leprosy will afflict the Raja and Rani, and they will die howling and screaming like dogs!'

Everyone gasped as soon as they heard these words emerging from the donkey's belly. Dumbstruck, they all exchanged glances. Poor kumbhar baba! What else could he have done after hearing such a message? Would the king have believed him? But now that the Raja had heard everything with his own ears, who could he vent his anger on? God knows what had cast this magic!

The voice continued, 'Baba, I will repeat it once more. Don't you forget.'

The same message once again. The Raja began trembling with fear. The Rani began to sob. How could the princess be married to a donkey? And if that did not happen, what tragedy would come to pass? What was this predicament!

The older princess was cunning and malicious. She said, 'By sacrificing one, all shall live. What is fated to happen will happen. Who can avert it?'

When the younger princess was asked, she said she would do as her parents commanded. 'We all live our own karma,' she said. 'If my sacrifice can guard the well-being of the entire kingdom, then so be it. Why, most men are anyway worse than donkeys!'

The younger princess helped assuage everyone's pain. Even so, the king returned to the palace with a heavy heart.

At dawn the next day, the donkey gave birth to a foal. The kumbhar cleaned and bathed it and had him sent to the palace. At sundown, a wedding canopy of moist green bamboo sticks was made, the toran[29] was tied, and an elderly priest made the Rajkanwari go through the wedding rituals with the donkey. The Rani could not even bring herself to look at them circling the sacred fire. In full sight of the Raja, what a tragedy had befallen them. And he

---

29 Toran: A decorative door hanging made of wood, with carvings of birds such as parrots; it is hung at the entrance of the bride's home.

could do nothing. If the ruler of the kingdom had to bow down to such a twist of fate, what were ordinary folk to do?

Seeing such misfortune come upon the younger princess, the whole kingdom wept, sighed, shook their heads. She had stepped forward to accept suffering and had saved the kingdom. Everyone praised her bravery.

What is a wedding without pomp and ceremony! Wedding songs were sung, and the daughter was bid farewell. But where would the daughter go? No groom, no wedding procession, no marital home! The bride's friends escorted the girl and the baby donkey to the rangmahal and locked them in. Even if it was to a donkey, it was a wedding after all. There was no question of anyone eavesdropping. So the princess's companions put golden padlocks on the doors and left without further delay.

The Rajkanwari sat with her head bowed. She had accepted her fate of her own will, but on this night to be with a donkey in her rangmahal instead of a man! She couldn't even bring herself to look at the donkey. Since the creation of the earth, such a wedding night could not have been experienced by any woman…

Just then, she heard a human voice speak: 'Rajkanwari, why do you sit with your head bowed? Where is the shame in looking at your man? Do not worry. No one has a husband like yours on this earth. At least look at me!'

The voice made the Rajkanwari forget her worries and her grief. She unveiled her face and stood facing the donkey. Nodding his head, the animal said, 'Ah-ha! What beauty! Are the apcharas of Inderlok any match for this?'

Then, the donkey came by her side and, raising his head, said, 'Pull my ears and peel the hide off. You will get to see if what fate has in store for you is good or bad…'

The Rajkanwari took him at his word. She did as she was told and began to pull at the animal's ears unhesitatingly. And the donkey's hide actually began to peel off! No sooner had the skin come off entirely than an astonishingly handsome man with a face like the sun appeared in front of the princess! Such beauty, such luminescence – it could not belong to a man of this world. The Rajkanwari was astounded. Was this a dream? She blinked and looked again. If the sun and moon were to smile, how pleasing would they look? On the lips of the man played a smile as radiant!

'You still take this to be a dream?' he asked. 'It is indeed as if it were a dream. But you stepped forward for this marriage, so I will keep no secrets from you. I am the son of Inder, the king of Inderlok!'

Still holding the hide in her hands, the Rajkanwari heard the whole story from the mouth of Inder's son. She had not imagined this could be the reason behind all these fantastic events. Her joy knew no bounds.

In the end, he said: 'My life dwells in this donkey's skin. You must take care of it more than you care for my life. I will have to suffer the life of a donkey for twelve years. I will remove this skin at night, only for you. And during the day, I will go back into it. Hide it away in a trunk. If you don't make me wear it again before daybreak, my entire body will burst into flames. No one else can know this secret. Ask the Rajaji for the nine-storeyed palace in the gardens. Tomorrow onwards, that will be our home. We must ensure this secret reaches nobody's ears.'

And no woman before the Rajkanwari would have celebrated their wedding night the way she did! For years, the world had only heard of Lord Inder. But when his own son slept on the marriage bed, if that did not add nine hundred thousand stars to this story of love, then what could?

The Raja and Rani would not have refused even if the Rajkanwari had asked for the entire kingdom. She had saved the entire kingdom after all. Then what was a nine-storeyed palace in the gardens? If she wished, a hundred-storeyed palace would be made for her, and that too in gold!

So the very next day, the Rajkanwari and the donkey moved into their new home. All night they would play chaupad-pasa.[30] Not even for an instant would the princess sleep. To tell you the truth, the night itself seemed to pass by in an instant. The Rajkanwari would cook with her own hands. And then, both she and her husband would sit and eat together. Every day, she would prepare new delicacies.

---

30 Chaupad-pasa: An ancient Indian board game and a precursor of ludo.

Her friends and sisters-in-law sniggered when they saw the light from earthen lamps filled with cow ghee burn through the night in the palace. This, upon being married to a donkey! Had she married a man, she would have needed four suns at the four corners of her bed! Ram knows how she spends an entire day with a donkey. The Rajkanwari could barely be seen outside. She did not emerge from her palace even when her elder sister got married! Such arrogance after marrying a donkey! What if she had married a prince? She would have buried the very sky in the ground, wouldn't she? No wonder her fate had led her to this!

But the Rajkanwari was very happy with her life. She did not care for the world outside. In that newly built palace in the realm of mortals, she would listen to stories from the realm of gods. She would feel as though she lived in Inderlok herself. And days started to pass by in the blink of an eye!

One brilliant, full moon night, like an innocent child, she asked, 'Do these stars, the sun and the moon all shine down from Inderlok? Those living there surely play with the objects in the sky!'

'Not at all,' said the son of Lord Inder. 'We used to think that the sun and the moon shone from the world of mortals. In my world, these things never felt as beautiful. Neither did the moon shine this way, nor did the stars twinkle in this manner. Even the sun did not blaze thus. There were no clouds, no lightning. No flowers and trees.

This dust is not there either. For the fine sand of this world, I would give up Inderlok and heaven a hundred times over! I have not quite been able to fathom why mortals hanker after heaven, why they thirst for Inderlok ... I miss nothing at all from there!'

'Not even that apchara?' asked the Rajkanwari flirtatiously.

By now, however, the son had become adept in the art of love in the world of mortals. Shaking his head he said, 'That I won't tell you!'

Annoyed, the Rajkanwari said, 'Ni, ni, tell me the truth. I will not be angry at all.'

'But you are already angry!' said her husband.

Then, fondling her golden hair, he said, 'It doesn't matter whether I miss that apchara or not, but I certainly thank her. Had she not made love to me, how would I have got the chance to love you? I say this once again: there is nothing to do in Inderlok but make love. Even then, the beings there do not know the art of love that is found here. Where else can one find the sulking and caprice of this world? Lord Inder's curse has proved to be a boon for me.'

The Rajkanwari had been meaning to ask a question for some time. Tonight, she thought, the time was apt. 'After you live out the twelve years of the curse, won't you go back to Inderlok?'

'Why do you worry about such things?' replied the prince. 'I won't even think of going back there for thousands and thousands of births. Better a mortal donkey here than a god there. I have realized this from my time in this world, that death here is better than life there. The graveyards of this world are better than the realms of heaven. A thousand times would I choose a breath as a mortal over immortality there. The darkness here over the brightness there. Why, a speck of dust here is more valuable than pearls there! Rather a soldier here than a king there. Mortals have only one flaw: they desire heaven and Inderlok. They think the gods are better than men…'

Inder's son was new to this world. He had just arrived here. That's why he found everything very pleasant. He had not yet come across its failings, its malice. The inhabitants of the mortal realm have some big flaws: They cannot stand another's happiness. They want to get their hands on each other's secrets. And the worst of them all is that their greed knows no bounds.

And so it happened that the light in the Rajkanwari's palace began to hurt the eyes of onlookers. They began to think that under this light must surely lie darkness. And they began to fervently search for that darkness! If someone asks for help, sheds tears, and begs them, people go out of their way to help. But if someone manages just fine on their own, without even letting another know, this cannot be digested by people. More than helping a troubled soul, people want to hear of their troubles. The Raja and the Rani were a little annoyed by the Rajkanwari's silence. The elder sister was very annoyed because her sister had not been present during her wedding. She particularly enjoyed spreading lies about her sister. And people began to hatch schemes to uncover the darkness surrounded by the light.

A middle-aged spy-woman took on the task of unearthing the secret. That woman appeared as innocent as a lamb. She had large, guileless eyes, a soft smile, a sweet voice. Laughing or crying was child's play for her. Her lies were so good that they could beat even the truth. The listener could not help but believe her. Such people are the most cunning.

At midnight, she went and sat in the garden near the new palace. With just two hours left before daybreak, she began to cry loudly and would not stop. The new palace was awash with light. The husband and wife were engrossed in a game of chaupad-pasa. As he threw the dice, Inder's son said, 'Two years have passed in this fun and revelry. We could not even tell how quickly time flew. Don't be impatient. Ten years will also pass by in an instant. Living two lives in one birth is also a great pleasure.'

Then, folding the chaupad, he said, 'It is your ninth month. You should not sit for so long. Go and lie down on the bed.'

'What good will lying down do?' said the Rajkanwari. 'I won't get even a wink of sleep. There is more pleasure in revelling with you than in sleeping. I don't think there is any problem in sitting. And there is scarcely any pleasure for a woman that can match the pain of the womb. Why do you worry so?'

Just then, the princess heard the sound of someone crying. It would not stop. She opened the jharokha doors and listened carefully – it was a woman. She strained her eyes to see where the sound was coming from and saw that it was indeed a woman weeping with her head between her knees.

The Rajkanwari turned to her husband, 'Who sits and cries in our garden? What must have happened to the poor soul?'

He said that the only way to find out would be to ask her. 'Let me go and ask.'

'Of course,' said the princess. 'My heart writhes at the sound of the sobs.'

Lord Inder's son stepped out and consoled the woman. He asked her why she was crying. Upon hearing the reason, his own eyes turned moist. Without even asking the Rajkanwari, he brought the woman into their palace.

The unfortunate woman explained that she had come here from fifty miles away. It was her only son's death anniversary in seven days. Her husband had died when she was seven months pregnant. The son had worked here as a labourer when this palace was being built. It was his dreadful fate that, one day, he slipped and fell while at work. His head was smashed. His bones were broken. He could not even drink water. What else was to be done but shed tears? 'So I cry. I come here for seven days every

year, to feed the crows[31] my son's favourite foods. Last
year, I could not. I fell ill. But even death won't come to
this unfortunate woman. What use is a mother's life after
losing a son? But what to do, I cannot even commit the sin
of killing myself...'

As she said this, the woman began sobbing again. The
listeners' hearts melted. They comforted her and managed
to calm her down. Not seven days, she could stay at the
palace for twenty-seven days, they told her – it was her
home. The couple thought this to be a nice coincidence as
the date of their baby's birth was close. It would be evil to
even think of doubting this poor sonless mother!

That wretched woman would spend most of her
time on the roof of the house, feeding the crows her
son's favourite delicacies, but her eyes and ears were
everywhere. In a matter of just two days, she was able to
figure out the whole secret. She did not even have to ask
anyone, but she had found out everything. And she did not
let them learn anything about who she really was and what
deceit she had planned.

The Rajkanwari was now in her tenth month. She was
lost in her dreams, and her husband was lost in his. But
they were the same dreams! The dreams of a child born of
the union of the realms of mortals and gods. The light from
the sun would wish the child joy. The moonlight would play

---

31 A ritual where crows are fed, usually with the departed soul's
favourite foods.

with it. There would be thunder in the clouds and lightning in the skies. And the earth would burst forth with greenery!

And there, that spy-woman was engrossed in her own dreams. When she would give the Raja and Rani this excellent news, they would be so pleased with her that they would cover her in diamonds and pearls. They would give her the keys to the royal treasury. Whatever she was given would not be enough!

One day, she took permission to visit the grounds on which her son had been cremated. She wanted to pray for him. Once out, she surreptitiously went to the Rani instead. The spy was a woman after all – for how long could she keep a secret? After greeting the Rani with much ceremony, she said with visible delight, 'It is such good news that you will want to give me a prize even before I tell you what it is!'

And with great relish she relayed to the Rani the news that her daughter could not have found such a husband in this world – the donkey she had married was, in fact, the son of Lord Inder! What could be a greater fortune than this? If the Rani gifted her seven villages upon the birth of her grandson, even that would not suffice! And in ten years, the curse would also be broken. Besides, Lord Inder's son was so content with the life he was living in the gardens, the nine-storeyed palace, and with the Rajkanwari, that he considered Inderlok to be as worthless as dust.

The Rani said that the woman had pulled off a miracle! Indeed, even if she gifted her seventeen villages it would be less! But if she could somehow get hold of the donkey's skin, it would be perfect. The king's son-in-law roams about all day in the skin of a donkey – how bad that looks! If the skin was gone, he wouldn't be able to assume the form of a donkey again. Such is the greatness of the gods. Us mortals cannot understand such things. He will not go against his father's curse of his own volition. This is the foremost virtue of the gods. But if the woman could get the skin, then he would come to no harm nor be in any danger.

The woman had to agree to the Rani's proposal. Delighted, the Rani filled her lap with gold mohurs and told her that if she was able to do the task assigned to her without any hitches, she would get the Raja to gift her seventeen villages. The queen would not forget what the woman had done for her for several lifetimes.

When she returned to the Rajkanwari's palace, the woman's clothes were full of dirt. She had, after all, gone to lie on the ground where her son had been cremated. She climbed up the stairs, sobbing. It was not easy to be where one's child had been burnt until nothing but ashes were left. It had been ten years since her heart had been set ablaze along with her son, and it was still burning. She cursed death which had taken her son away but kept her alive!

But today, a mother was about to give birth to a child. To cry for the dead would not be apt on such an auspicious occasion. The Rajkanwari explained this to the woman, and she immediately understood. Smiling, she left from there.

Stroking the Rajkanwari's hair lovingly, Lord Inder's son said, 'Today, a golden sun shall rise in the realm of mortals, and the earth will burst forth in bounteous bloom!'

The Rajkanwari lay on her bed, weaving dreams: a golden sun in her womb; a golden moon in her womb … Just then, she began to feel spasms in her stomach.

Quickly, she sat up. Looking at her husband, she said, 'Now you should leave. Men are not made for such things. Send the woman inside. I am trembling. Please don't come unless I call you.' As Lord Inder's son began to leave, she added, 'It is well past midnight. I am not well today. Don't forget to wear your hide.'

'Is that something to forget?' her husband replied.

He came outside and looked, but the woman was nowhere to be found. He called out two or three times, but she did not come. When he heard the Rajkanwari groaning, he started to panic. He looked on the roof, ran around the gardens, and looked again inside the palace, but she was nowhere to be seen.

But how could she be found if she wasn't there! She had taken the donkey's skin with her, hidden it under her arm, and headed straight for the Rani's. The queen was overjoyed to see it. She rewarded her with a tray full of pearls and said, 'Now you go ahead and light a fire immediately. Ensure that not even a single hair of this remains!'

Why hold back once the Rani had given an order? The woman lit a fire at once. And the Rani, without a second thought, set the donkey skin on fire with her own hands. And the crackling flames engulfed it.

The light that precedes dawn had begun to burst forth. And from the nine-storeyed palace, emerged a blood-curdling scream. 'Haaye ... haaye ... I'm burning ... I'm burning!'

The body of Lord Inder's son was engulfed by flames. Mad with panic, he kept searching for the skin. But only if it were there would it be found! Burning, he rushed towards the Rajkanwari's chamber, but hearing the cries of a newborn there, he turned around at once and went to the roof, still in flames.

A red sun emerged from the earth's womb. Perfectly round and pleasing. Exuding light. Exuding warmth. And facing the sun on the roof of the nine-storeyed palace, he was swallowed up by the fire. However, he did not utter a single sound. Such screams are not befitting accompaniment to the cries of a newborn. The golden sun began to rise in the sky. And in the palace, a new life was born.

Lajwanti

SHYNESS IS GOOD WHERE NEEDED. Itches disappear when treated. A reign, as one should reign. And true beauty need not feign. And so, at a certain crossroads in time, nestled in the lap of nature, was a village. One moulded in the same mould as any other village. The same old and new thatched huts. The same plastered pillars. And the same reluctantly peeling paint. In every home, the same earthen stoves. The same smoke, the same colour of sky. The same knotted turbans on men's heads. In their hands, the same sequinned sticks. And on women, the same motley skirts, the same madder-stained bangles. The same veils drawn low to cover their faces. The same bleating of goats and the same dust kicked up by hooves. The same simmering anxieties. The same quotidian worries. The same millstones, the same urns for grain, and the same pegs. The same sheds, the same cud-chewing animals, and the same piles of dung.

The same large and small wells, and the same water. Those same thakars and the same thakaranis...

As would befit such a village, it was situated at a considerably high altitude, atop a hill. A mile and a half or so away was a lake. It would hold water only during the monsoons. Once the lake dried up, the village folk would begin using the wells. And then, the same whirring of the wheel. The same ropes and the same buckets. The same women – the paniharis – filling their pots with water, and the same pots. Hearing the sound of their anklets, the very path which they trod would swell! The wind would dart around them as they sang. The rays of the sun would flirt with their beauty and the bloom of their youth. The stout and woody plants in the bushes would sway and dance.

As soon as the paniharis would leave the village, it was as if they had sprouted wings. Wings in their throats. Wings in their hearts.

There was one panihari, though, who was the very personification of shyness! Even in the midst of her friends, and beyond the borders of the village where there was not a soul, she would keep her face veiled. Neither would she giggle and chuckle, nor would she shoot back sharp retorts. She would respond only after she had been spoken to twenty times. Pink wrists and a yellow pomcha – it appeared as if two colours from a rainbow had fled from the skies and taken shelter in her being. The copper pots, resting on the colourful idhani atop her head, glimmered, as if the coppersmiths had found pieces of the moon to make the pots out of! The group of friends had tried all manner of teasing and pranks and given up. Had the pair of pots on her head ever slipped that she would? She would just smile behind her veil.

Once, one of the women made a cutting remark: 'If a veil is the measure of a woman's chastity, then we must all be shameless whores!'

Even the sting of that taunt did not succeed in making her open her mouth. She turned to face her friend and then turned away again. Then, another friend who was walking beside her said, 'My dear, don't ever unveil your face. If this drunken sun leaps out of the sky to catch a glimpse of it, the entire world will be left in darkness for eternity!'

'What if a male bird pecked your cheeks?' said another.

Yet another said, 'She seems more worried around women than around men! Something very dreadful must have happened during her childhood...'

A mischievous friend, who was walking with her shoulder to shoulder, said, 'Can't remember who, but someone was saying that she emerged from her mother's womb with her veil drawn all the way down to her navel!'

'You can keep mocking her as much as you like,' said a middle-aged panihari, 'but it won't pierce her thick skin. I am going to grab hold of her hands. Will one of you be bold enough to lift her veil so that the thirst of our eyes can be quelled?'

'What if there is a mole on one of her eyes?'

'What if there are pockmarks on her face?'

'What if she has a cleft lip?'

'What if she is snub-nosed, like a frog?'

'What if the teeth…'

But when her companions saw her face, they bit their tongues and their faces fell. They had never seen such beauty, never heard of such beauty! May the poor soul be blessed with good fortune a thousand times over, for she had saved their honour; otherwise, their husbands would have turned their backs on them! Indeed, such beauty should be hidden away behind seven locked doors!

Then, when the friend who had pulled off her veil pulled it down again, it was as if clouds had covered the moon. 'If this moon shines so by day,' she said with a sigh, 'Ram knows how it must glow by night?'

'More than Ram, it is her husband who would know…'

The women stood still, unable to move. The middle-aged one who had caught hold of Lajwanti's – the shy one's – hands said hesitantly, 'It is only if one has such beauty that the nectar-crazed bee will not leave to go to another flower even in its dreams.'

'I will never understand this race of men even if I die trying!' said one. 'They find opium sweeter than sugar…'

'Maybe, but we did not think of one thing at all,' chipped in another. 'If all the bees begin hovering over a single flower, what fate would befall the others…?'

One of the companions grinned and said, 'The fate of that flower would be no better either!'

Just then, the paniharis saw a man coming towards them. He was lost in his own world. In each of his hands was a spotless white dove. He kept speaking to them as he walked. As he chatted with the doves, he looked up, and his gaze fell upon the women. It was as if he had spotted a clump of shrubs. He cared no more for them than he would for a pile of stones. He changed course and passed at quite a distance from them. Even Lajwanti stared after him through her translucent veil. White turban, white angrakha, white dhoti. Jet-black beard. She could not quite see his face, but he was well built. The man kept walking. Let alone actually turning around and looking at the women, even the thought must not have crossed his mind!

All the women stood mute, staring at each other. After some time, the middle-aged woman broke the silence: 'We will know that you are truly beautiful if you can spin this bee around!'

The woman who had pulled the veil off Lajwanti's face said, 'This man is blind despite his eyes. Even the eyes of his heart are shut tight. Who knows what kind of a man he is!'

Another said, as she tossed back her head, 'I think there must be something missing in his manhood!'

Another wondered aloud, 'And when did you get the chance to check that?'

Suppressing a smirk, the former replied, 'In my dreams!'

A few others surrounding her said at once, 'Even then, lucky you! Your husband is quite powerful...!'

This time around, Lajwanti's lips parted and a voice many times sweeter than that of a koel emerged: 'Don't you feel ashamed to indulge in such gossip behind the backs of your menfolk?'

A retort escaped impulsively from one of her companions: 'It will be our turn to feel ashamed if you were to let go of shame for just one moment!'

It was futile arguing with her companions, she thought. As it was, she spoke little, but she pretty much swore to be silent after that day. At the time of her wedding, she had truly felt as if the earth and the sky had come to be united forever. How could those unbreakable vows witnessed by the flames of Agan Devta, the god of fire, be forgotten?

Meanwhile, they continued to see the man on the path, returning with two white doves in his hands and, every time, he continued to change his path in the same way.

Lajwanti kept peering at his white form and his white doves from behind her veil. One day, one of the women said, 'If this fool is ever willing to take marriage vows, I will renounce the body of a woman and become a dove! Then he will chase me and catch me with his own hands!'

Pat came the response from another woman, 'If this were to reach his ears, he might give up catching doves altogether!'

Ram knows what struck one of the women, for she turned to Lajwanti and asked, 'So, do you desire to become a dove or not...?'

To which Lajwanti replied softly, 'Why would I desire to leave the pleasures of this human existence and want to become a dove and peck at stones? In this land, how many are more handsome and intelligent than my man?'

'Another's pewter glistens brighter than one's own gold! Who can rein in this wayward heart?' said the middle-aged panihari, explaining a profound fact of life.

After this, the companions concurred with one another that this shy one did not have a heart or soul at all. She may speak and move and even breathe, but she was a statue made of stone!

After this, every day the same taunts, the same teasing. As they walked. As they lowered the rope into the water. As they strained the water. With the pots empty or full, the same chitter-chatter. As if all the other gossip in the world had dried up....

Finally, one day, Lajwanti had had enough and opened her hitherto pursed lips: 'It would be most unbecoming of me to stay with you lot for even a second more!'

Quite pleased to hear this, her companions said, 'Do as you wish, do as becomes you. But being a woman, and one of matchless beauty and youth, will you be able to guard your honour in this soulless wilderness? We are so many of us in a group and we still tremble within!'

'One who doesn't have deceit in her heart has no need to fear the light,' Lajwanti replied fearlessly. 'My man trusts me fully. My in-laws don't have any doubts about me. Then

what is this fear you speak of? Fear of what? Why, this is
the first time I'm hearing this word *fear*!'

From that day and that very instant, all her friends
abandoned her. And yet, she felt no remorse. Nor did she
arrange for another companion. With a pair of pots on her
head, she would walk alone to the well without fear, and
walk back alone with the pots full of water. When the sun
god keeps vigil from above, then what is there for humans
to fear? If she met the man with the doves, so be it. He
would anyway change course and keep his distance. He
would never so much as raise his eyes to look at her. If he
bore her no ill will, why would it bother her even if he were
to run around with two naked swords instead of two doves?
But the other men of the village had filth in their minds.
Despite being married, they were so depraved it was as if
they had never seen the face of a woman. They'd not even
refuse the roasted meat of a beautiful woman!

There was talk of that deranged man in every home
in the village. Such a madman could not be born even
from the womb of one's foe! Ram knows what pleasure he
found in his solitary life. He had frittered away the whole
of his inheritance just like that. But yes, the fool must
surely have been the head of the clan of white doves in
his past life. He had sworn to collect a thousand of them.
Never had he listened to anyone in the past, nor would he
do so in the future. He coveted nothing but doves – not
cattle, not farms and fields, not wealth and riches. He

took birth in the human form and spent his life in the company of doves.

As a rule, he would catch two new doves every single day. He would not even drink water before he had done so. Ram knows where he found the doves, but once he lay his hands on them, it was as if he had seized the very sun and moon! And once in his yard, those innocent birds would not want to leave; it was as if they had returned home to their parents. And why just doves? Even hawks, eagles, vultures, crows and snakes seemed to know him the moment they saw him. But he never apportioned his love to any other creature but the doves. He would feed them grains with his own hands. He would make them drink water from his own hands. He would pet each of them with love.

Ram knows what came over that shy one one day, but she asked her young nanad[32] to accompany her to the well. After listening to everything carefully, the nanad offered an immediate explanation. 'There is no need at all to be frightened of that crazy dove-man. He would not harm anyone, not even in his dreams. If even innocent doves trust him, then what are you afraid of?' Without arguing any further, Lajwanti picked up her shining pots and left quietly. If one has truth in one's heart, what are even twenty such men?

And then, every second or third day, either close to where the well was or on the way up there, her path would

---

32 Nanad: Husband's sister.

cross that man's. When she would not quite be able to see him through her veil, she would turn around, lift her veil and gaze at him. But the man, fully engrossed in his own world, would never look at her. She would scowl and then go her way, muttering, 'Wretched fool! Burdened his mother's womb for nine months in vain. A man, and he changes his path like this? Does he have anything to fear like women do? A complete crackpot!'

One day, after having filled water in her pots, she was pulling the rope out of the well when she saw the man on his usual route. When the lake was dry, there was a clear path by its edge. Were it another man, he would surely have come to ask for water pretending he was thirsty. But this one saw nothing apart from doves! As he walked past the well, she made a 'tch' noise and beckoned to him. He turned around and looked at her. Then she gestured that she needed help with raising the pots on her head. But he would not move at all. From where he stood, he said like a guileless child, 'But I'm holding a dove in each hand. They will fly away if I let go of them.' Saying that, he started to walk away.

And Lajwanti stood there, like a stone statue, glued to the ground! And when, in a few moments, she came to, she felt as if her youth and beauty were being scorched in some invisible fire ... Surely, this was worse than death! As she forced herself to hoist the pots on her head, she felt as if she was hoisting two boulders on her head.

The next day, Ram knows what came over her, but she searched out two large pots from the store and left to fill water, an hour or so before her usual time. As fate would have it, she had just pulled the rope up from the well when she spotted the man heading in her direction. He was about a couple of fields away. He must surely be on his way to look for doves. As he came closer, she unconsciously started to raise her veil, as if that hand and that body weren't hers but belonged to some other woman.

As soon as he was close to her, she said to him, 'This time, both your hands are free. What excuse will you make now?'

He jumped on hearing her nectar-like voice, and as he regarded her, he muttered, 'Now, there are only twenty-one doves left!'

'Yes,' Lajwanti said, smiling. 'You do what you must, but at least help me with the pots first?'

'Who helped you yesterday?'

'You refused yesterday. So I got annoyed and helped myself!'

'Where is that annoyance today?'

'But today, even if I get annoyed, I won't be able to help myself.'

'Why, what is new today?'

'Can't you see? These pots are so much larger than the ones I brought yesterday.'

'Who did you think you could trust to help you with such large pots?'

'I had faith in some decent person, one who doesn't have doves in his hands right now.'

The man nodded and said, 'If you have such faith in me, I will most certainly help.'

And that half-mad man lifted the pots and hurried away. He spoke no further, nor did he turn around and look at her.

It would have been better to have stayed behind her veil! Since the creation of this universe, no beautiful woman must have suffered such a slight! The way back seemed very long that day!

The next day, she somehow convinced her nanad, and together they left for the dove-man's yard. With her veil pulled all the way down to her chest as usual, she opened the gate to the yard and entered. What a strange and wondrous sight! Countless white doves waddled and pecked around the man. Their fair wings fluttered to the rhythm of their throaty cooing. They would lovingly leap on and off the man's head and shoulders. Even as both the women went quite close to them, the doves did not seem to mind. Neither did they flinch, nor did they fly away. And that man's eyes could see only the dance of those doves! He was alive to nothing else.

The nanad raised her voice and said, 'My bhojai[33] has come to watch the carnival of doves!'

---

33 Bhojai: Brother's wife.

Even as he fed the doves grain, the man said, 'You should have come earlier. Is there anything in this world that surpassed doves? But you cannot see clearly through the veil. What shyness from doves?'

Even then, that shy one did not move her veil. Her nanad said, 'My bhojai has sworn never to lift her veil. Even I have not seen her face!'

They kept looking at what went on in the yard for a while, and then returned as they had come. And the man, absorbed in his own world, kept feeding the doves grain.

When Lajwanti returned home, that scene fluttered in front of her eyes, cooing sweetly. And at night, at the time of making love, again the same cooing! Those white doves began fluttering around the chamber such that they would not stop. As she stroked her husband's face, she said, 'If you keep a beard, it will really suit you.' And as she suggested this, she closed her eyes, and while she embraced her husband, it was the dove-man she held close – and the thought of his beard brushing against her skin made her take leave of her senses. Who cared, then, for how long the night lasted, and what was left to dream about!

Halfway to the bank of the lake, the next day, she saw the man from her dreams approaching her. They both walked towards each other. Empty pots on Lajwanti's head and a dove each in the man's hands. But how was it that, today, the man did not change track and scurry away? A chill ran down Lajwanti's spine. There is evil in this rascal's heart! Not a soul to be seen in this vast expanse. No one to even hear her screams. What should she do now?

But nothing happened to cause her to do anything. Even as he was twenty steps away, he began muttering: 'Only two more to go! Tomorrow, my oath will be fulfilled. In the midst of this happiness, I forgot to change track. But there is no need to be scared of me at all. Have I spent so many years in the company of innocent doves without reason?'

As soon as the dread in her heart receded, she said from behind her veil, 'The company of doves has not made you start pecking among stones, has it?'

Crestfallen, that man replied, 'I did try, but I failed. My stomach bloated like a dhol! I barely managed to stay alive.'

Lajwanti was more at ease now. Smiling a soft smile, she said, 'The male dove does not leave the female for even a second, and yet you have still not gotten married? You scurry away at the very sight of women!'

Beaming a milk-white smile from behind his jet-black beard, the man said, 'Once my oath is fulfilled tomorrow, I shall give it a thought. But is it in my hands to find the dove of my dreams? It is for that dove from my dreams that I have lived this oath. Twenty years ago, I saw this strange dream. I have not let that vision leave me ever since…'

The lone panihari giggled and said, 'Indeed, fools needn't have horns! Will you squander away your life on the back of a dream?'

With the fervour of an invisible conviction, the man excitedly said, 'With the blessings of a thousand doves, will I not find the *one* dove of my dreams?'

Lajwanti did not venture a response to that question. As she left, she said, 'Only you know and your dream knows! I am getting late. I must fill the pots now.'

Then she did not even turn back to look at him. But the questioning look on the man's face kept dancing around her like the colourful tassels plaited into the edge of her veil.

The next day, their paths crossed again at the same spot. He held out the two doves in his hands towards Lajwanti and said spiritedly, 'Today, my oath is fulfilled! Now these white doves will certainly honour my dream.'

Half-crazed, he had just looked up at the empty pots on her head, when Lajwanti, flicked back her head, unveiling herself, and said in a sharp voice, 'You seem to have also learnt the treacherous ways of cats while in the company of doves! I can plainly see the evil in your eyes! You want to take advantage of me in this wilderness?'

'But I have doves in both my hands!'

'So what? Can't the doves be put in the large pot and its mouth be covered with the small one?'

As soon as she said this, the man clapped his hands. 'The very same dream! I remember it like I saw it last night! The dove of my dreams! You have appeared in front of me after twenty-two years. That must have been the night of your birth. Now, if these doves fly away, so be it. The sky stretches out before us…'

As these much-craved-for words fell on the woman's ears, she blushed with shyness.

'The dove of my dreams!' the man said again. 'I cannot bear to stay away from you for even a moment more!'

This time, experiencing the touch of his beard on her skin for real, Lajwanti lost all control of her senses. 'How did you bear to stay apart for so many years?' she asked.

'But my dream came true only today!' replied the dove-man. 'Then what parting...'

As he let go of the white doves, they fluttered and flew away, never looking back. Only their wings or the infinite sky know how far they went...

Repayment

THERE WAS ONCE A BAAMAN more handsome than even Kisan Bhagvaan,[34] but by nature, he was the very incarnation of Bhisam Pitamah.[35] He thought of women younger to him as his sisters, and those older, as his mothers. There was no greater sin in his eyes than debauchery. He would rather be condemned to death than sleep with a woman to whom he was not married.

But Kisan Bhagvaan's playful heart did not like this Baaman's righteousness. Which was why it was the poor man's fate to cross paths with an extraordinary woman. The woman's beauty was one in a thousand, and so were her ways. Her husband imparted many a good teaching and moral to her, but she would not mend her bad ways.

---

34 Kisan Bhagvaan: The Hindu god Krishna.

35 Bhisam Pitamah: Bhishma. A character from the Mahabharata who swore to lifelong celibacy.

One day, that Baaman saw her with the village thakar doing that which should not be seen. And thereon, he no longer felt at peace in the mirage of domestic life. So wounded was his heart that he resolved to never inflict this hurt upon another with his actions. There is no greater sting than the stab of this dagger! Neither did he stop his wife, nor did he confront the village thakar. He renounced the world then and there, in broad daylight, like Raja Bharthari.[36] He left his family and his people, and sought refuge with a guru.

The guru's ashram was near the city. After some days, when the guru came to know his pupil, he said with pride, 'Beta, I may be known as your guru because of my age, but in your conduct and qualities, you are more than a guru to me.' Hearing his guru's words, the pupil lowered his eyes bashfully. Instead of responding to him in words, he smeared his forehead with dust from his guru's feet.

The pupil would go to the city to collect alms every day, and his beauty drove the women crazy. Thus far, they had only heard of Kisan Bhagvaan's dusky complexion, but seeing the colour of the pupil's skin, they finally discovered how enchanting it could truly be. Fair skin seemed dull in comparison. On his head was a crown of

---

36 Raja Bharthari: Also known as Bhartrihari. The hero of many myths and folk tales in North India. He was reputedly the ruler of Ujjain, and renounced his throne for his younger brother Vikramaditya.

curly, jet-black hair. His teeth were like pearls. And in
his eyes, a heaving ocean of wine! Women would fall over
each other to give him alms. They tried to seduce him in
myriad ways, but there was not a flutter in the Baaman's
heart. One would not find a man so completely blind even
if they were to search the entire world! Faced with the
Baaman's innocence, the women themselves began to feel
ashamed. There was pleasure in seducing someone who
could be seduced, but to flirt with a stone would only cause
embarrassment!

Upon seeing the Baaman's beauty, the daughter-in-
law of one wealthy seth lost hold of her senses. She would
not allow him to go to any other home to collect alms. She
prepared for him a variety of delicacies and implored him
no end to eat at her house, but there was no way he would
agree. He would go back to the ashram, serve his guru and
only then consume a morsel.

When the beendni looked at the pupil's face, her eyes
wild with yearning, he would close his own and begin to
chant the name of Ram. He would hear her sighs but not
understand them. Strange are the ways of women! All the
enchantresses of the city were crazy about the Baaman,
and yet his own wife desired another! Indeed, the hearts of
women do not know what it is to be content. The Baaman's
heart, however, was in his control. The surest way to avoid
indulging in bad deeds is to not do to others that which
pains one's own heart. To treat the other as one would
oneself is the only thing that can keep the wheel of this

world turning. When his own wife's betrayal could have singed his heart so deeply, how could he inflict the same suffering on another? Where was the need to think any further about this? Surely it was quite plain and did not need to be said out loud. But humans do not comprehend things despite being told.

One day, the beendni began chatting with him about this and that, and then said, 'I am a householder and I give you alms every day. But you are a monk, and yet you cannot grant me a small wish. What kind of a monk are you?'

The Baaman replied with a clear heart, 'We monks possess nothing that could make us feel the empty pride of giving. We only have knowledge and devotion to offer, if you will take them. We do not even know the name of any third offering.'

The beendni smiled at the Baaman while inflicting on him a stinging taunt, 'Do you know anything at all!'

The Baaman accepted his ignorance and said, 'I know nothing. Which is why I have sought refuge in my guru.'

The beendni bit her lip and said, 'Then ask your guru whose maya is greater – God's or woman's. Ask him, too, if a monk can know God when he does not know a woman.'

The pupil replied softly, 'The day these doubts arise in me, I will ask him unhesitatingly. There is no riddle in this universe that my guru does not know the answer to.'

The beendni would be immensely frustrated by this obstinate ox, and yet, every day, she continued to give him alms with great eagerness. She spent every moment in anticipation of his arrival, longing to catch a glimpse of him.

One day, during the month of Saavan, it started to rain and, up until mealtime, the pupil did not come to ask for alms. Usually, the beendni would not eat until she had given alms to the pupil. Later that day, the Baaman arrived, drenched in the rain. The beads of water on his body seemed like invaluable pearls to the beendni. How could she explain it to this fool? 'See how beautifully falls the rain!' she said. 'There is nothing more enthralling in this world than the rain.'

The monk agreed. 'This is quite true, yes,' he said. 'What can match this rain that adorns the dry and unsightly earth in green? It is God's mercy that pours forth as rain. If one has true light in one's eyes, then in its every drop they can see the beauty of God!'

How could one illuminate the eyes of this blind man, the beendni wondered. In that very instant, numerous koels cooed at the same time. The beendni felt her heart quiver. Not only was this pupil completely unseeing, but he was also an utter fool! 'Do you hear the sweet calls of the koels or not?' she asked.

'Why would I not?' the pupil replied merrily. 'If I do not hear these sweet incantations of God in this birth of mine, when will I? It is as if there is nectar in every one of the koels' calls!'

The beendni felt an anger so fierce that she wanted to chop the Baaman's head off with an axe! Even a stone does not remain dry in this rain. And yet this fool was as dry as dry could be! What further hints could a woman give a man?

The Baaman, after having received alms from the beendni, was about to step off the threshold of her house, when she called out to him. 'If a lion dying of hunger asked you for your body, would you give it to him?' she asked.

'What could be a more meaningful use of a human body than that?' said the Baaman. 'If an animal's hunger can be sated by consuming mine, how can I refuse it?'

Here, thought the beendni, she could trap the pupil in his own words. She gathered her courage and said, 'If I asked you for your body to sate my hunger, you would not refuse, would you?'

'Humans are forbidden from eating the meat of their fellow humans!' cried the pupil. 'It is a sin to even hear such things!'

The beendni tried yet again to make herself clear. 'If my hunger is sated without killing you, what then?'

The pupil who had plunged head first into matters of spirituality and the soul could not quite comprehend this. Hesitant, he replied, 'Whose hunger can I help sate, when my own is sated by the generosity of the people of this city?'

Hearing the pupil's response, the beendni felt as if a hundred snakes had begun to sting her body all at once. She smiled venomously as she said, 'Your guru and you possess knowledge of only the soul. To gain knowledge of this body, you will have to accept one of us householders as a guru. Neither you nor your guru realizes that, for a woman, there is a hunger far greater than the hunger of the belly! Listen to what I say – make me your guru to gain knowledge of the body!'

The pupil turned around and left for his ashram without offering a reply. This monk had turned out to be worse than an animal, thought the beendni. He was certainly different from all other monks. The others grasped such things even without the hints!

The next day, when the pupil arrived at the beendni's asking for alms, she kept staring at his eyes. Surprised, the pupil asked, 'What is it that you see in my eyes that you bore yours into mine in this manner? These eyes are for regarding others; there is nothing worth seeing in them.'

The beendni sighed deeply and said, 'How beautiful are your eyes! Once my glance falls upon them, my heart does not want to see even God.'

The pupil asked in an anguished voice, 'So these worthless eyes of mine are a hurdle in seeing God?'

Without giving the pupil's words careful thought, the beendni said yes, and then repeated, 'How beautiful are your eyes! Poor God! How can he even compete with these goblets of intoxication?'

Without saying or hearing anything further, the pupil left the beendni's house. She kept gazing after him. It seemed to her as if the Baaman's feet were absorbed in some thought. Struck by a quandary of some sort, they were contemplating something. And so staring, her eyes got entangled in thoughts of his feet.

The following day, the beendni was sweeping the courtyard when she heard the sound of a stick against the door. She turned around to see who it was. It was the same monk who came every day for alms, standing there with a stick in his hand, blood oozing from the pits of his eyes!

The beendni's head began to spin, darkness descended upon her eyes. Was this some horrid dream? She rubbed her eyes and looked towards the door again. The exact same spectacle greeted her. She moved, her legs unsteady, towards the monk. Holding the stick, she said in a choked voice, 'So this is what you finally made of this black-tongued woman's words? For the wrong done in which past life have you punished me?'

The pupil tried to smile and said, 'What use are eyes that cast a shadow on God!'

Then, unfurling the fist of his other hand and holding it out before the beendni, he said, 'What offering can I presume to give to my sister? But if she is keen on my eyes, these silly orbs are not more important than her. I have washed them with water and have taken great care to bring them for you. Take them.'

Lowering her head at her brother's feet, the beendni said, 'My eyes are open now. I was completely blind – until today. But to be deaf and blind like my brother is a rare thing in this world. Your eyes have never seen what is not worth seeing. Your ears have never heard what is not worth hearing.'

The pupil let go of his stick and caressed his sister's head. He said, 'If gouging my eyes out has made the light glimmer in yours, then this birth of mine has not been wasted!'

Jaraav Masi's Tales

I KNEW THAT AS LONG as Jaraav Masi[37] spun the charkha, she would not stop telling stories. Left alone, she would sing songs to herself. I came by, so she began to share a tale with me. If I had said anything, she would surely have given me an earful. So let I her go on. I felt as if, just like the charkha Masi was spinning, a charkha of stories too was going round and round in her head. She began:

'This is a really old story. In a certain village lived a young man. He would never let go of a chance to ridicule the gods and mock the deities. The villagers were peeved with him, but they would refrain from telling him off out of respect for his father who was known for his devoutness. Alas, it must have been the deeds of his past life that caused such a worthless and thoughtless son to be born to him.

---

37 Masi: Aunt. More precisely, the mother's sister.

'One time, the young man had to visit a distant land with the hundi of a certain seth. On his way back, he came across the ashram of a sage under a banyan tree. Partly because he was thirsty and partly because he was in the habit of jesting with monks and ascetics, he turned towards the ashram.

'But he couldn't see any sage there, nor any pupils. Dejected, he was about to turn around when he noticed, in a corner, something resembling a large idol made of clay. He went closer and inspected it. Now it looked more like a termite mound. Once he started to brush the dust off the figure with his hands, it seemed like there was a man behind it! He was extremely astonished. He continued to wipe the dust and grime off the figure, and found underneath a sage who sat cross-legged in meditation, like a statue made of stone, holding his breath, but with a beating heart. The young man began to press the legs of the sage.

'Presently, the sage opened his eyes and looked around. Then, in an irritated voice, he said, "Who interrupted me while I was meditating, and ruined my penance of eight years? There was just one more year to go for me to attain salvation…"

'"Lord," said the young man, "I have made the blunder. Punish me as you will."

'Because the man owned up to his mistake, the sage calmed down. Softening, he said, "Perhaps it is the will of God. No use blaming you."

'The darkness in the young man's mind began to clear slowly. How could he disbelieve something he had witnessed with his own eyes? It takes a very, very long time indeed for such a thick layer of dust and grime to accumulate. This sage was surely the very manifestation of God. To believe in the unseen without proof is inappropriate. And for so many years, he had never seen any such evidence. But what power had kept the sage safe from even a scratch? Could a mere mortal accomplish such a wonder with the force of devotion? Had the young man wasted so many years, living out the life of a dog? Let alone eight years, if he could manage to meditate in this way for even eight days, this birth of his would be meaningful. But caught in the web of domestic life, he could not even dream of this emancipation. A whirling mass of thoughts began to swirl in his head. He had interrupted a penance so severe, and yet the sage had felt no anger. This is devotion, and such is a sage! Praise be to such miracles!

'After this, he bowed and touched the sage's feet with his head a hundred and eight times, and then confessed that he did not believe in God. "Lord, for so many years, I have not missed a single chance to poke fun at gods and deities and religion. But just the sight of you has lit up the darkness in my heart. I do not understand how years of murk has vanished in the mere blink of an eye."

'The sage replied affectionately, "Beta, you see with your own eyes how, every day, the darkness that hangs around all night vanishes as soon the first rays of the sun touch it! So what's there to wonder in this? The touch of light can destroy the darkness of ages."

'The man prayed with folded hands. "But Baapji,[38] does darkness too not have the same power? Such that, as soon as it appears, the light goes into hiding? It takes the same time…"

'The sage smiled and said, "I know what you mean, beta. But the light of devotion is something else. Even if waves of darkness come crashing down, they cannot diminish this light in any way. Instead, the darkness itself turns into light and begins to shine."

'Then the sage gave the young man many new pieces of knowledge and said, "Beta, if just the sight of me has made an avowed atheist like you a devotee of God, this is better than even my own salvation. I'm certain now that, through you, God has sent me a blessing greater than salvation itself. This is a very big thing!"

'The young man prostrated at the sage's feet and said, "Lord, your salvation would have meant deliverance only for you. In this world live countless sinners like me. You must deliver all of them. Today, I have realized how misguided the people of my world are. And I will not forget the knowledge I have gathered today for as long as I live. This surrender is not momentary. I will wander the mountains and set myself free. But first, I worry no less for the ignorant and their salvation. Let me get them to do

38   Baapji: A respectful term to address elders, superiors.

your darsan,[39] so that they see for themselves what devotion truly is. I can see plainly that you have been sent to this world for its deliverance. Even in my village, many foolish people are entangled in a web of false religiosity. I have no faith in that illusory devotion. You must rescue them. I am also convinced that this was why God sent me to interrupt your penance in this manner. And I'm not so selfish as to savour this pleasure alone. You must give my godforsaken village the opportunity to see you. There are many who are caught up in rituals and appearances, but none possesses real faith. Today, I take pride even in my lack of belief; at least I believed nothing without first seeing it. It was better to have been an atheist until I saw you."

"'What you say is absolutely true, beta," said the sage. "God never delivers anyone directly; it is the guru who shows the way. Never has knowledge dawned on anyone without a guru. My own devotion is my guru's blessing. But beta, why do you push me back into this mayajaal, into the illusions of this material world? I have bestowed upon you the knowledge I possess, and now it's best that I go back to my prayer and penance—"

'The young man broke in, "Baapji, this would be pure selfishness. You must deliver the entire world from this mayajaal, and only then think about your own salvation.

---

39 Darsan: Darshan. Literally, sight or vision. The act of visiting and beholding a god / an idol / a holy person in order to seek their blessings.

Without a true guru, what will happen to this tumultuous world? The mere thought makes every particle of my being tremble. It is the knowledge that you have bestowed upon me that makes me think this way. But lord, if you also forget about this godforsaken world, what horrible fate will befall it?"

'The guru consoled him, "Beta, don't worry so much unnecessarily. Your wish will be fulfilled. If it is God's will, then how can I defy it? I will obey his orders, of course."

'The sage had not ventured outside his ashram for as long as he could remember. Yes, nothing about the spirit, devotion and God was hidden from him. But he knew nothing about the inhabitants of the material world. He thought worldly beings were also like him. When he saw the man wearing clothes, along with surprise he felt a measure of pleasure too. Truly, clothes do not look bad on humans. There must be something more in humans than in animals and birds after all. He himself was a digambar, like the animals and birds – the sky above his only attire. That must have been the reason why God had smeared dust on him once he had reached a state of trance.

'As they set off for the village, he asked the man, "Do the people of your village wear clothes like you? Or do they wander stark naked like other creatures?"

'"Lord, among us householders, even newborns do not stay unclothed," replied the man. "Even they wear a loincloth."

"'Would it then be appropriate for me to go in this state?" asked the sage. "What was it you called that piece of cloth that you drape your head with? A turban, yes, a turban. So if you give me a few yards, then even I can tie it around my waist. Otherwise, people will get annoyed."

"'Us householders corrupt everything we see," said the man in response. "So don't bother about it. Everyone is naked inside their clothes. For sages as great as you, what does it matter if you wear clothes and what does it matter if you don't? But if you still command me to, I will take off all my clothes and give them to you."

"'No, no, what will I do with all your clothes?" said the sage. "Just a couple of yards from your turban will do."

'Promptly, the man tore off a portion of his turban and handed it to the sage. The sage felt strange once he wrapped the cloth around himself. He experienced something new. Even as he walked, he looked down at the cloth a few times. Wearing clothes wasn't all that bad, he thought. His own guru kept some half a dozen loincloths. What would he even do with any more? One was enough. Beyond that, whether you had five or you had seven, it was all the same. Having gone some distance, he said, "As we enter this village, this will suffice. Later, you get me a loincloth."

'The man agreed instantly. On their way, the sage spoke of matters related to knowledge and salvation in the form of parables and metaphors, matters of which the man was not aware. He wanted to go no further. Somehow, the sage managed to restrain him. "Accompany me to the village at least. Who would know me there?"

'"They are not so blind that they won't be able to recognize you," the man said. "And where can one find company such as yours? To satisfy this greed alone, I will come with you."

'Upon returning to the village, when the young man told everyone the whole story, they were surprised. It was the good fortune of the village to be able to behold such a sage! To the seth who had given him the hundi, the man said, "That your hundi would have borne such fruit, I would not have imagined even in my dreams. A sworn atheist like me has become a devotee. And now, I cannot bear to take even another breath in this village."

'The villagers thought that if such an atheist had become a devotee, then the sage was truly no less than God!

'But in the evening, when his family members heard from him what he intended to do owing to his new-found devotion, they lost their minds. He was going to set off for the mountains the next morning – he was going to renounce the world. Surely his impiety had been better off than this devotion! At least, the son was home. His parents tried very hard to change his mind, but the knowledge that he had obtained from the sage had such a profound impact on him that there was no going back. When his parents gave up, it was the turn of his wife. His parents hoped that no thoughts of detachment would survive in front of such a beautiful woman! But with renunciation on his mind, he honoured his wife like he would his mother. The wife cried and cried, but the man's heart would not melt. He did not spend even that last night at home. He spent it at the feet of the sage. And at dawn, he went off to wander the distant mountains.

'And here, the villagers committed themselves wholly to the sage. They would stand there with folded hands. Where one was needed to serve the monk, ten would be present. Only the fortunate get the opportunity to serve in this way. People would fall over themselves in his service.

'One day, the sage said, "Since I have only one loincloth, it is bothersome when I have to take a bath. While the loincloth dries, I have to remain inside the cave. I have to hide from my devotees."

'The devotees were ready to do anything. The very next day, seven or eight loincloths were stitched and presented to the sage. He inspected them one by one. In his heart, he was quite pleased. At night, he would check on the loincloths quite a few times. One day, after giving the matter much thought, he expressed his desire, "It does not matter to us sages, but one has to think about the mothers and sisters of the village. A bago[40] to cover the torso would be great."

'Eager as they were to please the sage, the devotees would do anything he asked. Nowhere in this world would

---

40 Bago: A flared angrakha, or choga-like upper garment for men.

they find a holy man who had spent eight years in meditation. The following day, the followers prepared seven or eight saffron robes and offered them to the sage. He was quite delighted with them. At night, he tried on all the robes, one by one.

'A few days later, there was an incident. The sage's garden was infested by rats. One robe was chewed to pieces by them. Other loincloths were also nibbled at here and there. The sage did not know what to do, but the devotees did at once. This was something for householders to know after all. "Baapji, this is the work of rats. No other cause for concern. Why do you worry? Let them gnaw and nibble away. It is their job to do so. Why should we care for them? If they destroy one robe, we will ready a thousand others."

'But from the next day onwards, the sage began to be mindful of the rodents. No matter what he was doing, his heart would be stuck in those robes. Tired, he finally said one day, "Isn't there any solution to these rats?"

'"Of course there is, Baapji. They won't even come out of their holes if they were to smell a cat."

'The very next day, a cat was placed in the garden. The sage was surprised to find that the devotees had indeed been right. Householders knew these things quite well. The rats caused no further damage. But the cat would come to the sage every now and then and go meow-meow; it would not leave him even for a second. One problem was solved, but a new one was created. Finally, he confided in his devotees. They smiled. "Why worry about these petty problems which us householders can concern ourselves with? The cat goes meow-meow in hunger. We will arrange for it. Nothing for you to be concerned about."

'The following day, five lactating cows were tethered in the garden. How much milk could the cat drink? The sage started to drink what was left over. He did not even ask his devotees for this. He would gulp down a full five litres of milk! His body began to glow.

'But the devotees could not manage the daily fodder and care. Sometimes, the cows would be left hungry, and then the milk would fall short. The sage was not pleased with this. One day, he disclosed his wish to the devotees, "If a man is left hungry, it is no big deal. Why, I have stayed hungry and thirsty for eight years, did not as much as breathe in air. But my heart aches to see our cows being left hungry! Better you take them away."

'The devotees said, "For you we would not refuse even our lives, and these are just cows. How could you even suggest we take them back?"

'The devotees discussed the matter among themselves and arrived at a solution. Ten of them donated five bighas of land each, and so, fifty bighas of land was put together for the cows. That very year, those fifty bighas produced so much fodder that even two hundred bighas elsewhere could not have. This was what miracles looked like! People began prostrating in front of the holy sage with greater devotion.

'The store filled up with bajra and jowar. Stacks of hay and straw piled up. With good fodder, the cows started to give more milk. But what would the sage do with so much milk? One solitary being – neither could he properly feed the cows, nor could he properly milk them. He could not even look after them properly: he did not know how to set curd, and he did not know how to churn curd for butter.

'The headaches for the sage began to grow by the day. The devotees were ready to lay down their lives for him, but none came forward for the grunt work. What a terrible quandary! With the cat, the cows, the fodder, the milk and the dung, he would barely be able to take time out for his prayers. However, he began to find pleasure in this fretting. Even if the devotees offered to help out, he would still want to do all this with his own hands.

'One day, he bared his heart to his devotees, "Who does all these chores at your homes? Do you do them or someone else…?"

'The devotees said, "At home, all these annoying everyday chores are taken care of by the women. If you suggest, we will make such arrangements for you too. That won't mar the sanctity of a sage as accomplished as you. You won't get soiled by it the way we householders are! You will always remain above it all, like a lotus in the mud."

'The devotees had thought that the sage would need a lot of convincing for this, but he agreed at once. The father of that young man who had brought the sage to this village was a part of this conversation too. What better match could be found, he thought. He got the wife of his son who had renounced the world, married to the sage.

'That night, a new knowledge dawned upon the sage – about why householders are not able to let go of this maya. Why would they? If one found something greater than God, who would ask after God? A waste of all those years spent in meditation and devotion! Either there is nothing such as God, or even if there is, it must surely be Woman. These bloody householders meet God every day and send monks and sages to wander forests and mountains! In search of what renunciation had that pupil relinquished all this pleasure and gone off?

'In a matter of days, there stood a large mansion in place of that garden. It seemed like a dream. The sage had become so engrossed in a life of domesticity that he did not have the time to even take God's name. The farming had increased substantially and so had the cattle. Even then, the devotees regarded him as a guru. They thought that this was God's manner of showing them the way. How could he, who had spent eight years in penance entombed in a mound of dust, be soiled in mud? This was just a divine game playing out.

'Day by day, that illusion began to thrive. Sons and grandsons were born to the sage. The way the vine of householders blossoms and flowers, this vine too blossomed and flowered. By the time he crossed the age of sixty-five, he began to experience shortness of breath. All night, he would keep coughing. He was a burden for his entire family. And his wife also became like his sons and their wives.

'Once, one of his young grandsons insulted him: "If you do not have the strength to wander about, why do you roam around so? You even spit wherever you feel like!" The grandfather continued to cough in response. There was no shortage of milk in the house, but no one would let him even touch anything except sour buttermilk! His condition worsened by the day. Meditation in the ashram was easier than this. But he was unable to let go of his attachment to this material world. Bearing the abuses and taunts, he would go around coughing in nooks and corners of the house.

'The real test of devotion lay further ahead. One day, his youngest son came and said, "That cow with both horns bent downwards will give birth at night. You keep watch in the barn. Don't you fall asleep. If the cow eats the afterbirth, it will be a disaster. She is special to me."

'That night, the old sage who for eight years did not as much as blink his eye while he meditated on an invisible God, fell unconscious from extreme coughing. And as fate would have it, that cow played a trick on him just then. By the time the sage regained consciousness, the cow had consumed the afterbirth. The old man grew feverish out of fear. At dawn, he was more terrified of his family than of even jamdoots.[41]

'When the youngest son darted towards him, mad with rage, he shut his eyes in fear. But the son's eyes were wide

---

41 Jamdoot: Yamdoot – a messenger of death.

open. He landed a kick on his father's waist and yelled, "You could not stay awake despite all my cautions? Would you have died if you did not sleep one night?"

'The once-beautiful woman who had married the sage had now turned red like the hide stretched out on a scarecrow. Who knows where her beauty had vanished, but the anger inside her glowed like embers. She pulled her husband by the hair, made him sit down, and screamed, "What did you do all these years? You have killed a cow that was perfectly all right! Why did you cause our son harm?"

'From having had his hair pulled at, the sage's eyes popped out and seemed to be floating in the air, and a gob of spit fell out of his toothless mouth involuntarily.

'Just then the voice of a stranger calling out to them was heard. The sage's wife beckoned him to step inside. Dressed in saffron robes, the man came closer and asked, "There once was the garden of my guru here. I have returned to this village after forty years. Did he set the entire village free and return to the forest?"

'The wife pulled down the veil over her face and stood up quietly. The owner of the mansion stared at that man's face, trying to place him, even as he continued to cough. But he could remember nothing.'

Jaraav Masi threw in a spool of yarn in the basket containing other spools and continued:

'And that poor sage – how could he remember even if he tried to? If only this craving for the material world would let you remember anything else! Only if this sorceress

would let you see anything else, there would be no reason
to weep. Can't my sons see that I kept them in my belly
for nine months, fed them from my body? I would keep
them warm and dry even as I lay wet and cold. Washed
their piss and shit. The stench has still not left my nails.
Those serpents don't even remember that the mother who
gave them birth and reared them lives alone, toils with her
hands. But against the enchantment of this material world,
neither could the sage see, nor can my sons. Otherwise,
would that godforsaken Baaman lead the snake to the gates
of moksa,[42] and himself return to live out a wretched life, all
for the love of wealth? If he had even the tiniest morsel of
a brain, he would have entered the gates of moksa ahead of
the snake. That blind man should have considered why, if
anything was more desirable than freeing oneself from the
cycle of rebirth, would the snake give away his invaluable
treasure to buy a passage through the gates of moksa?'

This time, I had to ask, 'Which Baaman? And how did
he return from the gates of moksa?'

Jaraav Masi looked at me, mildly annoyed, and said:
'So ignorant! You don't even know this much? What do
you know? Going around with your silly nose in the air. If
you had asked some fool, even he would know.'

Masi did not need to be prodded further. She
continued:

---

42 Moksa: Moksha. Liberation or release from the cycle of
    rebirth.

'There was a Baaman. He knew by heart all the holy books and scriptures – the Bhagvat, the Puraan, the Geeta, the Ramayan, the Garud Puraan and so on. I think, like the Baamans of today, he was in the business of sermonizing on these books, but possessed no real wisdom himself. Because if he was wise, why would he begin an affair with this woman? But of course, you men have no shame! You just make your own rules – so what if a man philanders, he can piss where he wants! And if women were to learn your ways, they'd be taught a lesson in no time at all. I learnt something about your uncle too, many years later. But he is no longer with us, so it makes no sense to talk about these things. His deeds have gone with him.

'Even that Baaman was able to hide this affair for days. But one day, the Baamani found out. It was as though a fiery dagger had pierced her heart.

'When he returned home late at night as usual, she said, "So where did you preach today? Tell me, I would also like to know."

'The Baaman realized something was amiss. The Baamani's tone was sharp. He had to respond. "I was preaching a katha[43] at a seth's home," he said, adding, "Came straight home after that."

'"When did I ask whether you came straight home or not?" his wife said. "But I have come to know everything without you telling me. You have fooled me for days. What

---

43 Katha: A story, often from a religious text.

should we do now? But at least don't waste your wealth. That whore loves your wealth, not you."

"'Who doesn't love wealth?" asked the Baaman. "I know that women of the house love wealth more than mistresses and whores. All this argument is in vain. She has a share of my love, so she shall have a share of my wealth."

'The Baamani's heart could reconcile with the division of her husband's divided love, but not with the division of his wealth. For this reason, there was a constant strain in the house at all times. The four sons and the mother were on one side, and the Baaman was on the other. He wouldn't budge, and his family wouldn't give up quarrelling either. Every day he would go and preach sermons at people's homes, make love to his mistress, and come back home and listen to his family's bitter and angry words.

'One day, the Baaman was headed to the Rajaji's to preach about the Bhagvat. On his way, he encountered a snake, coiled in the middle of the road as if waiting for him. The priest was about to turn around and run when the snake said, "Panditji, don't run. I have been waiting for you for a long time. Listen to me once, it will be for your own good."

'But the Baaman did not stop. The snake glided towards him swiftly and blocked his way again. Panting, the Baaman began to turn around and run the other way, but he fell. Then the snake came near him and said, "Don't be scared. I won't bite you. You know only too well that a snake never deceives others. Dust yourself and stand up!"

'The Baaman did stand up, but by now, he was shivering violently. The snake smiled. "Every day, you preach the knowledge you've gathered from the scriptures to all and sundry, yet you fear death in this manner! If it is fated, there is no way to avoid it. And if it is not, then there is no way anyone can kill you. But you don't seem to have any faith in what you preach! I think my poisonous fangs have less poison than your false words. Anyhow, no point in all this talk. Let's speak about important things. Where were you headed right now?"

'The Baaman replied fearfully, "To the Rajaji's."

'"Why?"

'"To preach from the Bhagvat."

'"What does the Raja pay you daily?"

'"One gold mohur and food."

'"If I pay you two mohurs to tell me the same katha, will you narrate it to me?"

'The first thought in the Baaman's mind was how would he escape from the snake. The second thing that struck him was that the snake was willing to pay two mohurs instead of one. Whoever gives me more is better, he thought. So he said, "Yes, yes, why not? This is my job after all."

'Then the snake asked, "Why, Panditji, is it true that he who hears the Bhagvat katha attains moksa straight away?"

'"Where is the doubt in that?" the priest asked in reply. "How can what is written in the scriptures be untrue?"

'Then the snake laughed aloud. "Do the priests who narrate the katha attain salvation too?"

'Seeing the snake laugh in this manner, the priest turned pale. He said softly, "If those who hear the Bhagvat katha attain moksa right away, who can stop the ones who narrate it? They attain it even earlier!"

'Then the snake said, "I was just asking out of curiosity. Your fate is yours to worry about. Start narrating the katha to me from tomorrow. Take these two manis,[44] far more valuable than the Raja's mohurs. You go to him after you have finished narrating to me. Come, let me show you where I live."

'The priest put the gemstones in his pocket immediately and left with the snake. He promised to come to the snake every day at dawn.

'The very next day, the Baaman reached there sharp on time with great eagerness. No one had paid him so well before this. The snake was far better than men, he thought. Every day he would finish his ablutions and prayers and head straight for the snake's. And every day, he would get two gemstones for his narration of the katha.

'But every day, when he came home, there would be a feud. How could he give such an invaluable gemstone to his mistress?

44 Mani: Mythical gemstone of great value and power, protected and carried by snakes.

'The Baaman would say without hesitation, "The way I give one gemstone here, I give one there! Everyone desires maya. You take your share, let her take hers. No need to indulge in this drama every day."

"How can you weigh us and that whore equally?" his wife would ask. "Do you feel no shame at all?"

'The Baaman would reply, "If I had any shame, I would not have a drop of water in this house. Compared to you all, she is better. Never complains about what I give here."

'Finally, in the midst of these daily rows, the Bhagvat katha came to an end. Even though he went about it very slowly and made elaborate commentaries, it had to finish some day. For the first time ever, the Baaman felt that it would have been such an excellent thing if the Bhagvat katha were twenty times longer. Why did its creator make it so short? But before the snake came along, he used to find this very katha so very long.

'Once the narration ended, though, the snake relieved him of this worry too. He said, "Panditji, I have an urn full of mohurs kept here. I want to offer it to you as a gift. But I would have to inconvenience you somewhat for it."

"Why do you worry about small inconveniences?" replied the Baaman. "I am ready to die for so many mohurs. Why, where is an urn full of mohurs to be found even in death? I am at your command."

'The snake said, "What you said has turned out to be totally true. After listening to this katha, I am sure there is nothing to stop me from attaining moksa. Whether narrating it will help you attain moksa or not is something you need to worry about. My salvation is guaranteed now. But I cannot reach the gates of moksa on the highest peaks of the Himalayas. I want to secure it in this very life. On the way there, if some human spots me, he will surely kill me. So, you need to take me in a basket on your head through the habitations of men. If maya can buy moksa, what better use of the mohurs!"

'The snake thought the Baaman would need some convincing. But he needed none. He went off and returned in no time with a basket from his house. When they reached the edge of the habitations of men, the snake said, "Panditji, some more mercy. How would I move under the scorching sun? Please carry me towards the Himalayas until evening. I will gift you another urn full of gold mohurs. In that same place, in another store, I have six urns full of mohurs. You choose the one you like. If you don't believe me, we can go back, and I can show you."

'But the Baaman believed the snake completely. It is men who lie. Birds and animals either don't speak, or when they do, they always speak the truth. The priest continued to walk with the snake until evening. He did not pause even to rest. The snake was so well-meaning after all. With the promise of another urn of gold mohurs, he took the Baaman to the very foothills of the Himalayas. There, the snake spoke of even bigger things. "Panditji, I have put you through so much trouble. I feel very embarrassed to say this. But if it is no trouble for you, please take me to the very gates of moksa. You know the route full well. I will just lose my way. All those seven urns are yours. For me, they are as good as dirt now."

'The Baaman was overjoyed. "Where is the trouble in that?" he said. "I will not let you be bothered at all. It is my responsibility to drop you to the very gates of moksa."

'Climbing the white peaks of the Himalayas, the priest finally reached the gates of moksa. He kept the basket with the snake on the ground and rested for a bit. The snake thanked him profusely, said he would be beholden to him forever, and happily gifted all his treasures to the Baaman.

'That done, he slithered past the gates of moksa. Turning around, he bid farewell to the Baaman, and then began to laugh out loudly such that he would not stop.

'When the Baaman asked the snake why he was laughing, the doorways closed! But he could still hear the serpent's laughter on the other side. He also thought the snake to be rather silly for having offered to hand over such an invaluable treasure against so minor a task. Climbing down the mountains, he thought how nice it would be if, instead of men, animals listened to the sermons he preached. These fit-to-be-burnt men are so miserly! Till the point he reached the snake's dwelling, he kept wondering if perhaps the snake had cheated him. But when he found the treasure, there was no doubt left. It was exactly as it had been described. Beside himself with delight, he reached home. He had the seven urns placed on a cart. Only when his family actually saw the treasure did they finally believe that this was not a dream but reality.

'The Baaman grinned broadly. "Let alone half, even a quarter of this treasure will last a hundred lives!"

'At night, all the members of the priest's family began to dream their own dreams around the treasure. All of a sudden, the Baamani woke up with a start. Then, waking her four sons, she said, "You have turned blind and foolish seeing all this wealth. You obviously did not hear what was said carefully. Half this wealth will go to his mistress's household. Your whole life lies before you. The duty towards one's stomach is greater than the duty towards one's husband. If Ram has not forsaken you, we can keep all this wealth here."

'When the sons heard their mother's scheme to keep all this treasure, this maya, they could scarcely believe her. But seeing her resolve, they were pleased no end. "We too had the same thought," they said, "but did not say it out loud because we were afraid of you!"

'The Baamani said, "With the aid of this wealth, all the women of this world can live out their widowhood. Then why fear me? Not much of the night is left. He always drinks water two hours before dawn. Get hold of some poison somehow and leave the rest to me."

'"No need to go anywhere," said the eldest son. "I have the poison already!"

'The youngest son said, "Let us all try to convince him. Maybe he will agree—"

'The mother cut him short, "He will not be convinced even in his death. Who knows what spell that whore has cast on him."

"'He will have no choice in death but to be convinced," the eldest one chipped in. "Now let us not go on and on. Let Ma do as she pleases. It is the son's duty to respect the mother's wishes."

'Just then, the Baaman called for water. His wife gave him a pot of cool water. Like every day, he gulped all the water down. As soon as he did, a spasm ran through his body. It felt like someone had drilled a hole in his head. He collapsed where he was. Every pore of his body seemed to be on fire. He tried to say something but could not. He kept gurgling incoherently.

'At this hour of death, the Baaman could hear the snake's laughter loud and clear. Some more time passed, and he could hear even the laughter no more. In his last moments, though, the meaning of the laughter became clear to him. But what use was it then? At dawn, the understanding that had revealed itself to him would be burnt with the rest of his body!

'The poison spread through every part of the Baaman's body. He turned black. His eyeballs appeared to pop. His veins swelled up. His four sons cremated him that very night. After this, the Baamani began to beat her chest and wail loudly.

'When the mother cried, the sons consoled her; when the sons cried, the mother consoled them!'

Just then, the yarn Masi had been spinning broke. And
with that, the story.

With her right hand, Masi then began to join the yarn
to her wheel again. And as she did so, she said, 'Against
the enchantment of this maya, the husband is nothing to a
wife, a father nothing to his sons. Let alone sons and wives,
one is nothing to oneself!'

And so the wheel of stories continued to spin like the
charkha Masi was spinning...

The Crafty Jaat[45]

WHAT CAN ONE SAY ABOUT the art of the Nats![46] You won't believe it if you hear it, but only if you see it with your own eyes. Such feats they perform using only their bodies! How they contort themselves, how they jump so high, how they run across a cloth in midair. How effortlessly they walk on ropes, perform somersaults, push a plough with their tongue, pull maunds of weight with their hair. Of all art forms, their art is the most difficult.

There was a Natni who was greatly sought after across the length and breadth of the land for the finesse of her art. She would not perform anywhere other than at the rajwadas, the royal houses. Raos, umraos, rajas and maharajas, all longed to see her performances. The

---

45 Jaat: A traditionally agricultural, landowning community; a member of the Jaat community.

46 Nat: Acrobat. Female: Natni.

opportunity to watch her would only come by once in a blue moon. Like farmers sitting in wait for clouds that bring rain, the rajas would wait for the chance to see the Natni perform.

One time, the Natni was to perform in Udaipur. The Rana of Mewar had been eagerly waiting for this moment for some years now. He was delighted to hear of her coming.

'Perform for us a feat the likes of which no king has ever seen before,' he told the Natni. 'Udaipur is above all other royal houses; the feat, too, should be above all others you've ever performed. Also, after today, no other raja can watch it ever again. Go on, show us.'

'Hukam,' the Natni replied, 'our feet can't but move to the beat of the drum. I know the acts I know. The only thing I need is an audience with the appetite for them. I can cross Lake Pichola on a tightrope if you like.'

The Rana could scarcely believe his ears. 'What! The Pichola?' he asked, astonished.

'Yes, the Pichola,' replied the Natni. 'The very Pichola you see here. I can cross it on a rope not once, but four times!'

The Rana thought it impossible. He said, 'If you can cross the Pichola on a rope even once, I will hand over half the kingdom of Mewar to you. And if you can't, then you will never perform in any other rajwada except mine.'

'It's easy to make a wager now,' the Natni said. 'But later, when giving away half your kingdom, you'll have a fit. Think about it carefully, and only then make the pledge.'

The Rana said, 'The Rana of Mewar doesn't need to think so much about such things. Get ready for your act.'

And in no time, a tightrope was suspended from long poles from one bank of the Pichola to the other. Vast crowds gathered to see the Natni's performance.

But just as the Natni was getting ready to begin her act, a thought struck her. It would take two to three hours to cross the lake. She was lactating. And her son would be famished by the time she returned. So she fed her son and put him to sleep, and only then did she climb on to the rope.

Countless eyes were fixed on her feet. The Natni started to walk on the rope as if she were walking on solid ground. The onlookers could barely breathe. They watched stunned, like dolls made of stone.

The Rana's heart was aflutter. The thakars surrounding him said, 'Even those who have offered more than a thousand heads in sacrifice have never had a claim on any part of Mewar. And here you have agreed to give this mere Natni half the kingdom! Your Highness, this is a crime!'

The Rana saw that the Natni was about to reach halfway across the Pichola. Darkness began to descend upon his eyes. She seemed sure to cross the lake. And if she did, half the kingdom would have to be handed over to her. But how could he refuse now, even though he wanted to! It would be a blemish on the honour of Mewar.

The Pichola was full to the brim. And it seemed like the Rana's heart had begun to drown in its waters.

Again, the thakars said, 'It is shocking, Your Highness. It is Mewar's great misfortune that it will now be enjoyed by acrobats.'

The Rana gasped as though he could not breathe, 'What can be done now! I am bound by the word I gave her.'

A Jaat, who was standing nearby, said, 'My lord, if it doesn't anger you, then I can propose a solution.'

The thakars said excitedly, 'If we have to sacrifice our heads during battle, we can do it without a thought. But our brains don't really do our bidding. If you can, then play your hand right away. Mewar's fate rests with you now!'

'If I can both preserve the terms of the wager and save your honour, then I will do so,' the Jaat said. He then headed quietly to where the Nats were camping near the bank.

Everyone's eyes were glued to the Natni's feet. She made it across the centre of the lake and moved towards the other bank. Her breasts were brimming with milk again. She thought of her son. Once she crossed the lake, she would feed him. As she moved along the rope, there was no sound except that of the soft ripples on the water. It was as if even sound itself was engrossed in watching her performance.

Then, suddenly, the shrill cry of a baby rang out. The scream reached the Natni's ears. She instantly recognized it to be that of her son. And as soon as the mother heard the scream, even as she walked on the tightrope, her concentration lapsed and she fell into the waters of the

Pichola … *Chapaak!* Just one splash. And then a mop of hair bobbed up and down in the lake a few times.

Fish play in the water and Nats play on land. The Natni did not know how to swim. By the time people gathered to help her, her act in this world had ended.

There, the Natni stopped breathing, and here, the Rana was able to breathe a sigh of relief. His heart calmed down. As soon as the Jaat came over, the thakars said, 'Even swords could not have saved the kingdom today, but this Jaat saved it by pinching a child. Had that scream not reached the Natni's ears, there was no way she would have slipped and fallen.'

The Rana patted the Jaat on the back and said, 'One can learn the art of the Nats, but the art of a Jaat cannot be learnt. The Natni's drowning saved me from losing face. It saved the honour of Mewar. It saved half the kingdom from drowning!'

Kanha the Cowherd

ONCE, THERE LIVED TWO BROTHERS who reared cows and calves for a living. The younger one grazed the cows in the forest round the year. He was like a new avatar of Kanha. Within three days of being born, the calves would begin to grow extremely fond of the cowherd. They would be more attached to him than to their own mother! They would understand his gestures without him having to utter a word. He would let the newborns drink milk to their hearts' content for the four fortnights after birth; he would not take even a drop away. Then, he would feed them leaves and buds with his own hands. They were soft and fresh, and tasted as sweet as milk. After that, the calves would not even look at the udders, let alone try to grab hold of them. At feeding time, the calves would only drink a fourth of the milk and then move away on their own.

The villagers called him Kanha – somewhat in jest, and somewhat because they truly meant it. Twice a day, when

it was time for milking, he would bring the full herd back
to the yard. Lest some wild animal cause them harm in the
forest, he would bring back even the dry cows along with
those that were milking. After that, he would milk them
with his own hands, and then take the herd back to the
pastures. It was as if his soul resided in each of the cows
and calves. He would tell people that if there was a heaven
in this universe, it was around his herd.

There were the choicest of cows from the Dhaat,
Swalakh, Sanchori and Ajmera breeds; white, grey,
dusky, fair, yellow, doe-hued, bushy-tailed. With shapely
horns, small muzzles, and soft skin. Thin hairy tails, a
bush of hair at the end as if trimmed by scissors, all four
udders the same size. Each cow with her own name:
Chhalar, Bugli, Jhoomar, Lebri, Koyali, Sinaer, Gegri,
Rendi, Bheendal, Kilangi, Roji, Bajoti, Todi, Kaleri,
Naleri, Mogri, Bhalri, Bheendi, Lakheri, and so on. Each
male calf, too, had his: Lichman, Bharat, Pailaad, Sankar,
and others.

There was only one bull in the entire herd. Named
Inder. When he grunted, people thought the clouds were
thundering! He had a white coat. A muscular hump tipping
to the left. A small muzzle, small ears, a long neck, a broad
back and strong legs. Was he a bull, or a piece of the sun?
And the calves, with dark hooves and waists, almost like
deer. And in the midst of it all was the cowherd who was
just as handsome and gainly, like a full moon among the
stars! A scarlet turban. An angrakhi fastened around his

torso. Pointed shoes on his feet, sudpis[47] around his ankles, lion-headed bracelets on his wrists, rings and chains on his ears, a golden necklace around his neck, and kohl-lined eyes. A sandalwood comb tucked in at the waist. A gaingan[48] stick in his hands. Slung on his shoulder was a goatskin flask. An alghoza at his mouth. Every leaf in the meadow would sway to its sweet melodies, ripples rose in the waters. The rivers, streams and springs gushed forth and danced, clouds thundered, lightning flickered, flowers smiled – so mellifluous were the tunes and rhythms that emerged from the alghoza of Kanha the cowherd.

The older brother, however, was as lazy and irritable as the younger brother was hard-working and amiable. When awake, he would either gamble or go around quarrelling with all and sundry. At night, he would grumble in his sleep.

The older brother was married. The younger wasn't. As fate would have it, the slothful brother's wife was clever, simple, understanding, deft and very hard-working. She would finish tending the cows, milking and feeding them, and the cooking and cleaning as efficiently as though she had twenty-five women standing around her in attendance. It seemed as though she would wrap up all the chores by merely moving her eyes instead of her hands. She was never

47 Sudpi: Anklets made of gold or silver, worn by men.

48 Gaingan: A type of bush or shrub found in the desert.

even an instant late in sending food over for her devar[49] with her daughter.

Often, one finds that those who set out to impress their wisdom on others can be evil. One day, it so happened that a neighbour came by to get some firewood when the bhojai was packing the meal for her devar. She remarked that surely such a meal could be for no one other than her man. But when she heard the response, wrinkles appeared on her forehead. She drew her eyebrows together in a frown. Scowling, and having expressed how shocked she was, she added, 'The silly and foolish don't have horns on their heads, do they? Even baseless suspicions can appear to be true. Stupid woman, the chaste put together such a meal only for their husbands!'

And after having imparted such a lofty lesson, the neighbour began to stare at all the food with her mouth watering: a bowl of churma, mushy with ghee and jaggery, rich curd, a small pot full of kheer, gawaarfali saag, and smoked and smashed green chillies. Clicking her tongue, she said, 'It is not your fault, though. Your devar's quite an eyeful. May such beauty be set on fire! Even an idol of stone would find its heart swayed. But silly woman, what is the use of letting slip such secrets?'

Wringing the sieving cloth dry, the bhojai said, 'What is there to hide in a meal, and what is there to let slip? Let alone one's devar, I do not think one should serve even

---

49 Devar: Husband's younger brother.

farmhands poorly. And my devar bears the responsibility of all the household chores. Does the work equal to that of ten men. He is as obedient as Lichman.[50] Till date, he has not refused my husband even once. If I begin to discriminate in rotis, would I not be struck by the plague! And what are these cows for, after all? I have never had double standards even in my dreams!'

Saying that, the bhojai chided her neighbour. However, the neighbour would not give up. Why would she stop herself from imparting her wisdom? She would inflict some taunt on the bhojai every day. Eventually, the poison began to course through the bhojai's veins. Just as a spoonful of curd can cause maunds of milk to curdle, the pearls of wisdom from the neighbour coursed through every pore of the bhojai's body. One day, she told her husband, 'You think of nothing but your gambling and your quarrelling. Where do you have the time to think about your grown-up brother's marriage? People have begun to suspect things that are not true because I serve the two of you the same food!'

The husband said, 'True. It indeed is something to be suspected. I held back from saying anything all these days.'

'If you had harboured any doubts, you should have at least spoken to me,' said the innocent woman. 'After he is married, it won't matter if his woman serves him sweet seera twice a day! We have no shortage of cattle and milk

---

50 Lichman: Lakshman. Ram's brother in the Ramayan.

after all. But if nothing else, one must maintain appearances in front of outsiders.'

Even though the husband did not trust his wife fully, he had complete faith in his brother. There was no reason to have any misgivings about him. But now that the opportunity had presented itself, why let it go?

The very next day, he directly broached the topic as his brother was milking the cows. 'You should get married now. Or are you planning to marry in your middle age?'

Even as the younger brother squeezed out streams of milk into the bucket, he replied, 'I do not care for marriage at all. You speak of marriage in this birth? I would not make haste for it even in seven births. Why should I abandon this reign of heaven and suffer in hell? If I have ever disobeyed you, though, then tell me...'

The elder brother responded at once: 'If this is not disobedience, what is? You might as well have smacked my head with a shoe. Your brains have become like those of the cattle you graze all day long!'

But Kanha's heart was as pure as fresh milk. He said, 'If the minds of men did indeed become like those of cattle, what more could one wish for? One would not desire heaven even in one's dreams.'

The elder brother reprimanded him, shouted at him, to no avail. Finally, he gave up, went to his wife and said that no one could argue with his brother. One could have gotten through to him if only he were a human being.

After that, the bhojai went over to convince her devar. When there was no way he would agree, she blabbered angrily, 'I cannot keep grinding away like this my whole life! My very bones have become hollow having to do all this work.'

Emptying a pitcher of milk into a bucket, her devar replied, 'I don't sit idle either. If you can get even ten hands to manage a herd so large, then you can smack my head with your shoe. Who wants to get married and have a leash tied around one's neck? I graze the cows, play my alghoza and—'

'So I am a leash around your brother's neck?' the bhojai interrupted. 'Getting churma and kheer twice a day has turned your head. Had I sent over dry scraps and crumbs, then your alghoza would have gone out of the window. If I stop toiling, you will forget all your airs and graces!'

Kanha had no clue what his brother and bhojai wanted. He had never heard such sharp and harsh words in his life. Today, they felt like daggers piercing his heart. He retorted, 'I don't sit loafing about that I should eat dry scraps and crumbs! The entire village knows whose arms toil to get all this milk and ghee. In any case, I don't get even a second's respite from looking after Chhalar and Jhoomar. Who wants to get stuck in this mess of marriage on top of that?'

The bhojai was infuriated at the devar's sharp words. The scoundrel definitely had deceit in his heart! She said, 'If your father had not fallen into this mess of marriage, then this herd would have died of hunger! Who would have cared for them? Today, your brother and I are fussing over you, but if you do not fall at our feet begging to get married in a matter of days, then shame on my name!'

Saying this, she slammed the door and went inside. Now the bhojai's life would be meaningful only if the devar's pride was broken. That day onwards, poison began to course through her heart. All these years she had given the devar the same food she had given her husband, and in return she had had to hear such stinging and horrid words. Even the milk a snake gulps becomes poison after all.

The very next day, she consulted her neighbour and sent her devar batiyas of husk, porridge of jowar and a pot of sour chhaachh. When her devar saw this, he could not believe his eyes. His niece too was shocked and pained. But what could she do? The earth began to spin in front of Kanha's eyes. From which corner of this heaven had these flames arisen? He had never thought his brother and bhojai to be so mean. He threw away all the food, out of his niece's sight. He did not have even a bite to eat.

In this manner, Kanha went without food for seven days. He would go off, milk the cows quietly, and return to the pastures. There, he would graze the cattle and play the alghoza.

On the eighth day, the cow named Chhalar came near him and said, 'Every single leaf here will get scorched hearing these tunes from the alghoza. No, not just these leaves, even the stones will shrivel. It's been seven days since I've been able to have even a blade of grass. What has happened? You have never hidden anything from us in this way.'

Hearing these words from the cow, tears began streaming down Kanha's eyes. Chhalar began to cry too.

Kanha loved every single cow in the herd. He knew them like his own soul. But Chhalar was like a mother to him. She was the queen of the herd. She could read Kanha's mind. Kanha shared with her the conversations he had had over his marriage and added, 'I have not eaten even a morsel of food for seven days. My heart just burns and burns. Were it not for this alghoza, it would have been reduced to ashes by now.'

Weeping, Chhalar said, 'The anguish in the melodies of the alghoza had reached my ears on the very first day. I thought you would confide in me on your own. Finally, on the eighth day, it was I who had to ask you. Our udders brim with nectar. What, then, is the need to suffer hunger?'

'No, I would not even dream of that,' said Kanha. 'I have never had even a drop of milk without the knowledge of my brother and bhojai. How can I start doing so now? Some day, surely, they will value me again.'

'As you wish,' said Chhalar.

Then she turned to face a kadamb tree and said, 'There is a large stone under that tree. If you leave a bowl in the hollow by that stone and, after a while, pull it out, you will find in it whatever delicacy you wish for. Partake of as much as you please. If you do not agree to this, I will not so much as look at a blade of grass for as long as I live.'

Kanha accepted Chhalar's request straight away. What she said turned out to be true. Thereon, he got to eat the choicest delicacies he wished for every day. One day, it would be laapsi, the next, kheer–malpua, on another it would be churma, on another seera; sometimes, it would be motichoor ra laadu, and at others, it would be syrupy sweet ghewar.

Hearing the music emerging from the alghoza, the parched and singed leaves turned green again. The heaven in that pasture was saved from being burnt to the ground.

No one raised the topic of marriage again. The bhojai thought that her devar would surely tire of eating such rotis day after day and make a fuss. And then, she would give him a piece of her mind, telling him that if he liked soft and thin rotis, he ought to get married and bring his darling home – she would not be able to concern herself with him any longer. But the devar did not bring up the matter at all. Every day, she would check if her devar was losing weight. But instead, he began to glow more and more as time passed. The husband and wife began to wonder what was going on and got flustered. Kanha would come, milk the cows on time, and leave quietly.

One day, Kanha was eating motichoor ra laadu and ghewar from a bronze bowl when his niece came to him with the usual meal. He did not think it would be right to hide the bowl from the child. If he was upset and quarrelling, it was with his brother and bhojai. What was the fault of that innocent child? He fed her the laadu and ghewar affectionately. And what was left over, she took home along with the bowl.

When she told her mother all about it, the poison in the bhojai erupted! The scent of such delicacies can make even the dead come alive, so what was so earth-shattering if a living being was flourishing after eating them? The devious man was surely selling off the cows' milk and buying these delicacies. That was why the milk yields had dropped considerably.

For how long could an infected, pulsating ulcer survive in a woman's stomach? As soon as she spotted the laadu and ghewar, it burst. The foremost shelter of a woman is her deviousness. If she wants, she can make even stones squabble and mountains battle. Inciting a man, then, is something she can easily accomplish. So she hurried to her husband, raging like the goddess Chandi and flashing like lightning. Throwing the bowl to the floor with a clang, she said, 'See your dear brother's games! He has sent laadu and ghewar for his bhojai. What was he thinking? How dare he! I trample on such sweets seven times!'

Then, sobbing, that devious woman told her husband such things that, as soon as he heard them, his hand reached out for his spear. He sharpened it and left for the pastures quietly. His wife understood his intent without him having to utter a word.

As soon as her man left, she bolted the door and started picking up the pieces of laadu and ghewar that lay scattered in the courtyard. She stopped only when there was not even a morsel left on the floor.

Kanha and Chhalar were sitting under the kadamb tree chatting, when Kanha suddenly saw his brother approaching them. Never before had his brother come to the forest. He eagerly went to meet him. But when Chhalar looked at the brother's eyes, she saw in them the dance of death! She bellowed loudly. Here, she cried out, and there, all the other cows charged with their tails raised and surrounded the brother on all sides. Seeing this circle of doom around him, the spear-wielding brother began to tremble. He had come to kill, but was himself encircled by death! There was no way out.

Kanha signalled the cows to halt. Coming closer to his brother, he said, 'If these cows had not rushed here and surrounded you, I would not have even dreamt that you came to murder the brother born of your mother. But beware, if you so much as raise your spear here, these cows will rip you to shreds with their horns. It will be my good fortune if death comes to me by my own brother's hands. If you have decided to kill me after all, why should I stop you? Let us go to the riverbank where we will be alone, and you can do as you please.'

With the spear resting on his shoulder, the brother followed Kanha. By the time they reached the riverbank, Kanha had mulled over a few things. He then spun the gaingan stick thrice, called out Chhalar's name thrice, and turned into a bird and flew away. Astonished, the brother spun around, and in that very instant, all the cows in the herd too became birds and took flight, following Kanha! The bull became a peacock and took off! Even as the brother looked on, the flock of birds disappeared from view. He threw his spear into the river and returned home with a sullen face.

The birds continued to fly behind Kanha the cowherd until they reached the ghats of Ujjain. When they saw ample fodder in the meadows by the lake in the Baavna Jod, they alighted there. As soon as he touched down, Kanha assumed the form of a human again. The flock of birds became a herd of cows. The peacock turned into a bull and began grunting. At the Baavna Jod were so many varieties of grass: dhaaman, jheraniyo, karad, maakhaniyo, barvadi, gandeel, ratadiyo, sanvo, mothiyo. And with the cowherd's alghoza, heaven descended on the Jod.

Kanha would savour five delicacies twice a day. The cows grazed on the meadows and enjoyed themselves. When faced with any hardship, Kanha would spin the gaingan stick thrice and call out to Chhalar, who would come running to his side like the wind and fulfil his wish.

Another wonderful thing happened after coming to the Baavna Jod. The hair on Kanha's head turned into pure gold! It began to glisten! If he did not keep it covered with his turban, it would give the illusion of a sun by day and a moon by night!

Every day at dawn, Kanha would take the cows to the river for them to drink water and he would bathe there himself. This was his daily routine. One day, as he was bathing in the river, a strand of his golden hair fell off and began to float away, but he darted and caught it. Then he put it inside a little box encrusted with glass, and keeping it on the riverbank, began to swim again.

After having finished his bath, when he looked for the box, he could not find it. Eventually, he gave up and followed the cows back, and began to play the alghoza with not a care in the world.

It is not as if stories are conceived in a flash of lightning. They are created by the light of day, in the darkness of night, and under the rays of the moon. It was the infinite caprice of fate that, at that time, two princesses came to bathe in that river. As soon as they stepped into the water, they saw something shining. The elder princess eagerly exclaimed, 'What shines is mine!' And the younger princess said, 'What lies inside it is mine!'

Soon, that object floated towards them, and the older princess grabbed it swiftly. It was a glass box! When they opened it, they found a strand of golden hair inside.

For a long time, the younger princess could not take her eyes off it. And as soon as she was able to look away, she glanced at the older princess and said, 'If I am to be married, it will be to the man to whom belongs this golden hair. Else I will remain an unmarried maiden.'

The older princess tried to warn her. 'Don't take such a vow,' she said. 'Who knows if this hair belongs to a man or a woman?'

The younger princess replied, 'I can tell. The scent of a woman's hair is completely different. A woman's hair is not as coarse as this. Once water leaves the cloud and once words leave the mouth, there is no turning back.'

The younger princess did not even bathe after this. She returned to the palace in her soaking wet clothes and lay down sulking. When the Raja and Rani asked her the meaning of such behaviour, she bared her heart and proclaimed that if she was to be married, it would only be to the man with the golden hair.

'You have not lost it, have you!' exclaimed the Raja. 'Have anyone's ears ever heard of a man with hair of gold or have anyone's eyes ever seen such a person? How will this vow of yours be fulfilled then?'

The Raja and Rani kept trying to convince the princess to give up, but to no avail. Only if they promised to accept her vow would she partake of food and water. If their daughter was hungry and thirsty, how could the parents eat? Finally, when they agreed, she stopped brooding.

Scores of riders travelled in every direction but failed to find a man with golden hair. How could something so bizarre even be found? Eventually, the Raja gave up and summoned four exceptional spy-women. One said that she could wrest the stars from the sky and bring them down for him. The Raja replied that he did not want stars from the sky. The second said she could grow mustard on her palms. The Rani said that she did not want her to grow mustard on her palms. The third said she could steal a child from the womb of an expecting mother and the mother would never know. To which the Rani replied that she did not want something so detestable. The fourth said that if she were given anything that belonged to someone, she could find its owner whoever or wherever they may be. If she were to get even a tiny piece of someone's fingernail or a scab from a wound, she could not be stopped from finding them, even if they dwelt in the underworld!

The Raja and Rani liked this fourth spy. They gave the other three a gift of a taka each and sent them away.

As soon as she opened the glass box and saw the strand of golden hair, the fourth spy said, 'The owner of this hair grazes cows at the Baavna Jod. He seems to be the very avatar of Kisan Bhagvaan! The beauty of even his shadow can barely be contained!'

The Raja ordered a chariot driven by sixteen horses to be harnessed and sent his diwan to fetch the cowherd. However, Kanha did not come. He declined straight away. Why ask the way to a village to which one does not wish to go, he said. If he did not want to get married even in his dreams, what was the need to go meet the Raja? Besides, he was not in the habit of leaving his cows unattended for even a second.

Many a person came beckoning, but Kanha would not listen. Finally, the Raja grew exasperated and entrusted the spy-woman to get him to come to the palace. The ways of spies are unique. She harnessed bulls by their tails. Harnessed at the wrong end, that cart trudged along slowly and reached the Baavna Jod. Seeing this spectacle, Kanha could not stop laughing. 'I have seen a cart with bulls harnessed by their tails for the first time today!' he said. 'What an extremely silly thing to do!'

'Brother,' said the spy-woman, 'if you are so clever, why don't you harness them correctly and show me? In my village, they harness bulls like this only.'

Kanha untied the bulls and harnessed them the right way. Then, the spy-woman said, 'Brother, how does one ride these bulls? Help move them along some distance, show me how.'

Kanha got on to the cart. As soon as he made a 'tich-tich' sound and touched their tails, the bulls shot off like cannonballs. There was no way he could disembark. The woman taunted him. 'You did not come when Rajaji himself summoned you. Now let's see how you can get off!'

At this point, Kanha understood everything. At once he spun the gaingan stick thrice and shouted, 'Chhalar ... Chhalar...'

As soon as he took the cow's name, along came Chhalar and the entire herd galloping behind her. They rammed the bulls with their horns, broke off the harness, and rescued their owner. The woman just about managed to save herself.

The Raja, however, sent the spy-woman back again. If she refused, she would be crushed alive in the oil mills. If she went, it would be her end, and if she didn't, it would be her end!

This time around, she disguised herself as a man, tied a saddle on to a camel the wrong way, with the front end hitched to its tail, and reached the Baavna Jod. When Kanha saw this spectacle, he laughed loudly in the same way as before. Laughing, he said, 'I have seen many a camel rider, but never have I seen or heard of one so silly! Silly, how come you tied the front end of the saddle to the tail and mounted it the other way round like this? You are not drunk, are you...?'

The rider said, 'Brother, in my village, everyone rides their camels in this way only. If you know the correct way, why don't you show me? I will be grateful.'

Kanha got the camel to sit and placed the saddle in the manner it ought to be placed. Then, running the front rope through the camel's nostrils, he tied it to the contraption and handed it to the rider. Feigning ignorance, the rider asked, 'How will this camel move, now that it is harnessed the other way round? Show me at least.'

Kanha quickly put his leg in the stirrup, and climbing on to the camel, sat on the front seat. As soon as he tapped the side of the animal with this ankle, the camel stood up with a start and began to run fast like the wind.

The rider sitting in the back seat dared Kanha. 'Go on and shout for your cow Chhalar, let's see if she can rescue you! Is it every day that one is sent for by the king? How much the poor man has entreated you!'

Right away, Kanha understood what was going on. Once again, he spun the gaingan stick thrice and shouted fearlessly, 'Chhalar … Chhalar…'

And as soon as he hollered, Chhalar flew in like a shooting star. Behind her was the whole herd. They caught up with the camel in no time at all. With their javelin-like horns, they tore the camel to shreds. The spy-woman just about managed to save herself from the jaws of death and fled.

After reaching the palace, panting and crying, she narrated all that had passed. The Raja and Rani heard everything with a great amount of surprise. The man with the golden hair seemed to have magical powers. What an onerous vow the princess had taken on!

Eventually, left with no other option, the Raja and Rani set out themselves, barefoot, to persuade that man. When they reached the Baavna Jod, they saw Kanha engrossed in playing his alghoza. The cows stood surrounding him.

Entranced by the sound of the alghoza, the Raja and Rani began to sway. They forgot what had brought them there. They forgot everything for as long as the alghoza played. As if a sorcery had taken hold of every fibre in their being. They forgot that they were the king and the queen, the lords of the land. They felt as if the man who was playing the alghoza was some celestial being. Even after the alghoza stopped, the pair continued to stand for some time, lost for words. It was only after a long while that they came to their senses.

When Kanha saw the two strangers standing in silence, he approached them and asked who they were and what had brought them to the Baavna Jod.

The Raja and Rani tried to fold their hands, but they could not quite do it. Folding hands in prayer was something commoners did! When they folded their hands, they forgot to speak, and when they spoke, they forgot to fold their hands. Somehow, stuttering and stammering, they managed to say: 'We are the king and queen of this land. We come here for a reason.'

After this, they paused awhile. And then they told Kanha about the princess's vow.

Upon hearing everything, Kanha burst out laughing. 'I had to leave home and come here because of this mess of marriage,' he said. 'And now that I am here, the same ordeal! Such is destiny! Anyhow, you are the lords of this land. I cannot make enemies of you. I am not going to marry even if I die. My cows will suffer. I will gather my herd and head elsewhere today itself.'

As soon as they heard this, the faces of the Raja and Rani fell. They had heard of his feats on two occasions from the spy-woman. This man was most certainly a mystic of great accomplishment or some wizard. Who else could dare to flatly refuse the king? Surely even God thinks twice before saying no to a king. This man was an avatar, definitely a divine avatar! Declining to marry a princess whom even the gods would fall for!

They beseeched Kanha, but he would not give the matter another thought. This time, when the Raja folded his hands, they stuck properly. He implored, 'We have understood what you say. Make the princess understand too. Then it will be the end of the matter! If she agrees, then I have no objection. You will have to bear the inconvenience of coming with us to the palace just once.'

Kanha turned down the request bluntly and said, 'The palace indeed! I would not leave the cows unattended for a second, even if I were to be gifted the reign of Inderlok.'

What could the Raja and Rani do? They were very powerful, but here they were pitiably helpless. What a vexing vow that delinquent princess had taken, that the king and queen had had to fold their hands in supplication – and that too in vain. They turned around and left as they had come, in silence, and with disappointment writ all over their faces.

As soon as the Raja and Rani stepped into the palace, what struck them was the extent to which they had begged and pleaded in front of a mere cowherd. Their pride was shattered. They lost their minds. This was surely worse than death. Their wounded pride flared up and rose like a tempest, and this ire was vented on the daughter.

The Rani said, 'If I had birthed a stone instead of you, I would not have had to go begging at least!' The Raja said that, because of the princess, he was as good as dead now. For the first time ever, he had spoken words of such helplessness. If a lion has to fold his hands and mutter impotently in front of a sheep, then shame on his roar.

And then, they angrily recounted to the princess all that had passed; they told her how they had begged and begged that cowherd, but he would not budge once he had refused.

After giving everything careful thought, the princess said that she was proud that she had not taken a vow in vain after all. It was because of the pledge that they had found that man with golden hair. Such a man is born once in aeons. She would go meet him herself. If he refused still, she would stay an unmarried virgin for life.

'Shameless girl,' said the Rani, shocked and enraged. 'What is this rubbish you are thinking! We went and were insulted. Now you want to go and get disgraced too? Will you force yourself on someone who has refused you?'

Both of them were the same: neither would that cowherd change his mind, nor would the princess. And when the Raja ordered the sixteen-horse chariot to be readied, she said that she would go alone and on foot. Utterly powerless, the parents gave in.

Clouds of excitement pouring in her heart, the princess reached the Baavna Jod. At that moment, every blade of grass in the meadow was drowning in the boundless tunes of the alghoza. Birds were glued to the branches they were perched on, as if they were toys made of wood. Lions, cheetahs, tigers, bears, hyenas, foxes, deer, monkeys, jackals, rabbits, pythons, cobras and many other animals sat immediately behind the cows. Either they had been sculpted out of stone, or they were lifeless! The snakes stood erect on their tails. None of them was aware of the other. Even though they could see, it appeared as though their eyes were devoid of sight.

Kanha was sitting on a branch of the kadamb tree, playing his instrument. The cows stood encircling him. The princess also came and stood beside a majestic lion. Suddenly, clouds began to drift in the sky and gather from all sixteen directions. It seemed as if they were racing against each other. Even as one looked, a new sky full of dark clouds had formed. It began to thunder. Streaks of lightning began to glimmer. Rain began to pour down. Even then, not a single creature moved. The princess remained standing too, like a statue made of stone, getting drenched. What was this maya! What was this enchantment!

The all-pervading melodies continued to echo for a while. It continued to pour. But as soon as the music came to an end, the clouds disappeared, it stopped raining, and the sky reappeared, shining and pristine, as if it had returned after taking a dip in the ocean. The birds began to chirp, and some took flight. The cows left to graze in the meadow. One by one, all the creatures went their way.

Only the princess stood where she was. When Kanha's eyes fell on her, he was astounded. The light of her beauty almost brimmed over the meadow. This apchara had surely been conjured out of the boundless melodies of the alghoza or had descended from the sky along with the rain. The colours of the sky and the meadow became a thousand times more vibrant. The sun grew brighter. Kanha had never imagined, not even in his dreams, that a woman could be so beautiful.

Both of them continued to gaze at the other's beauty for a while. The princess said in her mind, 'I am your Radha. Why did you reject me so?' The cowherd said in his mind, 'I am your Kanha. Why did you make me suffer so?'

All of a sudden, the princess spoke up. Words seemed to emanate from within her. 'Why did you refuse marriage?'

Words tumbled out of Kanha's mouth. 'I had to refuse as long as I did not find you. But our love has been and will be, for birth after birth. Then what's there in this artifice of marriage?'

'No, I won't listen to you,' replied the princess. 'You have deceived me in this way for aeon after aeon. Now, our love will bear fruit only if we marry.'

'What is this new insistence?' said Kanha. 'Listen to what I say, Radha. Don't besmirch our love with the smoke of the holy fire. It will turn black! Let it bathe in the light of the sun and the glow of the moon!'

Kanha tried to reason with her, but the princess would not listen. 'The world still taunts us,' she said. 'How can one trust love without marriage?'

Kanha tried to persuade her one more time. He said, 'Radha, do not persist with this demand. Our love flows in rivers, gushes in waterfalls, smiles in flowers, swims in moonshine, sparkles in stars, pours from clouds, shimmers in lightning, and blossoms in every leaf! Do not encumber it. As soon as our love is shackled, the sun will set, the moon will wane.'

Radha continued to stand her ground. 'No problem. Let the sun set, let the moon wane. I will bind our love in the ties of marriage.'

Eventually, Kanha gave in. 'Have it your way, then,' he said loudly.

After this, Kanha was married to the princess, accompanied by the sound of drums and nobat-nagaras, and the glimmer of diamonds and pearls. From that very day, the moon of love began to fade, the sun began to set every day...

On the night of the wedding, Kanha went to sleep in the rangmahal and the night passed by in an instant. For his herd in the meadow, though, that night felt as long as a year. Kanha had promised that, as soon as he would leave the wedding canopy, he would return to the Baavna Jod. But what had happened? He was not in some trouble, was he? All the cows, including Chhalar, wept and wailed, and died. Kanha had forgotten about them on the first night of his marriage itself! Once he is entranced by the beauty and sensuality of a woman, a man can think of nothing else. The cows had never borne even a moment's separation before. Then how could they have lived out an entire night? By the time the sun rose, there was only darkness in their eyes.

In this way, in the palace, three dark nights passed, each in an instant. And there, at the Baavna Jod, vultures and crows were having the feast of their lives. The carcasses of so many cows at one go! All the vultures and crows in the land assembled and tore off every piece of flesh that was available. Only the cows' bones were left. Apart from the bull, there was no way to tell which skeleton belonged to whom. In death, all distinctions were erased.

On the fourth night, at midnight, the princess gazed into a chandelier of seven lamps and said, 'How these three nights have flown! It is only when darkness falls that love truly shines. Three nights have passed by like three seconds. I could not feel them at all—'

'What did you say?' interrupted Kanha, agitated. 'It has been three days since we came here? No, no! Not even three seconds had passed, I thought. I became so blind and crazed in love! What must have happened to my cows?'

Saying that, he rose from the bed with a start. He flung the door open, and wailing and calling out 'Chhalar, Chhalar', he left the palace, the princess rushing behind him.

Kanha reached the Baavna Jod barefoot and searched everywhere, but could not hear the cows mooing. He stumbled upon bones a few times, but he did not realize they were the bones of the cows from his herd. At daybreak, at the sight that befell his eyes by the light of the sun, he lost consciousness and collapsed. Every hour following that, he would weep and utter the same lament, 'This was the reason why I always refused marriage! My cows died howling and sobbing, and I was enjoying myself in the rangmahal!'

He was clutching the gaingan stick in his fist. Kanha, barely conscious, turned the stick thrice and took Chhalar's name thrice. And as soon as he did that, all his cows came alive! They straightened their tails and mooed all at once. Every speck of dust in the meadow seemed to bear meaning again!

As soon as Kanha heard the mooing of the cows, he sat up straight. Calves suckled and cows mooed in merriment. Tears of joy and pain began to pour out of his eyes. The cows too began to shed tears. Kanha sought forgiveness for the mistake he had made.

The princess stood watching this spectacle, stupefied.

Just then, the Raja and Rani also arrived at the Baavna Jod in a golden chariot. The Raja approached Kanha and said, 'It does not look nice at all that my son-in-law grazes cows like this. I hand over half my kingdom to you in dowry. Rule in peace! For the cows, instead of one, I will keep twenty attendants. This is why I've come in my golden chariot – to take the two of you back.'

Smiling, Kanha the cowherd said, 'Then you have troubled yourself in vain! In each of the hooves of my cows dwells the kingdom of heaven! How can you tempt me with this vision of half a kingdom? I would reject even Inderlok seven times over!'

'Will our princess graze cows and live in the pastures?' asked the Rani.

Even before Kanha could offer a response, the princess broke in: 'Ma, what is there to think in this? It is the good deeds of my last birth that I have got such a husband and such a herd of cows! I do not want to stay anywhere else but in these pastures, not even in heaven!'

The Raja and Rani tried to cajole them and lure them, but the couple would not agree. At last, helpless, they had to turn back.

The two built a hut under the kadamb tree and began to live there happily. They would graze the cows together. Kanha would play the alghoza and Radha would listen. The entire meadow would listen. Even the inhabitants of Inderlok and heaven were envious! They, too, longed to live there.

All the delicacies they could wish for continued to appear in that bowl given by Chhalar. They knew no lack. Plentiful cows. Abundant milk and ghee. Soaked in the melodies of the alghoza, the days were peacefully passing by when, one day, a man and a woman arrived with heavy loads on their heads, asking the way to the city of Ujjain. Their clothes were torn and tattered. Their hair dishevelled and lips chapped. And all over their bodies were splotches and blisters. Kanha regarded them for a while and recognized that the pair selling wood were his brother and bhojai! So this was how their fate had eventually played out. In his heart as pure as milk, there arose pity. Without any bargaining, Kanha paid them two–three times the price of the wood they were carrying on their heads. They were saved the trouble of having to try to sell it elsewhere, and were delighted.

They would bring wood every day in the same way, and each time Kanha would buy everything without any haggling. He gave them good clothes to wear. He summoned the barber and had the man get a shave. One day, quite a few laadus and ghewars were left in the bowl he had eaten from. So he gave them to the wood sellers. To his great surprise, when the wood sellers saw the laadus and ghewars, tears began streaming down their eyes.

While Kanha understood the meaning of the tears at once, the princess, amazed, asked why they had started sobbing at the sight of the food. The wood sellers avoided answering the question a few times, but when the princess insisted, the woman said as she sobbed, 'I had a devar. One time, he had sent us such laadus and ghewars. After that day, many a hardship has befallen us. Ram knows what other difficulties will come our way.'

Kanha consoled them and said, 'Don't you be scared. Do not worry about anything. No hardships will befall you now. But where is your devar?'

This time, the man replied, 'That day, he became a bird and flew away. We have not heard from him since.' Then, turning to look at his wife, he said, 'If this murderer of a woman had not provoked me, would we be wanting in any way today?'

After this, Kanha hid nothing from his brother and bhojai; he told them everything. The brothers hugged each other. The bhojai regretted her sins and asked for forgiveness. The couple had reaped as they had sown. They had married their daughter off, and since then, had been wandering here and there.

From that day onwards, their wandering stopped. They built another hut, and all four of them began to live together in peace. Never again was there any discord among them.

One day, the bhojai teased Kanha. 'Devarji, if you would have agreed to get married that day, our home of plenty would have been destroyed.'

'Indeed,' Kanha teased his bhojai back. 'If that day my fate had been wrecked on the pretext of marriage, how would I have been able to marry Radha? For birth after birth, I have loved only her. It is just in this birth that I have been able to marry her.'

Behind her veil, Radha began to smile with such tenderness that the meadow gleamed even more than before!

Mortgage of the Next Birth

THE ESSENCE OF THESE FINE, subtle and omnipresent tales spreads from flowers as fragrance, oozes from udders and breasts as milk, pours forth from thunderclouds as rain, shimmers as lightning, and illuminates the whole wide world as rays of light.

So may Ramji bless us all, there was a poor Rajput[51]: stricken by hardship, defeated by fate. Once, as it happened, around midnight, there came a storm so terrible that his decrepit hut began to sway. It seemed as if it would be blown away like a feather at any moment! The howling wind, the swirling cold gusts, the sonorous thunder of the clouds, and the ghoomar of the rain to the beat of the thunder. As if they were all feuding. The wind howled that it was the greatest. The clouds thundered that they were. The lightning rasped that it was the foremost. The rain

---

51 Rajput: A Hindu martial caste. Female: Rajputani.

screamed that it was. And caught in the crossfire between these all-powerful forces, was that old, leaky hut.

The Rajput and the Rajputani began to look at each other, their faces morose.

Even as her insides twisted themselves into a knot, these words escaped the Rajputani's mouth: 'The night of destruction they speak of – it's not tonight, is it?'

The husband replied, 'And if it is? What more can we want!'

'What do you think?' the wife asked playfully.

The husband sighed, 'Are we that fortunate? But you have a true heart. Tell me what you think.'

As soon as the lightning subsided, the wife's face slid back into the pitch-black darkness. 'Does even death come when the luckless wish?'

This brief exchange over, both husband and wife sat without uttering a word, like statues made of stone. That pouring, dark night passed. And the sun rose on its own, just where it was supposed to. Gradually, the hut lit up. The Rajput and the Rajputani's clothes were soaking wet. The hut was dripping. They might as well have spent the night outdoors!

They unbolted the door and stepped outside. The sky was still pouring steadily. The Rajput turned his gaze towards his field. 'I can't remember a time when our lakes and basins have filled up like this,' he said to his wife. 'As if molten silver has engulfed everything till waist-height.'

'There will be a boundless harvest of wheat!' she replied with delight, as if stacks of harvested stalks had come home already.

'There will, there's no doubt about that,' he said. The very next instant, however, his face fell. 'But what can we do with just water? Where is the plough? Where are the bulls? Where are the seeds?'

'Where's the need to think so much about this?' asked the Rajputani. 'Listen to me. Go to the village on the hill. The wealthy seth there lends whatever amount one asks for. He makes no entry in his books, nor does he ask for the money back.'

'That is his game, silly! That's why I can't borrow from him. The seth lends against one's next birth. He asks for nothing in this birth. How can I rely on the next birth and borrow from him? I don't mind death, but—'

'Go to some other lender then,' the wife interrupted him, as tears gathered in her eyes. The countless drops of the falling rain seemed to dance in front of her eyes.

'If only there was some other lender to go to! This seth's lending business has become so popular that all the other baniyas in the region have shut shop. Tell me, what else can I do?'

'When do you ever listen to what I say? Go to that seth once. At least this birth will be bettered! We were born as human beings – let us savour *some* of this life's pleasures! Who has seen the next birth? I beg of you – go to that village on the hill for my sake. I don't want to die with this wish unfulfilled!'

Water glistened in all four directions. The Rajput's eyes could see nothing else. 'If that is your heart's desire, I will go,' he said, not without some hesitation.

As soon as she heard these words come out of her husband's mouth, the Rajputani felt as if the rain was pouring forth from her heart. The sparkle in her eyes began to frolic with the lightning. And the very next second, she became the mistress of the clouds and the rain!

The rain stopped as suddenly as it had started. And before their eyes, the water that was everywhere began to drain away. It was only the poor Rajput's field that remained flooded.

At daybreak the next day, he left for the village on the hill. His wife stood outside their hut, gazing after him. At least he had gone. If they could farm the land properly, everything else would fall into place. A web of dreams began to weave itself in front of her eyes.

Man's heart is beyond all understanding. Today, with every footstep, the Rajput was inching towards the doorstep of that seth whom he did not want to visit even in his dreams. Truly, who knows what the next birth will bring? And do the memories of the last birth linger and help us? Who knows what this intertwining of two births will lead to? I don't know what transpired in my past life, and I don't know what will happen in my next. This birth alone is the truth. Live each instant as it comes! Everyone desires happiness. One may or may not have their way, but who willingly accepts hardship? Buried deep in such thoughts, the Rajput reached the village on the hill.

At the entrance was a horde of people who had all come to borrow money. On a platform sat the seth, cross-legged. He wore a slanting yellow turban. He had a pallid face, shining white teeth, pink gums, and bloodshot eyes. Beside the seth sat the munim,[52] handing out money as per the former's orders. There also lay seven trays, all heaped with money.

If such a large number of people could clamour the way they did to borrow from the seth, why should I alone worry about the next life, the Rajput wondered.

Making his way through the crowd, he finally reached the seth, who smiled at him and enquired, 'Tell me, how much do you want?'

'Quite a lot. Two hundred rupees,' replied the Rajput. 'But about repayment—'

'No talk of repayment here, please!' the munim broke in. 'If you want to borrow by mortgaging your next birth, then speak!'

After that, there was nothing left to hear or say. The Rajput, his head bowed, thrust the money into a pouch and then tied it securely around his waist. He then turned to leave.

---

52 Munim: Accountant.

As soon as he was burdened by the weight of the money, he felt weightless. As light as a flower! Now for a pair of healthy bulls, a decent plough and quality seeds. Mounds of harvested wheat began to pile up in front of his eyes. So what if the seth won't take the money back? With so much of it, the Rajput could even keep aside an amount for charity. That way, neither would the grain for pigeons run out, nor would the grain in their stores. They had suffered hardship for so many years for no reason!

While he was walking back, the Rajput caught sight of a pond and felt thirsty. Eagerly climbing the bank of the pond, he saw it brimming with crystal clear water, as pure as a white lotus. He drank to his heart's content. Then, he felt like taking a dip in the water. So he took off his turban and began to unfasten his angrakha. He put the pouch containing the money by the bank, and immersed himself in the pond. What can match the coolness of water?

However, the very next instant, disaster struck. Around four or five buffaloes came to drink water from that very pond, and the pouch with the money got caught in one of their hooves and was dragged some distance. What's more, one of the buffaloes shat all over it! The pouch now lay somewhere, fully covered in dung.

Done with bathing, when the Rajput looked for the pouch, it was nowhere to be seen. His heart was in his mouth. What misfortune was this! Distraught, he looked along the entire bank, but the pouch was not to be found. What a mess! Who would believe him? His dreams had

been shattered even before they had begun to come true.
One can't fight a wretched fate! Reluctantly, the Rajput
turned around to head back to the seth's.

At that hour, the doorstep of the seth's house was
deserted. The seth and the munim were sitting on the
platform right in front of the house, chatting. When
the munim saw the Rajput heading towards them, he
exclaimed, 'Fools don't come with horns on their heads
after all! Imbecile! Looks like he has come to return
the money.'

But did the seth have any patience? Hurriedly, he
stepped out to greet the Rajput and told him with a smile,
'My dear fellow, why sully the tradition of this place? I'm
not going to take the money back even if I die.'

The Rajput narrated to him the whole unfortunate
incident to him in detail. 'It's my fate that's useless! Who
do I blame? If you don't trust me, you can search me.'

The seth laughed and said, 'Where do I have the time
to mistrust anyone? And who am I to search anyone? Here,
no one can lie even if they want to. Take however much
you want once again and go back.'

A little less flustered, the Rajput said, 'I had come here
with this very hope.'

'The privilege is ours,' said the munim. 'But you will
have to stay here for the night. The seth has wrapped up
his business for the day, and will now partake of food and
drink. First thing at dawn, you will have your money.'

Happily, the Rajput stayed on at the seth's for the night. He had an early supper, and then the munim brought him to the garden. He laid out clean sheets on a bed and placed a pot of cool water by the pillow. It is one's good fortune that brings such unexpected treats.

As soon as the munim left, the Rajput lay down. He was about to lapse into a contented sleep after what seemed like years, when he heard someone talking. He sat up with a start and looked around. There was nothing, no one. In the shed was tethered a buffalo, and beside her was a young male calf. Even as she chewed the cud, the buffalo said, 'You are listening carefully, no?'

'Why would I not?' responded the calf. 'I'm not deaf, am I?'

The buffalo continued: 'Finally, my debts are discharged! Now I owe the seth only five more litres of milk. At dawn, I will let them take it in exchange for a bale of hay, and leave this body. Freed of my debts, I'll get to see my next life tomorrow. Do forgive me if I've ever been mean to you. Now it's only you, the seth and the garden.'

'The time of my repayment is still quite a way off,' said the calf. 'This debt is like heartburn; it lets me digest neither straw nor grass. I grow weaker by the day. The seth keeps me very comfortably, but the disease of debt is a horrid one. I still have to pay him back a thousand rupees.'

As soon as the Rajput heard the calf's words, the sleep of contentment he had felt envelop him a short while ago fled. His heart wriggled in his chest. This loan against his next birth was quite worrisome. He had been better off with his troubles! For which birth had his wife taken revenge on him?

The calf continued: 'Now, if I can somehow arrange to compete with the royal elephant, then I can be rid of this burden! That elephant owes me a thousand rupees. That amount will be placed as bet. If the elephant loses, the thakar will pay the seth a thousand rupees and I will stand freed. And I will leave this body that very instant.'

Laughing, the buffalo said, 'Silly, what match is a measly calf for a mighty elephant! You haven't lost your mind, have you?'

Shaking his head, the calf said, 'The lender is always more powerful! No one can surpass the strength of him who is owed money!'

He wasn't hallucinating, was he? The Rajput stood up and stretched. He then stroked the buffalo and the calf, and understood everything in detail from them.

After this, the Rajput could not sleep a wink through the night. The stars that had been twinkling until sometime ago were covered in a mist. Nothing seemed to be clear any more. It was as if a porcupine had bored its way and was crawling around inside his skull. Ramji knows in what way the seth would claim repayment in the next birth! Against this burden of debt, even the weight of the Himalayas seemed bearable.

But as a human being, could he believe the words of mere cattle! What was the point of worrying before making sure if what he had heard was true or not?

Before the crack of dawn, the milkman arrived at the garden. After getting the buffalo to suckle the calf, he started to draw milk from the buffalo into a copper bucket. The bucket was frothing over in no time. Then, keeping the milk away, the milkman placed some bales of hay in front of the animal for her to eat. The Rajput stood rooted to the spot, staring with his eyes about to pop out of his head. As soon as the buffalo finished eating one bale of hay, she collapsed where she stood. The milkman darted towards her. The buffalo's eyes were blank. No breathing, no movement. She was dead. Glaring at the Rajput, the milkman shouted, 'You evil-eyed man! You killed a buffalo who was fit and fine! Never seen milk before, have you?'

'Why would I have not seen milk?' the Rajput replied gently. 'What's so special about it? There was a time when even we had cattle who'd give buckets and buckets of milk.'

Just then, the seth and the munim arrived in the garden. As soon as they came near the dead buffalo, the munim looked at the Rajput and asked, 'Why did you delay coming over? We have been waiting for you for a while. Both breakfast and money are ready.'

The Rajput shook his head. 'I want neither breakfast nor money,' he said.

'He killed a buffalo worth a thousand rupees!' the milkman cut in excitedly. 'Why would he want breakfast now?' He then told the seth about the buffalo's death, adding, 'What has happened is really unfortunate. The buffalo collapsed as soon as he cast his jealous eyes on her.'

'First, measure this milk,' said the Rajput softly. 'Then I will tell you what all this means.'

The milk weighed five litres. Then the Rajput recounted the entire conversation between the calf and the buffalo. The seth and the munim listened to him, stunned. The Rajput said, 'Seth, there can be no default in lending against one's next birth! Earlier, like an ignorant man, I took two hundred rupees from you. There is no way I will borrow against my next birth now. Not even if I were to die.'

Despite knowing everything, the seth feigned ignorance and said, 'Those who are born must die of one cause or another. I think you are hallucinating...'

The Rajput spoke animatedly, 'What about the matter of this royal elephant? Is that true or not?'

'A face-off between an elephant and a calf!' the seth replied. 'People will laugh if they hear it! You take the money you need and go back. This is like your home. If you leave empty-handed, I will feel hurt.'

'How can I spoil two births for the sake of your pain? I am not capable of returning the money I lost, else I would not have kept even that.'

This time, the munim said, 'If our calf loses in the face-off with the elephant, then you won't have any objection to taking the money?'

'But that will not happen. I am certain the calf will win,' the Rajput said. 'Seth, you've created an excellent business model! No risk with the next birth mortgaged. You can sleep and snore peacefully.'

Eventually, the munim went to the royal household to place a formal request for the duel. When those at the household heard him, they began to laugh so much they wouldn't stop.

Still laughing, the kaamdar said, 'Seems like pride has gone to the seth's head!'

The caretaker said, 'Looks like the seth has gone mad.'

The thakar said, 'No medicine for this save a good lashing!'

The choudhary said, 'The poor calf will surely be reduced to a pulp.'

At daybreak the following morning, a huge crowd gathered in the fortress to witness the spectacle. An immense elephant under the intoxication of drink! As if a small cloud hovered there! When the elephant saw the calf come towards it, he trumpeted loudly and charged forward. The earth seemed to tremble under his weight. Kicking up dust, he closed in on the calf. But the calf was not scared. Looking at the elephant, he laughed and said, 'Shame on you! You've not paid me the thousand rupees you owe me, and are showing me your face again! I am the one who lent you money. Take your pride elsewhere. If you want to live with the rightful pride of an elephant, first give me back my thousand rupees!'

But the elephant did not have even one paisa. Seeing his creditor, he began to tremble. He turned around and fled. The calf in pursuit, the elephant running ahead! After all, what is a debtor in front of a lender? And the throng that had gathered to watch them battle stared at this spectacle aghast!

In the end, the thakar had to part with a thousand rupees. And as soon as he gave the seth the money, the calf slumped to the ground, lifeless! In death, he attained immortality. And here, the living elephant was as good as dead. That measly calf had caused him insult enough.

After this, the seth and the munim argued no further with the Rajput. He returned to his village as he had come – empty-handed.

On his way back, when the Rajput saw the sparkling water of the pond, once again he decided to take a dip in it. As he reached its banks, he spotted a heap of dung. If it slid into the pond, it would make the water dirty. Why not pick it up and throw it away elsewhere? One peculiar turn of events was straightened out by another peculiar turn of events. And as soon as the Rajput picked up the dung heap, he spotted the pouch of money under it! So this was what had passed. After throwing the heap away, he scraped the dried dung off the pouch and washed it properly. Then, without further delay, he went straight to the seth's haveli.

After having wrapped up the business for the day, the seth and the munim were heading inside when they saw the poor Rajput. The seth said, 'Let's deal with him first and then go.'

When the Rajput came within earshot, the seth smiled and said, 'Come in dear fellow, welcome. You went through all this trouble for nothing. Now, in exchange for this inconvenience, allow us the privilege of lending you a hundred rupees more.'

The Rajput thrust the pouch of money forward and said, 'It is my great fortune that I found the money I had lost. Now, accept the repayment and relieve me of the mortgage of my next birth!'

'What is the point of frying our brains in this way?' the munim said. 'We didn't go to your house and hand you the money, did we? It is not our custom to take the money back in this birth. You should have thought it through carefully before you came here.'

'This birth of mine is already ruined. How can I knowingly wreck my next birth too?' the Rajput said in reply. 'I implore you, take this money back. I have not the strength to bear this burden!"

This borrower was quite something, thought the seth. But it would not do his business any good if he were to deviate from its usual practices. And this lending against the next birth was extremely lucrative too. As his business had grown from strength to strength, so too had his wealth. In a patient and soft tone, the seth said, 'Once the money leaves us, you can toss it away, bury it or burn it, it is not our concern. What's done cannot be undone.'

But the Rajput too was insistent. With twice the defiance, he said, 'Seth, don't you be so sure! Throwing this pouch away will not relieve me of my debt, right? But if I don't get you to take the money back, then I haven't drunk milk from the breast of a Rajputani either!'

Vow made, the Rajput tied the pouch around his waist, bid the seth and the munim farewell, and left at once. He returned to his village lost in thought. His wife was waiting for him. As soon as he entered the hut, he ranted and railed at her. It was because of her that Ramji had deserted him, or he would not have spread his hands in front of anyone, not even if he were dying! He told his wife everything that had transpired over the past two days in great detail. In the end, he asked, 'Now you tell me, what am I to do with this money?'

Slowly and calmly, the Rajputani began to convince him that once the money was brought, it could not be un-brought. Now, timing was critical. 'Let us plough the field well and buy quality seeds. The greenery will burst forth on this bare earth! Birds will peck at the grain and their beaks will bless us. There will be a splendid harvest. After keeping enough to meet our needs, you can sell the surplus wheat. And once we have enough money to pay back our loan with interest, you can do as you wish.'

The Rajput cheered up. 'My dear,' he said to his wife, 'I've discovered today that you are quite clever! While you were speaking, an idea to relieve us of the debt owed to the seth came to me. Now you watch!'

After that, the Rajputani watched the events that unfolded in their household! Thanks to the money, Nagori bulls, a double plough, and the best seeds were bought, and the field yielded a remarkable harvest of wheat. There were heaps of grain and fodder. Their dreams came true.

And the poor Rajput began to act on his plan, slowly, gradually, day by day. Along with a hundred diggers, the husband and wife began digging a hole for a pond, and within a few days, they had made space for a nice, big one. With the first rain of Aasaadh, the hole filled to the brim. And then, Ramji knows what came over that poor Rajput, but he would not let any bird or animal drink even a drop of that water. He would remain standing on the banks of the pond day and night, bow and arrow in hand. Which bird would dare come within the range of his arrows? And animals would flee upon hearing the whoosh of those pointed sticks. They'd vanish in a matter of seconds!

As fate would have it, one day, a Lakkhi Binjara's[53] caravan was passing by the pond when the bulls hauling the carts, thirsty for two days, began mooing as soon as they sighted water. The Rajput stood up with his bow and arrow, and threatened aloud, 'Be warned, if your animals are dear to you, restrain them. Or I'll shoot each and every one of them!'

---

53 Lakkhi Binjara: A trader who owns a hundred thousand rupees, usually a travelling tradesman. A regular motif in folk tales.

Hearing the shouts, the Lakkhi Binjara alighted from his caravan and said, 'Brother, what is this dilemma you have created! The bulls are thirsty. After wandering for days, we've finally found this pond. The sin of cow slaughter will be on your head! What is this madness?'

The Rajput answered, 'The blame for this madness is not on me, but on the wealthy seth who lives in the village on the hill and lends money by mortgaging one's next birth! This pond has been dug with his money. If you want to save your bulls, then get his permission. I won't have any objections then.'

The Lakkhi Binjara realized that it would be futile to quarrel with this lunatic, so he rushed to the village on the hill in his chariot.

Undeterred, the Rajput remained standing near the pond with his bow and arrow. In no time, the chariot returned. Along with the Lakkhi Binjara, the hassled seth and his munim too climbed out of it, and they recognized the headstrong Rajput immediately. What a fight he had put up the other day to return the money! The munim came closer, and began to spit and shout, 'Why smash pots of infamy on our heads? This has to do with you, this pond, and the Lakkhi Binjara! Then what is all this fuss about the seth's permission?'

Meanwhile, the thirsty bulls grunted and groaned in agony. They could not move even a step without the signal from the Lakkhi Binjara. A sea of suffering began to churn in the seth's ears.

The Rajput said brusquely, 'There was no way you would agree to take the money back. So, helpless as I was, I had to have this pond dug with that money. Free me of my debts and give your consent, only then will I let these bulls drink water. Otherwise, this sin is going to be on your head!'

The agonized howls of the bulls felt like throbbing pustules in the ears. If the seth remained unmoved by even this, ruin would befall his next seven births. What a tight spot the simpleton had put the seth in!

The seth's head was swimming. He came up to the Rajput and, shaking him by the shoulders, said, 'All right, I release you from your debts. I permit it. Don't make these bulls suffer any longer. Both of us own the water in this pond now.'

The poor Rajput kept his bow and arrow aside and said, 'Now I have no objection either.'

The Lakkhi Binjara mounted his chariot and let out a shrill whistle, and with that, the bulls rushed towards the pond. Before their eyes, numerous birds began to fly in and descend upon the edges of the pond. Hordes of animals, their throats parched, dashed towards it. No bird or animal could think of anything but satiating their thirst!

The Father of Sin

IN THE DURBAR OF A certain king was a special gathering of intellectuals and wise men. The king himself was not very bright, but he respected learned men and understood subtle matters when they were explained to him. From time to time, he would ask his courtiers new questions. Whoever gave the right answer was rewarded with whatever they desired. The king would always give the wise men time to ponder before they answered. But if he did not get a response before the time was up, he would mete out the strictest of punishments. The greed for the prize and the fear of the punishment made the intellectuals and wise men think deeply about the answers.

One day, the king asked: 'Who is the father of sin?'

It was a tough question; few even ventured to offer an answer. The king repeated the question a couple of times.

Then the Rajguru[54] stood up and said, 'My lord, I will answer this question. But I need a month's time.'

The king agreed. That very day, the Rajguru began leafing through the pages of the scriptures. He began consulting lengthy treatises. He would pose this question to every individual he met. A whole fortnight passed researching in this manner, but the exercise yielded no results.

Twenty days passed … twenty-five days passed … and still the Rajguru had not found an answer. By now, he was extremely vexed. Such was the grip of anxiety that he could neither eat nor sleep! The thought of not being able to get the right answer was sucking the life force out of him. Lines of worry cast a dark shadow on his once-glowing face.

Seeing the Rajguru so lost, the mehtarani – the sweeper woman – asked him, 'What is the matter, Guruji? I've been meaning to ask you for days. You seem to be engrossed in some thought. The very colour of your face has changed. What worries you so much?'

The mehtarani was stunningly beautiful. But as she was an untouchable, people were forced to keep their distance from her. Her smile was like a flash of lightning, and she had a voice so sweet that it seemed as if a koel dwelled in her throat.

Usually, the Rajguru would not even let the voice of an untouchable fall on his ears, but that day, anxiety made him forget his caution. 'How would you lowborn folk

---

54 Rajguru: Royal priest.

understand such serious matters? Something worries me, of course, but how will you be able to help me?'

Smiling, she said, 'The lotus blooms in the mud. Sometimes us lowborns can do what highborns can't manage.'

As the man on the verge of drowning tries to latch on to even a twig, the Rajguru confided his problem to the mehtarani.

As soon as she heard the question, the mehtarani began to giggle. She said, 'You have been stressing over such a trifle for so many days? I think all your learning has been in vain! What was the use of all your scriptures and texts?'

She laughed again. Her laughter dazzled the Rajguru. He forgot about all the precautions and distinctions he practised so diligently. His greed for the prize and the fear of being punished were far greater. He asked with the air of a beggar, 'So you can give me the answer to this question?'

Most definitely she could, said the woman. She knew it the moment she heard the question. If the Rajguru would come to her house that evening, she would make him see the father of sin himself. The Rajguru agreed right away.

When the Rajguru went to her house, she began to fry meat, seasoned with onion and garlic, in ghee. At first, he covered his nose with a cloth. But after some time, he removed it. The heady aromas made his mouth water. Such dishes were made in the royal kitchens every day. Such smells were not new to the Rajguru!

A short while later, the mehtarani placed a bottle of wine and arranged sparkling gold mohurs on a silver dish and kept it in front of the Rajguru. 'If you eat the meat and drink the wine, I will give you these twenty-five mohurs,' she said.

The Rajguru said, 'Ram, Ram! What outrageous things you are saying! If someone finds out, my dharam and karam will all be spoilt. Even coming to your house is taking it too far. Now don't distract me with these other things and quickly tell me the answer to my question.'

The mehtarani said coyly, 'Forget about people finding out. Not a whisper will reach a third pair of ears! But I will tell you the answer only once you have consumed these, not before.'

The Rajguru was helpless. He glanced around furtively and then, taking the bowl of wine from the mehtarani's hand, he took a sip.

The wine, her smile and her gaze cast such a spell on the Rajguru that he forgot everything else. He drank the wine from the bowl she had drunk from, and they both partook of meat from the same plate. He was in a trance. The intoxication of her beauty was stronger than that of the wine. And the intoxication of the prize and the gold mohurs was even stronger than the intoxication of her beauty! When the mehtarani offered him fifty more gold mohurs, the Rajguru even agreed to indulge in things that are best left unsaid...

Afterwards, he asked her, 'At least tell me now, who is the father of sin?'

'You still haven't figured it out? Then it is pointless to spell it out! What sort of a wise man are you? The father of sin is greed! Just look at the sins greed made you commit today. Whatever prize you get now, I am entitled to half of it. The rest and all your dharam–karam is up to you. Why, even I went to such lengths purely out of greed...'

The Truthful Thief

WHEN HAS THE GOOD IN man been worshipped? Can it be discerned? Are there those who can discern it? This is why, in our land, it is appearances that are worshipped. People bow to appearances, prostrate before them. Appearances hide all that is flawed in us. They are a signal of our worth, one that even the unlettered can read instantly. Sometimes, weaklings, idlers and good-for-nothings assume facades. It makes it easy for them to get scraps from those around them. And at other times, there are some who use false appearances to lay traps. No livelihood is as convenient. A business that needs no investment, this enterprise thrives as long as there are people who will bow down before appearances. Many an idler gets by with a facade alone, makes merry as he pleases on the strength of it. Hardship and pain make many take refuge in false appearances. For people so stricken, they bring a whiff of peace and happiness. The ancient wheel of religion keeps spinning on the backs of those ensnared in the delicate mesh of such appearances. Hence the saying: never trust an ointment that comes as a gift, or the shaved head of a monk! The truly wise do not trust appearances.

Once, a mahatma, who hid behind such appearances, came to a village and camped for the chaturmas.[55] He was accompanied by a party of followers – unlettered, guileless and ignorant folk, and on top of that, with an unshakeable faith in the atma, the parmatma and mukti![56] Where else in this universe could one find a people more susceptible to deception? It is not hard to convert those who are willing to prostrate at your feet without knowing you. An oil lamp does not budge from where it burns, but who can stop crazed insects that dart into it in a race unto death? Doesn't the flame shake its head and warn them? Over the past few years, that pretend-mahatma had developed a taste for this concoction of appearances and religion. The more he implored people not to spend time away from their jobs and everyday chores, the more they flocked towards him. He would keep refusing to accept new pupils all day, and yet the queues only grew longer.

---

55 Chaturmas: The four months of the monsoon season, when monks pause their itinerant lives and stay in one place.

56 Atma; parmatma; mukti: The soul or self; the supreme self; liberation or release.

Every hour, the mahatma would say, 'My dear people, I have no accomplishments. I liked the colours of these robes, so I wore them. Believe me, there is nothing more to it. I am a wandering mendicant. I must keep wandering in this way – it is written in the lines on my feet. You go about your work, and I will go about mine. I do not interfere with your activities. Why must you interfere with mine?'

What kind of a devotion would it be if people were to agree to such words? Even more people began to queue up to become his followers. One goes and twenty-one come. When might one get an opportunity to see such a venerable mahatma again!

That mahatma had another rule. Before accepting a follower, he would insist that the person give up eating something or the other. Some gave up consuming brinjals, some root vegetables, some pumpkins, and yet others, watermelons. Some pledged to give up drinking milk, while others promised never to eat curd, and one left eating amchur. Someone said that they would not eat after sunset. Others swore that they would not sit and eat with others. Some gave up having sweets, while others, savouries. But those who would give up their chillum, ganja, bhang and opium were few and far between!

There lived in that village an audacious thief. When he heard this clamour of aspiring followers, he too grew restless. He was used to doing his job at night and sleeping by day. One day, even as he slept, it occurred to him that he must go and find out about this mahatma. He awoke in the middle of the day, rubbed his eyes, and then landed straight at the mahatma's abode. At the time, there was a thin crowd of devotees at the sage's doorstep. The thief bowed his head at the feet of the mahatma and said, 'Please accept me as your pupil.'

· The mahatma said, 'You must be aware of this rule of mine – unless one vows to abstain from something, I do not accept them as a pupil.'

'What if I swear never to make anyone my guru?' asked the thief. 'Will you accept me as a devotee then?'

The mahatma had made thousands his followers, but never had one who had sworn such an oath come along. He felt as if he'd been smacked in the face with an old, withered shoe. But he was no less cunning. The very next instant, he gathered himself, smiled and said, 'Child, what is the need to become a follower after making such a vow? You must know that once one makes a promise not to do something, one has to give it up completely.'

Then, the thief said, 'If that is so, I hereon vow to abstain from four things. Most do not give up even a second thing after a first. First, as long as I live, I vow that I will not get into bed with a queen. Second, I vow to not eat from a golden platter. Third, I vow to not mount a golden howdah on an elephant. And fourth, and the most important, I vow that I will not become the ruler of a kingdom. Now have mercy on me and accept me as your follower!'

Hearing the thief's words, the mahatma was beside himself with rage. But what could he have said? Even the most mischievous buffalo stays tethered while he is watched. How could that wearer of appearances discard his facade and confront this thief? But he must be taught a lesson. A show of temper would only harm the mahatma. So he said again, with a smile, 'Never before have I had a follower who matches you. It would be my pleasure to be your guru. You have forsaken these four things as per your own wish. Now at least give up one more as per mine. I will not forget you as long as I live—'

The thief was impatient. He interrupted the mahatma, 'Why would I not give it up? If you suggest it, I surely will. I will give up breathing if you so command, and still won't die.'

This man! Deep creases appeared on the mahatma's forehead. He was so furious that he wanted to make the man take this very vow! But what would people say when they heard of it? He had to keep up appearances for many more years to come. What big pleasures had he even savoured yet? He was just about warming up to the pleasures of life. The mahatma started to ponder over an oath the thief could be sworn to, one that would straighten him out within a few days. It had been so many years since he had assumed this form, and in that time, he had seen many a great sage. Even sages could not get by without lying. Then how could a poor thief live out a promise not to lie? Either he would refuse to swear to the oath, or he would give up in a couple of days. 'Alongside these four vows,' said the mahatma, 'if you swear that you will not lie even in the face of death, that would be like fragrance from gold!'

The damned thief was unbelievable! He agreed instantly and said, 'Whether this gold will acquire a fragrance or not is for you to worry about. But from this day on, I swear to never lie again!'

Every hour, the mahatma would check again. 'See, if you cannot fulfil your vow, it will not only be you who will lose face – I will too. To not lie is not as easy as you think.'

The thief said with confidence, 'Don't you worry about this at all. If something else brings you dishonour, that is on you. But I will not bring shame on you even in death. And what loss of face for us thieves? We leave our faces behind in our mothers' wombs. I have lied a lot since the time I learnt to talk. I have lied without measure, as much as a thousand people would, and have still not found any peace. Everything I have said has been a lie; all that I have not said has been the truth. All I need to change is that, from now on, everything I say must be the truth and all that I don't say must be lies. Go ahead and make me swear to never utter a lie from this mouth of mine. I accept it.'

Then, despite his wishes, the mahatma had to accept the thief as his pupil. He tied a red string on the thief's right wrist, and the thief handed the mahatma a hairy coconut. Becoming a follower in lieu of a coconut was not a bad deal.

Even a baniya cannot go about his business if he does not lie; and this was the business of theft. But the thief had to have a means of livelihood after all. Just as businessmen leave for distant lands, he too would set off to faraway places to earn a living.

Wearing torn clothes and tattered shoes, he departed for foreign shores, his shoes dragging as he trudged along. He walked and walked until he entered a new kingdom. Dusk had set in by then. He heard the sound of bells emanating from a temple and joined the devotees. There was no devotion in his heart, yet he stood there. Soon after the prayers, the devotees left for their homes. But the thief remained standing there, in front of the idol of the deity. Where else would a thief spend the night if not in this beautiful temple? His eyes found the diamonds and pearls the idol was covered in more pleasing than the idol itself. For God, diamonds and pebbles were all the same. These distinctions lie in the hearts of men.

The pujari spotted this new devotee, with ragged clothes and shoes in tatters, gazing at the temple deity's idol, as if in a trance. 'Who are you, brother?' he asked. 'Never seen you all these days...'

Startled, the thief replied, 'I am a thief. I have come to this village only today.'

The pujari smiled. 'If you are a thief,' he said, 'then why have you come to this temple?'

'Why? To steal, of course. Besides stealing, what other job is there for a thief?'

The pujari smiled again and said, 'Silly, why do you lie to me? I have been the pujari of this temple for fifty years now. God alone can read the hearts of men, but I can

certainly read their faces. Thieves do not tell the truth even
when they are thrashed. You are surely an ardent devotee
and have come here to test me. But I am not scared of being
tested. I will come out pure. Look, your words make him
who dwells in all our hearts smile!'

The thief looked at the pujari's face. Long, white
hair. Luminous beard, and toothless mouth. A tilak
of sandalwood paste. And around his neck, a string of
rudrach[57] beads. The thief said again, 'I am a thief. If you
do not believe me, that is your wish. If God smiles at what
I say, that is God's wish. I would like to spend the night
here. You will not object to that, will you?'

Hearing the thief speak thus, the pujari, without
another thought, hugged him straight away. Shedding tears
of joy, he said in a choked voice, 'Omniscient one, today my
devotion has borne fruit! You have given me your darsan in
this form! My eyesight may have weakened, but the eyes
of my heart are wide open. Am I so blind that I would not
know it is you?'

The thief somehow stopped himself from bursting into
laughter. After that, the pujari left the temple to this very
reincarnation of God and went off and slept in the small
room at the rear. This devotee had offered the supreme
being such priceless diamonds and pearls, so he accepted
them. But how long would devotees continue to make

---

57 Rudrach: Rudraksh. Dried pieces of stone fruit that are
strung together and used as prayer beads.

such offerings if the divine being started to accept them in this way!

That thief was so audacious that he could take off the very clothes of men who were asleep and they would not even bat an eyelid. What was he going to leave behind, then? There was not much thrill in this robbery, but nevertheless, immense wealth came into his hands. Invaluable diamonds and priceless pearls and a parasol of pure gold! All his life he had lied, and as a consequence, he'd had to bear hardships. He had barely been able to eat rotis in peace. He had been beaten black and blue until his bones were hollow. Once he lied, he would never admit to the truth.

There are such profits to be made in faraway lands! That is why businessmen leave behind their homes, where generations of their people have lived, without hesitation. With four hours to go before sunrise, the thief left the temple, God and the pujari behind, and returned to the place he had come from.

Once he returned to his village, he melted the gold parasol into a large brick. He went into the fields, dug a deep pit, and buried the urn filled with diamonds and pearls, and made note of the trees at the spot, and then headed straight to a goldsmith. As was the rule in the business, the thief gave the goldsmith a share of his loot and got for himself chains, earrings, bulky bracelets, and a seven-strand necklace. Then he went to a tailor and had fine clothes such as those worn by rich men and nobles made for himself. And for five thousand rupees, he bought a fine horse.

Such is the miraculous play of maya! Earlier, people would be suspicious of even what little wealth the thief possessed, and they would ask him where he had got his hands on it. Despite knowing fully well that he was not going to tell the truth, they would not give up until they had broken his bones. And today, when he was ready to speak the truth upon being merely asked, not a soul questioned him as to where he had brought such a large quantity of gold from. Even the sun did not glitter like this gold! Could so much wealth be amassed by thievery? Surely, it had to be from some business, or gambling.

After resting for a few days, the thief again mounted his horse, which was as fast as the wind, and set off for foreign shores, a golden walking stick in hand. Astride such a horse, how long does it take to reach one's destination? The very next day, he camped in a gigantic city. He tied his horse in a garden and rested awhile. As the sun set, he left for a wealthy seth's mansion. Why rob the weak and meek? Big loot can be made only off big people!

The seth had finished his meal before sunset and returned to his garden. He was feeling a bit out of breath, so he had just stretched himself out when he heard someone clear his throat.

The seth asked, 'Who goes there?'

'Oh, I am a thief!'

The seth sat up with a start on hearing of a thief. Breathless, he could not even scream. But as soon as his eyes fell on the thief, the seth felt instantly relieved. He himself did not have as many jewels to wear. On top of that, there was the thief's golden walking stick. Smiling, the seth said, 'My good man, why scare me by speaking of thieves? One can tell a thief just from his shadow. What, you take me to be such a fool? I can deduce if one is a thief or an honest man by his breath alone.'

The thief broke into a smile and replied, 'Then your deductions are all wrong, seth! I hereby declare that I am a thief, and I am here to rob your mansion. If you do not believe me, that is your problem. Now tell me, who do you think I am?'

The seth caught the thief by his hand and said, 'Sit here, beside me. I am seeing you for the first time. But I have heard so much about you that I could recognize you as soon as I laid my eyes on you. My eyesight has weakened somewhat, so it took a bit of time. Don't you mind me.'

Then, the seth regarded the thief's face closely. What was the need to touch gold so pure? One could tell it apart as soon as one saw it! Smiling, he said, 'You are the fabulously talented jeweller of Ujjain! But pray, what have I done to incur your wrath, such that you never so much as turned your face towards my abode all these years? Nevertheless, you have done me the favour of coming here today, and that is enough. I will show you such priceless diamonds and pearls and emeralds and rubies that you will never forget them! Where else in this land will you find the five real gems of Sesnaag?'

After this, the seth dragged the thief to the mansion despite his protestations. Opening all three vaults, he showed him the rarest and most priceless jewels by the light of a lamp. 'Just glance over them once for now,' said the seth. 'You will be able to assess them by the light of the sun, tomorrow. You do not even need to quote me a price! I will accept whatever you hand me. You know the worth of these better than I do. What can I tell the sun about the light of a lamp? I think you are hesitant, as you do not have enough money on you. I am not so petty. One must treat a man as befits him. You can send me the payment within six months. You may leave with as many gems as you like!'

The thief said, 'I will take the gems I like, and I will take the gems I don't like! I won't leave a single one behind. You need not coax me so for this. It would have been harder for me to find them had I tried to search for them on my own, so you showed them to me yourself. For this, I am beholden to you.'

The seth smiled. 'For so many years, I had only heard of your mischievous nature! Today, after seeing it for myself, I know that none of it was untrue.'

The seth pampered him no end, so he agreed to spend the night at the mansion. He had thirty-two delicacies prepared for his guest and served them to him on a silver platter with his own hands. And the thief kept noting where the silver bajot[58] and the golden bowls were kept.

While the seth awoke quite early, the thief had woken up two hours before him, headed to the horse tethered in the garden, and made off. When the seth called out to him and went near his bed, he found it to be empty. He called out again, two or three times, but all he heard was the sound of a horse's hooves. The seth kept thinking that the jeweller had gone to the jungle and would return presently. But neither did he return, nor was he seen leaving! At daybreak, fate was to bring tragedy the seth's way – which it did! Almost driven out of his mind, the seth went to the Raj Durbar and wailed and sobbed. But upon hearing everything, the Raja plainly refused to pursue the thief. On the contrary, he berated the seth: Had not the thief kept saying he was a thief? Such an honest thief should be given a reward! These words broke the seth's soul. The scoundrel had left not a speck of gold behind!

Here, the seth was in a state upon losing all his wealth, and there, the thief was in a state on acquiring all this wealth! He would collect all his riches in one place and wonder what he would do with so much. Even if he were to give it away by the fistful, all day and all night, would it ever end? And how much could a man

---

58 Bajot: A low table on which meals are served and partaken of.

even spend? He got a splendid three-storeyed mansion made for himself, bought enough cows and buffaloes for milk, and had five or six mares of the finest breed in his stables. At home, there were adequate clothes, and pots and pans and blankets and bed sheets. He would even help the poor generously, now and then. No one who came to this mansion was ever refused anything. He set aside substantial sums of money to build rest houses and pyaus. But never once did he even entertain the thought of leaving his regular line of work for another. What could compare to this business? All these years, he had not quite understood the right manner of carrying it out. He would only have his bones broken then. It was hard to manage two square meals a day. Rotis were in short supply. And now, it was the same livelihood, but people accorded him such honour and respect! There was not a soul to question how so much wealth had come to be amassed and from where. Now he had found out that there was no crime in thieving and robbing. Who said it was deplorable? Poverty alone is the biggest crime. The foremost sin, a life without a dime! The grand design of maya itself is above all of it. All injustice and misdeeds get hidden in its shadow.

Now, he would feel some contentment if he could rob the royal treasury! So what if his wealth was overflowing? How could he bear to sit idle? How could he forsake his talent? And so, the same garb, the same horse, and that very same golden walking stick.

As he passed the walls of the fortress, he was stopped by a soldier who asked, 'Who are you? What brings you here?'

Then, even as he sat astride his horse, he said, 'I am a thief, and I have come to rob the royal treasury. Stop me if you can!'

Seeing his attire and bearing, the soldier had addressed him respectfully. If he were a thief, wouldn't he have sneaked in? And this man had not even gotten off his horse. And such princely attire! Invaluable jewels! Such a fine horse! Never had he seen such a thief. He must surely be the raja of some kingdom. The soldier folded his hands and beseeched, 'My lord, who am I to stop you? Command me as you will!'

After entering the fortress, the thief reached the first gateway. The guard there bowed down before him and greeted him with a 'khamma ghani'. He moved ahead. The seventh gateway was heavily guarded. One of the guards there folded his hands and said, 'No one can pass through here without the Raja's approval. If Your Highness so commands, I will go inside and seek his consent. Who are you? And what brings you here?'

Just like earlier, the thief replied seated on the back of the horse, 'I am a thief, and I have come to rob the royal treasury. Stop me if you or your Rajaji can. Do not regret it later.'

The guard got frightened. He thought that perhaps his question had caused the guest offence. He had heard of the new diwan. This must be him! Who else could arrive in such splendour? Folding his hands, he said, 'Forgive me, my lord, forgive me! Whose mother has given him the courage to stop you!'

The thief smiled and rode ahead. The guards were relieved that the new diwan had mercy upon them after all!

After this, he halted only once he was near the treasury. The khajanchi[59] heard the sound of the horse's hooves and came out and asked with folded hands, 'Didn't quite recognize you, my lord?'

'How would you recognize someone without having seen them before?' asked the thief. 'I am a thief, and I have come to loot the treasury.'

Upon hearing this, the khajanchi immediately understood that he must be the new diwan. He has come to test me and inspect the treasure. He is annoyed I did not recognize him and that is why he is speaking sharply. Now he was certainly going to lose his job! Trembling, he said, 'My lord, the blind and the ignorant are one and the same. The advancing years have somewhat weakened my eyesight.'

That said, the khajanchi untethered the keys to the vaults of the treasury that were tied around a ring and handed them over to the new diwan. Things had happened exactly as the thief had wished. He took the keys and headed inside. The khajanchi, still trembling with fear, remained standing outside. The thief had no dearth of

---

59 Khajanchi: Treasurer.

wealth. He only wanted to be able to say that he had stolen from the royal treasury. So, he chose five pearls and put them into his pocket, and then handed the keys back to the khajanchi.

As he left the fortress, not a soul stopped the thief. And as soon as he exited the fortress, he raced away on his horse. The soldiers stood watching the dust it kicked up.

Before locking up, the khajanchi rechecked the treasure vaults. Five pearls were gone! Perhaps he had made a mistake. He counted a second time. Then counted again, a third time. Five pearls were indeed missing. So he really *was* a thief! Ram knows what punishment the Raja would mete out! The khajanchi was just about to shout out, when a clever idea formed in his mind. He thought, there had been a theft already and all the blame would fall upon the thief anyway. Who believes thieves? So, he picked out five priceless pearls just like the ones that had gone missing, and put them in his pouch. And as soon as he hid the pearls away, he began to scream, 'Thief … thief … thief…!'

The courtiers in the Raj Durbar were always on the lookout for such things. No sooner did they hear the cries than they rushed in from all directions. There was complete chaos outside the treasury. Everyone got together and went to the Raja.

Howling, the khajanchi narrated the entire story, 'My lord, if thieves begin to ride up to the royal treasury in such splendid attire, fearlessly astride a horse, in broad daylight, even God cannot guard the treasury! What am I?'

All the guards concurred with the khajanchi's account. He then pleaded with folded hands, 'Your Highness, I cannot carry this burden any more. If such wealthy folk begin to steal, then who will bear the responsibility of guarding the treasury? And that too, announcing boldly that I am a thief, I have come to rob the royal treasury, do what you can? My lord, this is a new style of thievery! Who can catch one so fearless? And would he worry about being caught? Only the poor are caught! Even if one so audacious were caught, who would call him a thief? My lord, those who pull off robberies so huge are called kings! Who can dare call them dacoits? Those who would, wouldn't their heads be chopped off?'

That Raja was a mere occupant of the throne. He did not really comprehend the nuances of ruling a kingdom, or of justice. He would hear what was said in silence and would not offer a response easily. The day-to-day matters of the kingdom were handled by the Rani. The Rani was very cunning. She heard everything carefully and said, 'I do not think any of you are at fault. Even if the diwan were in your place, he would not have doubted the thief. What's done is done. But if this thief is not caught, who will care for the rule of law? It is the thief's generosity that, despite having the entire treasury at his disposal, he took only ten pearls. Just as he took ten, he could have taken everything! Who would have stopped him? But now he must be caught, even if he hides in the seventh underworld! This is about the honour of the royal treasury!'

As soon as the Rani finished saying this, soldiers from various parts of the fortress rode out. Following the hoofprints of the thief's horse, they reached his haveli straight away. Having succeeded in robbing the royal treasury, the thief was sleeping peacefully in his chambers. As soon as he heard the horses, he opened the doors of his mansion. And the soldiers instantly recognized him to be the rider! However, there was not a trace of fear on his face! What was this man? When interrogated, he admitted to having carried out the theft at once and said, 'My good men, why did you go through so much trouble? Did I not tell you clearly that I am a thief and have come to rob the royal treasury?'

When the soldiers asked him to come with them, he gallantly mounted the same horse and left with them. They had never seen nor heard of such a thief!

As soon as they reached the Raj Durbar, there was an uproar: the thief had been caught, the thief had been caught! The Durbar was convened as soon as the Rani ordered. Vast crowds gathered to catch a glimpse of a thief so accomplished. At last, the simpleton Raja arrived and, without a word, took his place beside the Rani. When he surveyed the crowd crammed into the Durbar, he was rather astonished. He looked at the Rani and said, 'So many people have gathered to see a thief! Not even a fourth gather to catch a glimpse of me. This thief is fit to be a Raja! Nay, he is fit to be a Badshah!'

The Rani gave him a look, so the Raja swallowed the words that were on the tip of his tongue. He would look at the thief and smile, and then look at the crowds and smile.

The Rani's keen eyes observed that there was not another face in the entire Durbar as handsome as the thief's. On that face, there was no sign of fear at being caught. The Rani could not believe it. She asked repeatedly, 'Speak the truth, a hundred transgressions will be forgiven. Who are you?'

The thief got mildly annoyed at having to answer the same question again and again. Shaking his golden walking stick, he retorted forcefully, 'How many times do I have to say that I am a thief, a thief! I told everyone clearly and came to rob the royal treasury!'

'How many pearls did you steal?' the Rani asked.

'Five!' replied the thief.

The Rani turned her gaze to the khajanchi and asked, 'You were saying ten pearls were stolen. Why the difference?'

'My lord, can you trust thieves?' said the khajanchi with folded hands. 'He is lying through his teeth!'

The thief said, 'I have told you everything as it is. I may be a thief, but I am sworn to never speak a false word! Your own truths and lies are your business. I did not even touch a sixth pearl!'

The Rani had full faith in the thief's words. And seeing the khajanchi's face, she read his mind. In a severe voice, she said, 'This khajanchi speaks blatant lies. Diwanji, take four riders and head straight to his home. Go and search for the pearls there!'

A thief has only so much courage! The khajanchi confessed at once. He got the pearls from his home and handed them over to the diwan with trembling hands.

The courtiers were surprised beyond words! The most respectable men in the land were no match for this thief.

He who had become the thief's guru was also watching his pupil's daring from the crowd, and now felt pleased at being his guru. He stood up and said with pride, 'My lord, he is my student and I am his guru. It was I who had made him swear to speak only the truth! That day, I had honestly not believed he would uphold the honour of his words in this way. If one is to have pupils, let them all be like him!'

When the Rani heard the guru's words, she was delighted. She said to the diwan, 'I am greatly pleased with this truthful thief. Gift him these five pearls!'

But that thief would not accept the Rani's gift. He said, 'I am not a Baaman that I will hold out my hands to receive gifts in this way.'

No one present could have dreamt that, in that Raj Durbar which was bursting at the seams, a mere thief would think of defying the Rani in such a manner. Silence descended upon the Durbar. Even a lion could not look the Rani in the eye when she was angry. If she got annoyed, she could have someone hanged as easily as she handed out gifts. That foolish thief did not know her nature. For a moment, she felt a rage so strong that she wanted to have his head chopped off! But the very next instant, she suppressed her fury, and managing a smile, she said, 'I knew that this thick-headed thief would say something like this.'

Then she faced the diwan and said, 'If the pupil won't take the pearls that were stolen, then give them to his guru. After all, it was he who got the thief to swear to not tell lies…'

But that thief really *was* thick-headed! 'I have earned these five pearls,' he said undauntedly. 'Who I give it to, who I don't, is my wish!'

This time, the diwan could not control his anger. 'This chandaal's[60] tongue has grown too long! It takes advantage of Raniji's mercy and wags too much! I have seen thievery and bravery together in only this man. He robs the treasury in broad daylight, and now boldly and barefacedly proclaims the pearls are his earning!'

The thief smiled and said, 'Diwanji, why get so angry needlessly? Man comes into this world empty-handed and leaves this world empty-handed! Are even our bodies our own? Everyone amasses as much wealth as their might lets them. Some are petty thieves, others are big. And the big thieves always punish thieves weaker than them. I ask you – from where did these pearls come into the treasury?

---

60 Chandaal: While the term has been used as an abuse here, it refers to a caste tasked with disposing corpses.

Whether it is a king or the poor – if they spit, both will only spit saliva! Everyone loots what they can. And what can one loot with empty hands? The more the power of land, wealth and weapons, the more the loot. That is all that separates petty thieves from big thieves! I will tell you about myself. Earlier, I spoke nothing but lies and the world also perceived them as lies. I would get blisters, merely trying to fill my stomach. Now I speak nothing but the truth, and yet the world thinks I am lying. They do not dare think I am speaking the truth. And immense wealth comes into my hands because of the strange ways of this world.'

All those assembled were stunned at the thief's words. The Rani seemed to be under his spell. The Raja just kept smiling to himself. The khajanchi was sentenced to a hundred lashes in public. The thief's guru was gifted five pearls, which he accepted with a bowed head. If he had not reined in his anger and accepted the thief as a follower that day, and if the thief had not honoured his vow in this way, how would these five pearls have come to him?

And the thief – he was bound in chains and imprisoned in the deepest dungeon. It was pitch dark even in broad daylight in this strange world. Those who possessed power would not let the weak have their share of even the sun or the breeze. Then how would they let the weak near even the shadow of their wealth and lands?

It got darker by the minute. Must be night, now. There was nothing but darkness all around him. Today, he had not been able to claim even a ray of starlight. Suddenly, the leaves of the peepul tree in the graveyard began to gleam in front of his eyes. The full moon was up. Endless moonshine, the whispering breeze, the song of fluttering leaves, and the moonlight that danced off them! In place of this vision, even if all the wealth in the world became his, what use would it be? Even as it shimmered in front of his eyes, this vision was so far, so out of reach ... The dancing moonshine, the soft alghoza-like melodies of the breeze! Today, amidst the darkness, the thief realized the worth of this spectacle.

All at once, his cell was unbolted. A little light trickled in. An attendant came in with a lamp. She was a special, trusted attendant of the queen. She said, 'Raniji summons you.'

'Why?' The question emerged from the thief's mouth involuntarily.

'To deliver the judgement for the theft of the pearls,' replied the attendant, even as she suppressed a smile.

And as she said this, she put the lamp down on the floor and undid the thief's shackles. The dungeon echoed with the clatter of the chains. He left with her without saying a word.

As soon as he emerged from the dungeon, he looked up, and then, all around him. The white gleam of the moon on the thirteenth day of its waxing had lit up everything evenly. And in its soft veil were numerous stars, dozing. Half awake. A pleasing, cool breeze, as if fanning those slumbering stars. If he had not been sentenced to darkness, how would this enormous, infinite, invaluable treasure of nature have fallen into his hands? Which wealthy jeweller in this universe could examine these countless diamonds and pearls, and pay the price of even a single one of them? But today, he had come to own all of nature's maya. No need to tunnel through walls for this!

He ascended the stairs behind the attendant and reached the Rani's rangmahal. Its corners were lit with oil lamps. The Rani was bedecked in all her finery. The fragrance of perfumes was all over. There lay in front of her a silver bajot, and on it was a golden platter. And on it, there were thirty-two delicacies in golden bowls. As soon the attendant entered the rangmahal, she started to fan the golden platter.

The Rani said, 'Listening to you today, I was so pleased that I cannot express it even if I tried. There would be no bigger injustice than punishing a man as honest as you. As long as I am around, such injustice will never be meted out in this kingdom. But you declined my gift too. If your Guruji had not accepted those pearls instead, I would have died of shame. Your Guruji saved my honour. If the pupil is such, why wouldn't the guru be so! I just about managed to conceal my anger. But now, do not refuse anything I say. If one can have a diwan as honest, decent and intelligent as you, then there will at least be some pleasure in ruling this kingdom.'

'But with such a fair king around, why do you even get into this muck of ruling and governance?' asked the thief.

'As soon as I saw his smile, I understood that no king on earth could have a heart so pure. Can kings afford to have hearts so uncorrupted and just? I found his smile to be more valuable than all his treasure.'

The Rani smiled. 'Then both of you are just the same. He sings your praises, and you sing his. No one knows what the Rajaji muttered into my ear upon seeing you. You will laugh if you hear it. If I had not gestured to him to remain quiet, then Ram knows what rubbish he would have spouted. He had decided to crown you king! If he had his way, he would have rested only after he anointed you. I am aware that, since this kingdom was founded, never have as many people gathered in court than did today. But of what use are crowds alone? Nevertheless, as soon as Rajaji saw the crowds, he bared his heart like a guileless child and whispered into my ear softly that, when not even a fourth of this crowd assembles to see him, then how could he be fit for the throne? The talented thief who such crowds clamour to catch a glimpse of should be king! A fistful is enough to test a whole cart of grain. This is your Rajaji's face. He is as naive as a child, and completely silly!'

'I do not believe what you say at all,' said the thief. 'It is not so hard to claim the throne of enormous kingdoms. But such a king is as rare as they come. It is your good fortune that you are the queen to such a king.'

Then he looked at the golden platter in surprise and asked, 'It is nearly midnight and Rajaji has still not eaten?'

'This platter has been set out for you!' replied the attendant.

Exasperated and incredulous, the thief said, 'I have promised to never eat from a golden platter! But what was the need of such indulgences for me? I cannot believe that a thief can be accorded such respect. I have eaten dry crumbs off my palms – such platters don't suit me! And for someone who has borne insults all his life, neither can I digest such honours! If you had sent in a few scraps at the hands of some servant, they would still have been as good as thirty-two delicacies to me.'

The Rani was exceedingly cunning. She tactfully said, 'Only the jeweller knows the worth of a diamond. For the poor sculptor who chisels stone, it is as good as a pebble. After knowing his virtues, it would be unfair not to accord a man the honour he deserves. I have never found anyone as decent as you in this kingdom. Being the Rani of this kingdom, if I do not respect the good in good men, then would it be in keeping with my position? Ask this attendant and she will tell you that I have thought so far as to take out a procession with you on a golden howdah astride an elephant, even as attendants fan you, during the next Devjhoolani Gyaras, exactly as the deity's procession is taken out!'

Hearing this, the thief could not stop laughing. Seeing the thief laugh like that, the Rani stopped midway. Once he stopped, the thief said, 'In case you do not believe me, you can confirm this with Guruji. I have vowed never to mount a golden howdah on an elephant. Just my luck! The logic with which I made these vows that day – and the serendipity of these events today, that here, I, a mere thief, stand, refusing point blank. I was only taunting my Guruji, and so I swore to abstain from things that would never come my way. Had I known better that day, I would not have tangled myself in these vows even in my wildest dreams. But now, how will regret help? Now I cannot break these vows even in death. Forgive me. Only in you have I seen the virtue of respecting the virtues of others. This great virtue cannot be found even in the gods. You have honoured my honesty, so, if I have any good in me, I will not forget this even when I am dying. Thieving is my talent, but I do not take away from the virtues of others.'

Hearing the thief's words, the Rani was even more pleased. She looked at her attendant and the attendant glanced back at her. When the attendant saw the delight in the Rani's heart sparkling in her eyes, she left without being asked to. And the Rani shut the door and came and stood by the thief. Then, looking him in the eye, she said, 'Thieves are so cunning that they can catch on to even the dreams of those asleep. And here you are, so simple-minded that, let alone what is in the heart, you cannot even catch on to what is on my lips. You still have no idea why I have gone to such lengths? You just confessed that I respect one's virtues.

What better chance will present itself? Do not deprive this bed any longer! It has been waiting for us!'

Even before she finished saying what she did, the Rani caught hold of the thief's hand and made to move towards the golden bed. And the thief felt as if a snake had coiled itself around his wrist. A shiver ran down his body! He jerked his hand away and said, 'If I laugh, I will incur your wrath. So I am somehow quashing the laughter that rises to my lips. But you will not be satiated with anything other than the truth. In all honesty, I have sworn never to get into the macha[61] of a queen!'

The incensed Rani hissed, 'Fool! Queens do not have machas! They have golden beds!'

The thief again replied in the same tone, 'But they mean the same thing...!'

It was as if an arrow had pierced through the Rani's heart. How to sway this stone? If the thief was really a stone, he would have been swayed by now. But he had become a stone despite being a man. What was the way out now? The Rani felt as though her body had been cut into pieces!

The Rani's biggest asset was that one's weaknesses never remained hidden from her. And so, she shot off an arrow to puncture this weakness! 'As you said, Rajaji is a god, not a mortal. Then wouldn't it befit him to reign in

---

61 Macha: A four-legged cot.

the realm of gods rather than rule here, in the world of men? Sending him to the godly realms and putting you on the throne – you can leave that to me! You will have to merely bear the trouble of sitting on the throne, nothing else. I am a queen, and I fall at your feet! Do not deprive me any longer!'

Even after hearing these words, the thief could scarcely believe them. Was he still dreaming in the darkness of the dungeon? He rubbed his eyes and looked around wide-eyed. He truly was in the Rani's rangmahal. In all its four corners were golden lamps aglow, there was a golden bed, and the Rani – she lay with both her hands around his feet! The thief started, and jerked his feet away. He held the Rani's hands, and getting her to sit on the bed, said, 'You are the rulers of this land. What is this silliness you indulge in? I will not lie even in death! I have also vowed to never become the raja of a kingdom! The accursed like us have just such deeds to their account. Even the goddess who writes our fortunes cannot change them!'

The mistress of the kingdom had become a beggar today! Sobbing, she said, 'I will not be able to change your fate or mine! I have left no stone unturned. If you won't give in, what can I do? If you had acquiesced, then no one would have been at fault. But since you have not, the blame is all on me. If someone asks, though, do not reveal what transpired tonight, even if you are dying. My honour hides behind your lips…!'

'But my Guruji has sworn me to never tell lies!' said the thief. 'I will not lie even in death…!'

As soon as she heard this, the Rani was furious again. It was as if someone had stepped on a snake's head! If this truth were to get out, it would sully her name. Every single person's eyes would pop out of their heads! Who could bear the very throne being shaken? How? She screamed, 'Thief … thief…!'

The people in court were always on the lookout for such a melee. And that too, from the rangmahal! In the voice of the Rani herself! Royal assassins dashed there from all directions, naked swords in hand. And the price for not uttering a false word was paid by being hacked by blades. How long could the might of truth last against the force of power? Even as the Rani looked on, they chopped the honest thief into pieces! There was not even an opportunity to speak – either the truth or falsehood.

This story should have ended here, but only if the Rani's heart would let it. It comes in the way at each step and stretches this story taut. The next day, there came again a moonlit night. Even more beautiful than the one that had passed! It was that very rangmahal, that very golden platter, and that very same attendant who ushered the thief's guru into the Rani's chambers by the light of lamps. But the guru was not bound by any vows! The Rani offered, and he agreed in an instant. The guru is always a step ahead of his pupils.

As that sensuous night slipped by, the sun rose again. And at an auspicious hour, that pretend-mahatma, in the guise of a holy man, was anointed Rajguru by the Raja himself.

And on this happy note, to the celebratory clamour of drumbeats, this story must end! Stories with bloody ends never feel as nice!

Sulking Raina-de[62]

THE SUN BLAZES ACROSS THE world but dims as soon as he enters Raina-de's rangmahal! What can he tell his own queen about his light, his warmth? And the queen – she is quite the queen too! One in a million! With endless black hair that cascades down to the earth, its every strand strung with countless pearls. And a blue veil that flutters across this boundless universe.

In the evening, when the lord arrives, there is a shower of gulal;[63] at daybreak, when he departs, there is the same shower of gulal. At the hour of love, a moonlike lamp is lit. Every morning, the queen sulks when her lover departs, and every evening, she must be appeased. And the lord has

---

62 Raina-de: The goddess of the night.

63 Gulal: A coloured powder, often pink, used in celebrations such as Holi.

grown used to this petulance. He finds the sulking queen even more beautiful!

~

Today, it was the same as every other day. Smeared in the gulal of love, when the sun arrived at the rangmahal in great anticipation, he found its door shut and bolted. The chirping of countless birds was his knock on the door. The sullen queen finally opened the door, but not before quite some time had passed.

Caressing her silken hair, the sun said, 'The same thing again! But what has the poor lamp done? You should at least have lit it.'

'Don't speak to me. Light it yourself if you want.'

'I don't know how to, that's why I plead with you. Only when I gaze at your beauty by the light of the lamp will my scalding body be soothed.'

Brushing his hand away, Raina-de said, 'I know your ways very well. Do you wander the world all day to learn these tricks? At night, when you wanted to have your way with me, you said you would be back after a quick round, in an hour or so. If you were going to arrive at your usual time, then why did you make empty promises to me?'

Laughing, the sun said, 'My dear queen, I have to look after the entire universe. I wake all living things with hunger in their bellies, but I do not let them go to sleep hungry. They rely on me alone. If I break my rule, it will betray their trust in me. The day is for the whole world;

the whole of the night is for you! And in spite of this, you complain! I don't get even a moment's respite from looking after each and every living being.'

Raina-de's anger was ebbing, bit by bit. 'Are you the only one who grinds and toils away?' she asked.

'If I grind and toil away alone, it won't be enough. That is why I bless different creatures with promise and strength, as needed.'

'I don't see any merit in this promise and strength you give,' said the queen. 'The farmers and labourers who work their fingers to the bone in your heat day and night, sweating buckets – they barely manage to lay their hands on scraps. And the rich and royal, who will not wander even close to your heat and light – they make merry, regale themselves!'

Turning somewhat sombre, the sun said softly, 'I have given up on man and stopped caring for him. He has grown too daring. He is now drunk on his own knowledge; he does not depend on me. I fulfil the hopes and needs of the birds and animals who rely only on me—'

Raina-de interrupted with a taunt, 'What great hopes you fulfil! One being eats another! Just today I was looking out of the jharokha when I saw a roaring lion gobble up a pregnant deer. The poor thing howled and wailed for her unborn child, but no mercy arose in that murderous lion's heart.'

'These are the ways of nature. It knows not the difference between life and death. As one lives, one dies.

As one dies, one lives. I nourish beings as they are, I don't change them.'

'When one is helpless, one has to console oneself by dressing up the truth in this manner. But, truly, doesn't even one small creature get left out of your care?'

Shaking his head, the sun replied, 'No, not even one. It is for these very creatures that I endure being parted from you.'

'And what if some creature does get left out? What then?' asked Raina-de, as if she were placing a bet.

'Then, let alone leaving this palace, I won't as much as cast a glance outside!'

'Don't give me that! I know well the worth of your promises!'

Embracing the queen, the sun said, 'If you won't, who will? You are the sole reprieve from my burning!'

Holding her pearl-encrusted hair in place, Raina-de said, 'At least don't make my priceless pearls come off and scatter all over for this empty affection!'

'The worth of these pearls is in our love alone!'

'That is true, yes...'

And after this, no one cared about the scattered pearls...

As the sun made haste to leave the rangmahal at dawn, Raina-de kissed her man's cheek and said, 'Stay back for just one day, upon my request. If I die, this wish will remain unfulfilled.'

The sun extricated himself from her embrace and said, 'The two of us are immortal. If we die, the world dies!'

'Still, stay for just an hour more. Don't you care for my love even this much?'

'It is because I care for it that I leave on time. If I delay for even an instant, then the world will erupt into chaos.'

Raina-de had to shower the world with gulal despite her wishes. Smiling, the sun set forth. And with his smile, light and more light spread everywhere!

Sulking, the queen took off all her pearls. Now, she would rest only once she had put her husband to the test. If she won the bet, she would never let him leave their palace. All-powerful, all-caring for everyone, indeed!

She came up with an excellent plan. She hid an ant in a small box of kumkum and tucked it away in her blouse.

As the day stretched out interminably, she counted each passing instant. There was no way she could be calmed today. The sun must be delaying his return on purpose!

The sun had tired of knocking on the doors of the rangmahal when Raina-de finally unbolted them. And as soon as she saw him, she put on a morose face and said, 'How come you are so late today?'

'I came back on time. But, of course, my brooding queen would feel it is late.'

Raina-de flung a jibe at him, 'No creature escaped your care, did it?'

The sun played along. 'If it did, then who would worship my heat and light?'

'Your heat and light indeed! Why sing your own vain praises?' she said. Then, taking out the small box from her blouse, the queen asked, 'Were you able to look after this ant?'

Smiling, the sun said, 'If you doubt it, then check the box. I put into the box half a grain of rice with my own hands. A tiny piece of it is still left over, after the ant nibbled at it.'

Raina-de could scarcely believe this. She opened the box impatiently and checked it, only to find there really was a small piece of grain close to the ant.

No end to her surprise and her joy! She bathed her lover in kumkum and said, 'If my pearls scatter all over now, so be it. I won't care even the slightest!'

And with these words of affection, she took her husband into her arms. And the pearls kept scattering through the night...

Only I Can Say No

ONCE, WHEN A CERTAIN MAARAJ[64] was out seeking alms, a newly wed beendni neither offered him flour nor gave him rotis. The maaraj turned red in anger. He was on his way back, muttering curses to himself when he met the beendni's sasu.[65] He said to her, 'Who does your beendni think she is, insulting a mahatma! Is a pinch of flour or a scrap of roti dearer than a sage? What a time we live in – the reign of beendnis in every home!'

Hearing the maaraj's words, the sasu flared up. 'Is that so? How dare she say no to a maaraj! Come with me.'

The maaraj was greatly pleased on seeing the sasu's reaction. He reached out for the pile of wood she had been carrying on her head and now carried it himself. The sasu

---

64 Maaraj: A version of the word 'maharaj'; here, a respectful address for a monk.

65 Sasu: Mother-in-law.

walked ahead, muttering and scowling. As soon as she reached home, she took the heap of wood from the maaraj and hurried inside. Then, she gave the beendni a dressing down. How could she have refused the maaraj? Fortune had smiled on him today, thought the maaraj. The sasu yelled at the beendni for a long time.

In due course, the sasu came to the maaraj. 'How dare the beendni turn anyone down while I am still around? If someone has to say no, it should be me,' she said. 'Go on, get out! You will get nothing!'

Double Lives

It takes two hands to clap!
And entangled clouds to thunder!
Touch arouses the fire!
Who can measure, who can order?
The waves crash, the fire rises.
Youth in youth's place,
who can see, who can trace?
So may Kamdev be sated,
so may each have lives unabated…

IN TWO ANCIENT VILLAGES TWENTY-FOUR miles apart, lived two seths, equal in years. Two so rich and so miserly were not to be found elsewhere in the land. Love unbounded, affection abundant! And as fate and that auspicious night would have it, the two seths were wedded at the same hour.

The hathleva[66] with their incredibly beautiful beendnis
was enjoined at the same moment. And it was at the same
time that pearls were conceived in both the oysters. Beside
themselves with joy, the seths vowed that should one have a
boy and the other a girl, they would be joined in matrimony
– the children were married off while still in the womb!

Intoxicated by their love for one another and crazed
by their wealth, the seths knew not about the caprice of
nature. In the ninth month, they both had daughters born
to them under the same alignments of the stars. Partly
obsessed with the promise made before the children were
born, and partly due to his habitual miserliness, one of
the seths tricked the other. Despite having a daughter, he
had bronze thalis beaten instead of the customary baskets
made of cane. He dispatched the nai[67] with the good news
to his friend's village. Festivities commenced in both their
mansions with the handing out of jaggery.

At first, the mother thought that this was a joke
between two friends. In time, everything would be revealed.
Until then, there was no harm in continuing with this
masquerade. In the innocence of childhood, what is a

---

66 Hathleva: A wedding ritual where the hands of the groom
    and the bride are joined during the pheras.

67 Nai: The barber caste. But their responsibilities could also
    include those that a butler does in a household, and they
    would also take care of all rituals.

boy and what's a girl! It is only in youth that these deep differences come to be properly known...

The father, however, knowingly or unknowingly, made no effort to put an end to this charade. He raised his daughter as a son. She grew up with a dhoti tied around her waist, an angrakhi draping her torso and a bandhej turban on the head. At first, all of it seemed to be in jest. But even when she was old enough and the father showed no change of heart, the mother began to fear the worst.

One day, she prodded her husband, 'How can you be so blind with your eyes wide open?'

'I'm not blind at all,' said the seth, a little annoyed. 'I can see all three realms of the universe!'

The sethani held her head and said, 'He who sees the three realms can't see his grown-up daughter dressed in the garb of a man?'

'Where do I have the time to care about such trivial matters?' the seth replied bluntly.

The sethani uttered spontaneously what she said every day, 'Father of our child, what is this foolishness? It is time to get our daughter married, and you think this is a trivial matter?'

'But I never refused to get her married. In fact, can anyone vie with my far-sightedness? I arranged a match for her while she was in the womb!'

The sethani came closer to her husband and said, 'What use is your arrangement? Has a girl ever been married to a girl, pray?'

'What's marriage! You get married, and that is that. But a vow cannot be broken even in death!'

The sethani began to feel faint. These weren't words said in jest. How could she explain to her husband what was as clear as day? Is this even something that needs explaining? She stood gaping for a while. But if she remained silent now, it would bring ruin! Finally, she braced herself and said, 'My good man, the promise you have made cannot honour the demands of the bed. Have some sense before you spout such silliness! I did not nag you all these years thinking it was all a joke.'

'But I never did anything for which I should be nagged! We will get a huge amount in dowry! With much pomp I will ride in my son's jaan.[68] A man's word cannot be changed. Why should I have to compensate for nature's error?'

The sethani was perplexed. Either her husband was still teasing her, or he truly did not want to step back from his promise. But today, she would not let the matter rest until a suitable solution was found. Mad with rage, she said, 'To hell with your gains! How will our daughter fulfil the needs of the bed having found a father like you? Does this thought never occur to you?'

'Why? Why would it not occur to me?' the seth replied, amused. 'When men go to foreign lands, good women patiently wait it out for eight to ten years. If they end up

---

68 Jaan: Groom's wedding procession.

with a slow, soft husband, wives manage in some way or the other. Child widows, too, somehow spend their days without anyone. Our daughter's fate is her own. She will live it out on her own too.'

The sethani was now convinced that this matter could not be overlooked another moment. The seth did not want to untie even one knot in this web. Her daughter's face began swimming in front of her eyes. In a choked voice, she said, 'We have given birth to her! How can we punish her like this? How will she live out her fate being married to another girl? I can't consent to this crime even in my dreams—'

Annoyed, the seth interrupted her: 'But when did I even ask you for your consent? I alone am enough for this. If you do any further meddling, I will kill myself! I'd rather die than go back on my word. Besides, do you not know how the deficiencies in the beds of seths are met? How your father's line has continued – that is hidden from no one in this entire village! Despite that, did I not swallow this fly with my eyes wide open?'

The sethani had not anticipated this searing taunt from her husband. She was dumbstruck. It was as if the blood in her veins had frozen up. Truly, this was hidden from no one. Her mother had not abstained from any man she had come across! While her weak father was engrossed in his trade and accounts, her wild mother had grown blind to even the caste of the male company she kept.

She would eat and drink with that Bawari[69] in full view of everyone. He was extremely well built and handsome. And the sethani was his spitting image: the same face, the same mannerisms. As soon as the seth lifted the lid of that pandora's box, the sethani was left speechless. Hesitantly, she ventured, 'Do as you please…'

Her husband had not expected his shot to land so perfectly! The whole matter was resolved with such ease. As fate would have it, the very next day, at an auspicious hour, a proposal for the wedding date was received at the seth's. The father accepted it with great joy. But as for the mother's heart, it felt like a dagger had pierced it. And yet, she did not open her mouth; she did not even make a sound. It was out of her hands now – it was up to the daughter and her fate.

The daughter was completely innocent, though. Neither was she aware of her youth, nor did she know what lay in her fate. Having been brought up as a boy all these years, she thought of herself as nothing but a boy. Without any knowledge of what a marriage actually stood for, she looked forward to this novel thing with great enthusiasm. Once married, hair would surely sprout on her slippery cheeks to form a beard, she thought. Her fingers itched to twist the pointy ends of a moustache. And seeing her daughter's naivety, the mother suffered in silence.

---

69 Bawari: Presently a 'denotified tribe', which has historically been subject to much discrimination.

And then, when a female friend accidentally saw the seth's daughter bathing one day, all the friend's misconceptions were cleared up. For years the friend had thought that the parents were working up some enchantment. But now, when she saw the seth's daughter eager to ride a horse during her wedding procession, the friend could hold herself back no longer. She took her into a room and began, 'My silly sister—'

'This is not something I have heard before,' she interrupted her friend. 'Why did you address me as sister instead of brother?'

'What why?' said the friend, with a snigger. 'You are a girl. So why does it sting you to be called so? What a fool you are, that being a woman you dream of becoming a groom! How long can it last by merely adopting the ways of a man when, in reality, you are not a man?'

'How long? It will last a lifetime! Do you see any lack in my manhood? This dhoti, this angrakhi. And this turban, sixteen hands long!'

A smile appeared on the friend's lips as she said, 'A sixteen-hand-long turban cloth does not quite compensate for the instruments of men! You should refuse this wedding outright. Your youth demands a groom for itself. What will two girls in wedlock do – sit and dig the ground? You are now of an age to be able to comprehend such things, and you still don't get these simple matters?'

And yet, that ignorant daughter born to the seth could grasp nothing of what had been said to her. Instead, she scowled at her friend and said, 'You are jealous of my beautiful bride! You can't bear my happiness!'

In response, her friend hugged her and said, 'What can I even tell you? You will learn only once you fall. But then, that lesson alone will not be enough. Your father is greedy for dowry. Did your mother tell you nothing, though? It is shocking how she has made peace with this.'

Then, that guileless girl said animatedly, 'I will go to my mother at once and ask her. She will hide nothing from me.'

'To not hide anything from you would be for the best,' saying so, the friend went back home. And the agitated daughter rushed to her mother and demanded, 'Ma, today one of my friends told me something very shocking – that I merely wear the clothes of a man, but I am not really one. I don't believe her! Don't you hide anything from me. Tell me, my friend is a liar, isn't she? I told her off to her face, saying that she is only jealous of my beautiful beendni!'

The mother turned away and wiped the tears from her eyes. After a while, when the torrent of emotions in her heart had subsided, she said, 'Yes, would I not have warned you if such a thing were indeed true? Sometimes our friends do pull our legs so.'

Then, the daughter confidently declared, 'Let them pull my leg! Do I care? If I were not a man and instead were a woman, even then I wouldn't have refused this marriage,' she declared with confidence. 'This is a meeting of hearts! If two hearts touch each other, can two women not marry?'

'Yes,' the mother replied softly, 'your father too says the same thing.'

'My father does not lack intelligence, does he!' the daughter said gleefully.

She had asked her mother what she had to. There was no reason to linger there any further. So, flicking the tail of her turban, she left prancing and skipping. And here, the mother, stifling the sobs which surged from within her, was lost in her thoughts like a statue made of stone.

The following day, when she met her friend, the darling daughter gave her a mouthful. She had not been born under such stars as to be fooled, she said. And then added, 'Even if I were not a man, I would still have married some woman and shown you! We would have made quite a pair!'

The friend had not yet borne a child, but she had been married now for two years. When she heard such silly talk, she could suppress her laughter no more. 'I think the well you drink water from is laced with bhang. Silly girl! Millstones can grind and chaff against one another all they want, but what good will it do? The need for a man can be fulfilled only by a man!'

'Does a man have a special magic wand? It is the grain that comes from being ground by millstones that nourishes the whole world. Grains become flour. We get dal.'

The friend burst out laughing. She clapped her hands, and in between guffaws she managed to say, 'The two of you must not leave any stone unturned in grinding dal, then!'

Ignorant as she was, the daughter felt annoyed at her friend's laughter. Forcing a smile herself, she asked, 'Why? Is there something wrong with grinding dal?'

Stifling her giggles with great difficulty, the friend replied, 'You will know when the time comes.'

'Surely you too must have found out something!'

'But there is no comparing your marriage and mine...'

'True, not even a shadow of resemblance. Your ancestors would not even have heard of a dowry as enormous as mine!'

The friend was not offended. Pinching her left cheek softly, she said, 'Why drag my ancestors into our spat? No one can make you see sense.'

And truly, that simple daughter born in the house of seths, could neither comprehend matters on her own, nor would she get it when others tried to make her understand. As the wedding approached, the joy in her heart began to surge and well over. At last, the much-anticipated auspicious hour arrived. After much feasting and revelry, the jaan finally departed. The father of the groom mounted on a camel, and the groom on a chariot pulled by Nagauri bullocks.

The jaan hurtled towards its destination. The bride's side greeted them at the edge of their village. Following the kanwar-kalewa,[70] at the appointed hour at dusk, the groom and bride sat under the wedding canopy. Two hands,

---

70　Kanwar-kalewa: Ritual breakfast for the groom.

both as soft, were joined together. And no sooner had one touched the other than a shiver ran down their spines! Two beings, unknown to one another, were being bound for life.

On a scarlet-coloured bed, by the light of a lamp, sat the turbaned groom awaiting his bride. At midnight, the tinkling of anklets and the whispering of women was heard. The bride stood at the threshold of the chamber, her face veiled. Flowers blossomed in the groom's heart.

When the new bride hesitated at the threshold, her friends pushed her inside the room and bolted the door from the outside. Slowly, she walked to the scarlet bed. Lifting her veil, the groom gazed at her face. Why, hidden behind the veil was the moon itself! The groom's anticipation could barely be contained by the pillars of the chamber. Caressing the bride's face, the groom said, 'I'd heard praise of your beauty every day, but I could never have hoped for such beauty even in my dreams!'

Parting her pink lips, the bride spoke in a soft voice, 'You are no less beautiful! My beauty is nothing compared to yours.'

Both continued to gaze at each other's faces and drank their fill of the other's beauteous radiance. The friends who stood outside the chamber door grew tired peering in through the cracks, but other than the flame of the burning lamp, they could see no other flame! Perhaps only once the thirst of the eyes was quenched would the thirst of the body come to mind.

The next day, though, it was the same spectacle! The onlookers' eyes began to hurt, but nothing they were eager to see came into view. Their tender legs began to ache too. And so, one by one, they left. Shyness is fitting where shyness is needed, but what use is so much shyness? What a waste of two successive nights that were meant for being spent in pleasure! And they aren't *that* young. Is there any end to the thirst of these fit-for-burning eyes! Whether they stare for a moment, or they stare all night long, it is the same thing! Well, to each their own thoughts and their own understanding...

Meanwhile, however, even after the bride came to her in-laws', the groom remained as shy as before; his understanding of the situation at hand did not change either. And there, the sethani grew ever restless. The anxiety over this strange marriage made her tremble even in the sweltering heat of the month of Aasoj. The seth asleep beside her snored away, but Ram knows where the sethani's sleep had vanished! How must those two girls be grappling with this nemesis called night? Once the bride's illusion cleared, when would her grief cease? And that naive daughter of the sethani understood nothing. She went to get married with such excitement. Walked into this with her eyes wide open. But the bride – she was still mired in illusion.

And there, the newly-weds' chamber was illuminated by the soft glow of the burning lamp. The bride, stroking the edge of the groom's turban, said, 'It's already very stuffy

in this room. Take off your turban and lie on the bed. I'll
fan you for a bit.'

That said, she began to wave a colourful fan at her
husband. The husband said, 'The turban is a special
adornment for men. Taking this off is a slight to one's
manhood. If you say so, I'll take off my angrakhi.'

At this point, the bride continued to roll her soft
wrists and fan her husband, and there, the husband was
unabashedly undoing the strings of his angrakhi. As
soon as he took off the tunic and the bride looked at her
husband's bare torso, she let out a scream! And with that,
she collapsed on the bed, nearly unconscious. She wailed
through the stupor, 'You too are a woman! For which birth
did you take this revenge on me?'

For the first time, the husband's illusion was pierced,
as if with a dagger. And with that dagger, the life spent
thus far enshrouded in the clothes of men began to dance
in front of his eyes like a Kavad painting! The meaning of
the friend's words now became clear. Being possessed by
illusion can make one deaf and blind. One can neither hear
anything nor see anything! On this curtain of illusion, one
projects what one wants to see, and one hears what one
wants to hear. The truth means nothing at all then.

After all these years, her ears began to covet the
truth. Beside herself, she took off her turban. Took off
the angrakhi she had been wearing and put it to one side.
Then she removed the bride's clothes and put them aside.
She was stunned. She kept gaping at the truth which

unravelled before her eyes. How could she not have realized it all this time? Both bodies were similarly sculpted. The unconscious bride was sprawled out on the bed like a pink fish. And another fish, just like her, was standing by her, fully conscious. Ever since the earth came into being, such a spectacle must never have been seen.

Then, something occurred to the conscious fish and she began shaking the unconscious one every now and then, saying, 'Open your eyes, beendni. My illusion has been completely shattered. I have wronged you! Punish me!'

After much shaking, the bride opened her eyes and looked around her. Then, she sat up with a start. Both fishes, cast in identical moulds, began gazing at each other's beauty. The fish posing as the groom accepted her blunder. She would be placated by accepting whatever punishment was to be meted out to her. She had walked into this with her eyes wide open, after all. But the bride had been pushed into these flames, unbeknownst to her. She had been deceived. And for this deception, no punishment was too severe.

The bride was clever and considerate. To accept one's wrongdoing and repent is itself the foremost punishment. She understood immediately that she had been wronged unknowingly. And even as she tried to stop her, the fish that had pretended to be a groom narrated to her the whole Ramayan of her childhood. The father had woven this web of deceit to uphold the false and hollow honour of the vow made at the time of their births and because of his greed for dowry. The poor mother had protested much, but she had failed to make him change his mind.

Having heard everything, the bride ventured in a soft voice, 'I have lived out this deception for a mere seven days. But you have been scalded by it for years! Your pain is much deeper than mine. The same trick has been played on both of us. Now we have to live out this hardship together.'

'But it was I who posed as a groom and tied the toran! It is all my fault. You have been deceived by me—'

'And you have been equally punished for this deception,' the bride broke in agitatedly.

'No, even death can't absolve me of this crime.'

Then the bride caressed the groom's cheeks and offered in a mellow voice, 'Now we will meet death together.'

In tears, she replied, 'If I had walked into this marriage knowing what I was doing, then I would have been free of the wrong I have inflicted on you. But the regret of this lie won't ever leave me. Else, I would have created an example of a marriage between two women like no other and shown the world.'

The bride consoled her, 'Nothing has been lost yet. Don't beat yourself up, silly. The path to our salvation will have to be sought by us. What is new in a marriage between a man and a woman? The sun rises every day in the east – that's common. The sun that rises in the west is the one which is extraordinary!'

That said, she opened her dowry trunk and took out a set of fine clothes. She decked the seth's daughter up with her own hands: adorned her with jewels and lined her eyes with kajal. After dressing her up, she wore her own clothes. Both of them glowed like the lighted wick of a lamp. The bride spat seven times to ward off the evil eye, and then kissed her partner's cheek. She affectionately said, 'Your name is Beeja and mine is Teeja.[71] It is our good fortune that this twist of fate has befallen us. Now never speak of regret in front of me.'

Beeja stared at her finery and said, 'This is not a dream, is it?'

Teeja wrapped her in a tight embrace and said, 'Silly girl! Never before has a truth shone more brightly!'

Once the darkness of night melted away, the sun rose in its place, as it did every day. But the sight which befell the seth's eyes when the door of the newly-weds' chamber opened that day left him blinded. Despite knowing everything inside out, he pretended to be aghast. He darted towards the two like a rabid dog. Recognizing his daughter, he looked at her and screamed, 'Why have you dressed up like this? Don't you care at all for the honour of this household and my vow?'

Beeja could not stop herself from laughing at the state of her father who was gasping in astonishment. She said, 'It was *I* who was going to ask about the meaning of this deception of yours! But now I will not ask anything, nor will I offer any answer.'

---

71 Beeja and Teeja mean the second and the third one respectively.

'Shameless girl, what answer can you even offer? I will not let you dress like this even if I die!' said the father, spit spraying from his mouth as he stomped his foot.

Hearing the commotion at the door of the chamber, the mother arrived hurriedly. She hadn't slept a wink all night. Seeing her daughter's elaborate clothes, she felt the sting of a scorpion in every pore of her body. News of the daughter's death would not have been as heartbreaking as this spectacle! When the truth, hidden for so many years, finally bared itself all at once, she could not take it. The daughter was about to ask her something, when the mother embraced her and began to sob copiously. In the midst of this, she said, 'Don't ask me anything, beti, don't ask me anything. I tried a lot, but just like you, I could not do anything. Even then, I beg you with folded hands, don't curse your father.'

This time, the glimmer of a smile lit up Teeja's lips. 'You still fear a curse?' she asked. 'Rest assured, neither will I condemn you, nor will any word of condemnation escape her lips. The two of us are, instead, thankful that we have been able to lay our hands on such an invaluable piece of wisdom.'

Hearing these words from the bride's mouth, the father did not know what to do. He took off his turban, and placing it at her feet, said, 'Beendni, saving our honour is in your hands now. Convince our daughter somehow to take off this attire and put on what she was wearing earlier.'

Chortling, the new bride said, 'You still address me as beendni? As for this claim you make of your honour – I don't understand how this false appearance will save it? And what is the point of saving such honour anyway? You did as you pleased, now we will do as we please. We merely want to accept your deception and accept it as a blessing for all to see!'

The seth just needed an excuse to reveal his true colours. As soon as he heard the bride's words, he slipped into the skin of his real self. With bloodshot eyes, he said, 'In this house, only I will have my way! If you want to have your way, then there is no place for you here!'

This time, the daughter spoke up, 'This place does not suit us any more either. In the midst of this talk, I got distracted. I had come to say this very thing. Give us your blessings if you want to. We are leaving now. My heart does not even permit me to rinse my mouth here!'

The seth's visage become more monstrous still. He screamed, 'Go away! Go! But I won't return even a paisa from the dowry. Don't you count on that!'

As he shouted and raged, the daughter could not help laughing. She said, 'We now count on no one but ourselves. Don't you worry, we don't want even a bit of the dowry. If it does not embarrass you, then we are ready to strip off even our clothes and leave from here!'

Forgetting the propriety that befits a relationship between a father and daughter, the seth said, 'I knew it! Now you will go around dancing naked! Do what you wish, but these jewels are all mine. If I had not brought you up, how could you have even dreamt of such a dowry!'

'Such dreams suit only people like you,' said the bride, and then both she and the daughter began taking off their jewels. In their extreme fondness for dressing up, both of them had completely forgotten about the jewellery. They began taking off all their ornaments one at a time. But when the bride began removing her rakhdi,[72] the mother's heart brimmed over. Weeping, she said, 'My dear, at least don't take this rakhdi off. It is a mark of your husband being alive!'

The seth's greed knew no bounds that day. In fact, more than greed, it was the honour of the lord of the mansion that was dear to him. When that honour, built over generations, was being shattered by the daughter, he lost it. His obstinacy and rage surged higher and higher. He thought the sethani's words utterly foolish, and again he flared up. Grinding his teeth, he said, 'What does the bliss of a husband being alive have to do with a rakhdi? The poor don't have gem-encrusted rakhdis, are the husbands of those women dead? I will not let even the smallest scrap go, even if I die!'

Smiling, both of them handed over their rakhdis. For the first time in her life, the sethani chided her husband. Coming close to him, she said, 'You have not been bitten by a mad dog, have you?'

---

72 Rakhdi: A small borla, or head ornament.

Beating his chest and head, the seth roared, 'Mad dogs have bitten these two! But why would you see that? If they want to leave behind all this wealth and wander about, let them!'

When it became difficult to even breathe in a situation so devoid of grace and respect, the two girls exited quietly, without saying or hearing another word. But the mother's heart was still full of delusions. She thought tears were an emblem of motherly love. In a choked voice, she asked, 'Beti, where have you decided to go?'

As she was leaving, the daughter replied softly, 'Wherever we get food and water.'

Such gossip can neither be outrun by horses nor contained by the wind. Up until now, the people in the neighbourhood had deliberately closed their eyes. When they heard murmurs, they covered their ears. Who isn't naked behind their clothes? Who would dare to meddle? Even a straw wielded by the powerful is as mighty as a stick. One can live without the sun, but cannot survive without the moneylender for even a second. Some lowered their heads while some scratched theirs, but who would take the lead? None of them had heard or seen anything so bizarre. Even then, not a sound emanated from anyone. Everyone pretended ignorance.

But when the seth's son left the mansion dressed in a bride's attire, along with the beendni, everyone's head began spinning. If God had not given one eyes, then why would they have committed the sin of seeing? Without anyone saying anything, a murmur spread with the wind! And with those whispers, the wind itself began to seethe. Every corner of the neighbourhood began to sizzle! How could such huge lumps be swallowed! How could an elephant pass through the eye of a needle? It was as if a hive of wasps had erupted. People gathered in every lane; the lanes were abuzz with their gossip. A marriage of two women! Two girls in wedlock! A taint on the race of men! If such new ways were adopted, then families and societies would disintegrate. The sun's face would be blackened! How did the seth sustain this deception for so many years? What could be a bigger fraud than this? If this matter was not brought to trial, who would ever care for the panchayat? This serpent could not be hidden away in anyone's pocket any more!

In no time at all, the panches from the neighbourhood surrounded the girls. 'Don't you dare take another step until the matter is brought before the panchayat for them to judge it!' everyone cried. 'If women begin to marry women, will men bore down rat holes!'

The beendni shot back an answer, but the clamour from the members of the panchayat drowned her out. The cry for the panchayat to look into this rang out from all sides. And then, the seth's daughter raised her hand and gestured everyone to stop. And with that, the words that had made their way up to everyone's mouths, fell back down their throats. Once a hush fell, she spoke out loud, 'I do not want to have anything to do with the panchayat! But despite that, if you all are dying to get the council involved, then I will just come back in a moment. Until then, wait here.'

Saying that, she instantly left for the mansion. People parted to make way for her. She did return in a bit, but not alone. She held a scarecrow in her arms: it had a pot as a head, on which were drawn a snub nose and a pointy moustache; and it was clad in the very turban, angrakhi and dhoti she had worn on her wedding day. Then, coming close to the beendni, she bent down to dig a hole in the ground. The people around the two girls continued to watch the spectacle unfolding in front of them wordlessly, while the seth's daughter planted the scarecrow in the hole. The tail of the turban trailed on the ground. Then she stood up and declared loudly, 'If I were scared of this scarecrow, I would be scared of you moustachioed men! You are all worse than this scarecrow! We will defy you and go ahead. Let me see which one of you men comes in our way!'

Such was the sorcery in those words that every man standing there began to see his own self in the scarecrow! In the scarecrow's pot-face, the panches stared at their own. Meanwhile, the two girls departed fearlessly, not once did they turn around or look back. Once they were out of sight, every man standing there felt as if the scarecrow was laughing at him. But what was there to laugh about, pray? How dare a scarecrow ridicule living men! All at once, the scarecrow's face began to sting their eyes. And everyone present pounced on it with such fury that they ripped into it. Some fortunate ones were able to lay their hands on shreds of the angrakhi, dhoti and turban, while others were not. Only once the scarecrow had been torn to pieces were the attackers appeased. And they left as they had come – disappointed. Looking at their loot, though, the men became lions again and began roaring at the women in their homes.

Beeja and Teeja, arms around each other's necks, left the village behind. Everywhere, the earth was bursting forth in verdure. Fields of bajri were swaying in the wind. Creepers were winding up in the gardens. A carpet of green covered with small bushes and big trees. Tufts of clouds wafted here and there in the sky above. The earth bloomed endlessly in every direction. Those daughters of nature encountered nature for the first time. They pranced up the hill like deer. Running with abandon, once they reached the top, they began to dance the ghoomar. The mud huts in the settlements of men seemed to them like the mould on the food offered to Sedal Mata.[73]

Clouds gathered over the mountain. Soon, it began to rain heavily. Drums of joy started to ring out in all four directions. Bolts of lightning shot through the sky, hoping to catch a glimpse of the beauty of the two friends.

Wiping Beeja's face, Teeja said, 'These bolts of lightning crave to see us. And from behind the purdah

---

73 Sedal Mata: Shitala Mata. A Hindu goddess, believed to cure poxes, sores, pustules and diseases, and most directly linked with the disease smallpox. Ritual offerings to her are always of stale food.

of clothes, there is little chance that their thirst will be quenched!'

'What purdah for us!' Beeja replied. 'Why make the poor lightning suffer?'

As soon as they took off their kurti-kaanchlis, the sky lit up with streaks of lightning! It was as if they had suffered for aeons and aeons within the clouds and their sores were soothed at the sight of this pair of lotus flowers. Once again, drums of joy rang out everywhere!

After a while, the lightning shimmered tremulously again. This time, for quite a while. Two figurines, like the velvet mites found in the desert, stood with their arms around one another, melting into one whole, enraptured. Their breaths paused as they drank the nectar from each other's lips.

And that picturesque mountain's lifeless existence was rendered meaningful! The lightning acquired a new glow!

Upon coming back to their senses, they got dressed. Thunder and lightning again, as if to protest against the clothes! And with the crack of thunder, they both held each other in an embrace once more.

They felt as weightless as flowers as they started to descend the mountain, playing in the rain. The joy they felt seemed to be flooding everything, everywhere. It was as though the contented earth had spread itself out to be caressed by the love pouring forth as rain from the clouds.

When they had climbed down the mountain, they realized how sublime and noble their love was. If anything in this world was purer than the clear water from the clouds, it was their profound love.

But love alone cannot sustain one in the world of men. Moreover, both were women. They wanted to set up their new home. But where? They had made enemies of the men of the village, and they wanted to never even turn towards that place again!

Without much thought or planning, and chatting merrily, they headed to the shelter of a bavdi[74] haunted by ghosts. It was getting dark. Meanwhile, the rain stopped, and the girls wrung their clothes dry.

A desolate forest. And a deserted bavdi. Where lived a hundred and twenty-eight ghosts. Not even a birdling dared to venture there. And whoever did, never returned home. Men feared passing anywhere in its vicinity, even in broad daylight.

Both friends were sitting on the bank of that bavdi, unafraid, chatting, while high in the sky, the teras[75] moon played hide-and-seek around the clouds. All of a sudden, Beeja said, 'The moon muttered a mantra in my ears unbeknownst to you. If you give me a kiss, I will tell you what it is!'

'If you give me a kiss,' Teeja replied, 'I won't even ask about it!'

'No, the mantra is certainly worth knowing!'

---

74 Bavdi: Stepwell.

75 Teras: Thirteenth day of the lunar month.

'Then tell it to me without me even asking.'

'The moon teases me every now and then, saying why I look at it instead of the moon sitting beside me.'

'Liar, that's what the moon told *me*!'

The two moons had just begun to savour each other's nectar when a deep voice fell in their ears. 'I knew you would definitely come here.'

They broke their embrace with a start and looked around. A man, clad in white, as if he had been moulded from moonshine, stood smiling.

He continued, 'Today our bavdi has been sanctified. But it is very surprising you were not even a bit frightened in coming to the bavdi of ghosts!'

The women stood up quickly. Beeja replied softly, 'One must fear men. What is there to fear from ghosts!'

As soon as the chief of the ghosts heard this, his smile grew wider and he said, 'What you say is absolutely true. Even we died, with our desires unfulfilled, because of the deeds of cursed men. Now we must live out the afterlife as ghosts. We scare the scared and take our revenge. We cannot stand even the footprints of men. Today, those rogues left no stone unturned in torturing you in the middle of the village—'

Teeja interrupted in astonishment, 'How do you know?'

The ghost continued: 'The furore around your wedding travelled through the mouths of men and reached our ears.

We were eager to watch a spectacle. Why should we be left behind? Unseen by the eyes of men, our entire community witnessed the racket. And as soon as we did, our hearts warmed up to you. It was us who ensured the scarecrow worked. Else would those accursed men leave you alone? We accompanied you right up to the mountain so that no one could deceive you.'

As soon as they heard this, the girls shrunk back, mortified. The chief of ghosts could not help laughing. 'You were not shy of the lightning,' he said to them, 'then why must you be shy of us? Seeing your love has made our lives worthwhile. I am the head of this congregation. The two of you can set up your home here without any hesitation. I will build such a palace beside this bavdi that the king himself will be envious. The kingdom's treasures might fall short, but the two of you will never want for anything. All your wishes, small and big, will be fulfilled. Seeing the pure love you share has given me such happiness, I can never repay your debt. Let any woman or man even look at you with disapproval! Now, in this Ekthambiyo Mahal,[76] you can make love without a care.'

When Beeja and Teeja turned towards where the chief's hand pointed, they beheld a glittering white palace, with extraordinary jaalis and jharokhas! The light from

---

76 Ekthambiyo Mahal: A palace that stands on one pillar. A common motif in folk stories.

inside the palace shone through. The moonshine outside bathed it.

They had never imagined their love to be so magical! When the two of them entered the Ekthambiyo Mahal, they were rendered speechless. The floor made of saffron. The pillars of gulal. The ceilings of vermilion. The beds of lotuses, bedecked with roses.

The girls began to sway with joy! Those scarlet-coloured birds were neither conscious of the world outside nor of themselves, so lost were they in the rapture of love. What could prevail against the spell of Lord Kama!

But finally, they emerged from their trance and life returned to them. Gazing into the light in each other's eyes, they broke into smiles. Beeja sprinkled that uncorrupted smile with words: 'Once again, the life of the chief of ghosts must have become worthwhile.' Teeja blurted out, 'Even the gods in heaven must have felt their immortality fulfilled!'

At dawn, when the two emerged from the palace, they felt as if the morning sun had risen to the horizon from their wombs. And from that night onwards, the sun left its ancient abode and began to appear in this new place instead. To this day, it has not gone back! The pleasure in all the world thirsted for the bed in that Ekthambiyo Mahal. And in that thirst was the thirst of the entire universe!

A fortnight of happiness passed as if in an instant. The chief of ghosts never faltered in looking after the couple. One day, he said to them, 'In the midst of all this self-indulgence, you have forgotten about the rest of the world. But the world has not forgotten you even for a moment. You can visit the village without any worry. There is no danger. I will be behind you, guarding you. The women of the village are free to visit you. Even the sun suffers when alone. The moon too wanes.'

'But we are two of us,' said Beeja and Teeja at the same moment.

The chief smiled and said, 'But your souls are one! And at the time of making love, even less.'

The girls were now as bold as brass. Hearing the chief's words, they giggled. The chief's smile appeared dull in comparison.

After this, the two of them wandered into the settlement of men, bouncing and darting like tassels. There were the same fences and pillars. The same sheds and roofs. The same fences and walls. Separate hearths. Each with their own fire, their own smoke. Separate heaps of dung and separate dung cakes. The same grinding of teeth and the same push and pull. The same piles of refuse here and there. The same struggle for well-being and prosperity. Scars of pain and poverty. Grappling to feed the many mouths that had been birthed. Stinking nappies. Drool leaking from mouths. Strife and chaos in every home.

How had they lived for so many years in this hell? How had they managed to grow up here? It was disgusting to even recall that past life! But the villagers were absorbed in their own world, as usual. Drawing red and yellow mandanas[77] in their courtyards. Painting the columns with scenery. Singing songs on special occasions. Preparing feasts for festivals. Moving back and forth on swings, and dancing and singing. No one seemed to find anything distasteful.

Upon seeing Beeja and Teeja together again today, no one called a panchayat to sit in judgement on them. Instead, trembling and shivering, the villagers went inside their homes and bolted their doors. Everyone was terrified of the ghosts of the bavdi. They could twist someone's neck in an instant! Each person's neck is dear to him! And these girls were just the kind to mix with ghosts! They had managed to befriend even the spectres. Only someone who was like them would want to face them. Therefore, whoever encountered Beeja and Teeja, lowered their heads and walked past.

Beeja's father was sitting with his accounts on a ledge when suddenly he saw his daughter and beendni. He nearly fainted. He stood up, shivering. The pleats of his dhoti came undone. He begged with folded hands, 'I am ready to give you all the dowry, with interest. But do give your blessings to my little hut!'

Beeja shook her head and said, 'I have no desire to take back the dowry. I came because I was eager to meet you. I don't want a single thing from this house.'

---

77 Mandana: Rangoli painting made on the floor of one's home for decorative and ritual purposes.

Drool gathering at the corners of his mouth, the seth asked, 'Why not? Are you not my daughter?'

'I know well enough that I am your daughter. And I know a father's love too! But now, if you even speak of any give and take, I will never return here.'

The father could think of nothing to say in response immediately. Once he had gathered his wits about him, he folded his hands and said, 'Now you reside in a royal household. How can you even stand this place? As soon as I receive a summons, I will come over myself.' He did not mention his fear of ghosts on purpose.

There was no end to the disgust and revulsion surging within the daughter. It was as if she had fallen into a cesspool! She turned around to leave. Teeja did the same, as she had no desire to step inside her in-laws' house.

With his dhoti in a state of disarray, the father followed the girls saying, 'Beti, you are leaving without meeting your mother? She has been crying her eyes out!'

As she was leaving, Beeja said, 'Send her to our home. There will be no danger.'

That said, Beeja walked away quickly, while Teeja caught up with her. She understood without being told what was going on inside Beeja's head. As soon as they left the village, Beeja scowled and said, 'Now I will feel relieved only if I bathe in a pool of perfume!'

Teeja tried to distract her. 'Why, does our breath smell any less than perfume?'

No sooner had she uttered these words than she embraced Beeja. The peacocks called out and broke into a dance. Frogs began to fill the air with their sweet croaking. Deer stared at their embrace, as if bewitched. Eager pigeons began to coo and dance as if entranced. And with the calls of the birds, it was as if a current of enchantment ran through the forest. It seemed like all of creation had found, in that embrace, the path to its salvation.

After some time, they desired the privacy of their palace and they hurried towards the bavdi. The hell of that repulsive village was left far, far behind.

The next morning, Beeja awoke with a start at hearing someone knocking on their door. She woke Teeja up, and after dressing hurriedly, they rushed downstairs and opened the sandalwood door. It was Beeja's mother, with her daughter's friend. Before Beeja could say anything, the friend smirked, 'Even married women don't wake up this late!'

Beeja was still sleepy. Forgetting her mother's presence, she said as she rubbed her eyes, 'Are we any less than married women!'

Once the two of them stepped inside, they completely lost their minds. Now they finally saw what they had only heard of all this while. Without having the colony of ghosts in one's control, who could make such a creation? But how had they managed this? Their absolute astonishment made the sight of the Ekthambiyo Mahal four times as wondrous as it actually was. The mother and the friend had arrived with much to say, but not even a syllable escaped their mouths. It was as though two crickets had been entrapped in a golden cage!

After taking in the entire spectacle, the flabbergasted sethani gazed at Beeja and asked, as if in a dream, 'Did I truly give birth to you?'

Beeja smiled and said, 'About that, either you would know, or the midwife would! How can I say?'

The sethani's silly question annoyed the friend. 'Did you come all this way to ask this?' she said softly.

'Was it worth it?' Teeja asked teasingly.

After this, Beeja served her mother and friend the choicest delicacies on a golden platter. And then, while the guests rested on the golden bed, the two lovers had some food together.

Beeja then came to check in on her mother. Both the sethani and the friend were fast asleep: faces down, eyes shut. They had tried very hard not to nod off, but even a wounded man would begin to snore on the soft sheets of the golden bed. What were two fatigued, hale and hearty women!

The two of them awoke with a start at noon. They looked around them. Even a king would yearn for such opulence! This dream, seen with eyes wide open, began to feel rather painful. The mother poked Beeja's friend. 'We will have to speak up eventually. If we stay quiet like this, how will they come to know?'

With a deep sigh, the friend said, 'The greatest of men would find their minds so numbed by the sight of such an extravagant palace, that they could neither see nor think!'

After the four of them had sat together and chatted for an hour or so, Beeja's friend gathered courage and ventured, 'The news of this palace had reached everyone on the third day itself. Such things need not be relayed by anyone – the news travels with the wind. Were it not for the fear of the clan of ghosts, a second Mahabharat would have broken out over marrying you. The king had ridden in to wage war, but he fled midway. Who else would dare, after the lord of the land had been chased away? Big and small, young and old, every man has begun to desire you—'

Teeja interrupted, 'What harm have we caused anyone?'

This time, it was the mother who replied. 'What can be a bigger harm than this? Your relationship has rained shoes on the race of men!'

Beeja looked at her friend and said, 'We do not have a solution to this problem.'

Now, the friend's resolve strengthened. She explained in a mellow voice, 'You do have a solution. That is the only reason we have gone to such lengths.'

Both lovers began to listen intently. The friend continued, 'You see, only the toontiyo[78] for your wedding

---

78 Toontiyo: A wedding ritual where women cross-dress and entertain themselves, while the menfolk are away in the jaan.

was carried out. Not a bead of sweat from a man has touched even your shadow!'

'Neither will we let it!' exclaimed Beeja.

'No, beti, one cannot even dream of this,' her mother said. 'A woman can live without water, but not without a man's touch. Many a proposal have come to your father. The richest men in the land are all ready to get married to you. To hell with this hollow vanity! Set up a nice household, tend to your family. May you bathe in milk, may you be blessed with many sons and get a chance to extend the family line. Your father is eager to give each of you double the dowry he got!'

Teeja replied sweetly, 'We got entrapped in this vine and we are still reaping the fruits. Now you want to uproot it completely. This alone is the biggest source of pleasure for us. There is no other answer I can give you besides clapping my hands and laughing.'

The mother's face fell on hearing Teeja's response. She looked at Beeja and asked, 'Beti, what do you have to say?'

'My answer is no different. You need not do anything more now.'

Seeing the colour in her daughter's eyes, the sethani felt astonishment and rage rising up inside her. But it subsided as soon as she remembered the ghosts of the bavdi. She looked at the friend and softly said, 'It is quite late. We should leave now.'

The friend rose quietly and left with the mother. This dreamlike visit to the palace was good enough, she thought. Beeja did not even come to the door to see them off.

The following day, a knock was heard on the door at the same time as the day before. A harried Beeja opened the door. The friend was standing there all alone, with downcast eyes.

Surprised to see her, Beeja said, 'I saw you in a dream last night, standing here just like this. I kissed you, and then you ran away. I called after you, but you did not so much as turn and look back. Let me kiss you again! Let's see how you escape this time.' And immediately, Beeja planted a kiss on her friend's left cheek. But no sooner had she done so than tears began streaming down the friend's face. Beeja's smile faded. Holding her hand, she asked, 'Are you upset by my kiss? I was only—'

'Why would I be upset by your kiss?' the friend broke in, in a choked voice. 'Tears that had collected over two years found release upon being prodded by your kiss. I have thought about it time and again, but I still cannot fathom how the two of you found so much courage. I have not the strength to even look at you. Yesterday, with your mother, I did not get the chance to say what I wanted. So today, I came alone.'

Seeing Teeja, the girl's heart filled up again. Gazing at the faces of the two lovers, she began crying copiously. It was only tears that could soothe the anguish in her heart.

So they didn't stop her from crying. And in every tear was the bitterness of all the water in the Luni river.

Once the tears abated, she articulated the bitterness of her heart in words. On being married, she had been sad to leave behind her parents' home but also eager for her marital home. But on that much-anticipated night in the chamber, her hopes were crushed. The man in whose hands she had placed hers for life had not in him a trace of what made a man! His family had every knowledge of this, and yet had led the jaan with much pomp in the hope that the touch of a virginal bride would rouse within him the fire that had been missing so far, that it would make him aware of his virility. But they were mistaken, and the innocent bride had to pay the price for their blunder. Further, because he could not have his way, the husband bit her body all over to demonstrate his manhood!

Narrating this tale of woe, the friend shed her clothes to show them her wounds. Her back, chest, arms, hips and thighs were all covered with dark, dull spots. Weeping and wailing in front of her parents had not helped. One cannot destroy the honour of a noble family! And who would expose what happened behind closed doors? How long could she protect herself from the advances of her susro[79] and jeth?[80] Eventually, she had to give in. Can a

79 Susro: Father-in-law.

80 Jeth: Husband's older brother.

lamb survive after entering a lion's den? Even after he came to know all that had passed, her husband did not so much as let out a whimper. He devoted himself more and more to his business. The bride's arrival had brought along with it much prosperity; the business was doing well. Everyone was content with the virtuous beendni!

Beeja snapped out of her stupor. She said with a deep sigh, 'And you also had to learn to make yourself happy with all this!'

'What else could I have even done?'

'Are you still happy?' asked Teeja.

'I was happy so far, I was. But seeing the two of you, the agony inside me is aflame again!'

'There is no need for you to go anywhere now,' Beeja said with impatience. 'The three of us together – who do we care for?'

The friend shook her head. 'No,' she said, 'I did not come here to stay. To have been able to pour my heart out to you both has soothed my scars. Only in death will I be able to leave my marital home. So much wealth! Abundant cattle and milk! Seven three-storeyed mansions! I cannot give all this up so easily. I am yet to bear a child. I will feel at ease only after I have produced an heir to the line. My devar has come to take me to my in-laws'. I will have to leave day after tomorrow. Being able to unburden myself of the weight in my heart will see me through the days to come. I have not the courage to live with you.'

She wanted to say much more, but could not. Her throat choked, her eyes welled up. After a while, she wiped the tears away and said, 'Yesterday, you made me sit separately. Today, I will eat with the two of you. Perhaps, if I partake of food that has been left over by you, I will also come to possess as much intelligence as you.'

'You have enough intelligence,' said Teeja. 'But it is the ghost of morality that haunts you.'

As soon as ghosts were mentioned, all of a sudden, the chief of the ghosts of bavdi appeared. But the friend wasn't scared in the least. She gaped at him.

'Why did you call out for me?' the chief asked.

Teeja could not stop herself from laughing. 'You are not the ghost I mentioned. You are the invisible light of the future!' she said. 'Even then, good you came. It is seeing you that sustains our courage!'

'Don't praise me too much,' the chief said with a laugh. 'I might puff up and float away!'

Then he looked at the friend and added, 'I have heard the full account of your hardships. You can now go to your in-laws' without fear. You will find that your husband has become quite the man. Your jeth and susro will not dare to even look at you. You will birth five Pandavs with your husband.'

The friend was overjoyed. Seeing how beside herself she was with delight, Teeja said, 'Careful, lest your heart bursts with happiness!'

Beeja turned to the chief and asked eagerly, 'You know these spells too?'

The chief replied with pride, 'What do we not know? What can we not do?'

In the midst of the ecstasy that followed this unexpected boon for the friend, all three girls sat together and ate with great relish. After chatting for a bit, Beeja and Teeja walked back with the friend all the way to the village. They reminded her repeatedly that no sooner had she reached home than she must send word of her new-found happiness.

On their way back, though, Beeja seemed pensive. Teeja prodded her, 'In what deep thought are you lost? Is it something you must hide even from me?'

Beeja paused and then said, 'How can I get by if I hide things from you? But it truly is a matter to ponder deeply. I will tell you only if you listen to me carefully.'

Rolling her eyes, Teeja said, 'You aren't out of your mind today, are you? Do I need to be told to listen to you carefully?'

Beeja gazed into her lover's eyes and said, 'Didn't something strike you after hearing of the boon granted to our friend?'

Teeja hugged her and said, 'What occurred to you, occurred to me too. But to even think about it is futile. Is the boundless happiness we feel not enough?'

'No, it is. But hearing of the boon, the regret in my heart has surfaced again. If you agree, we can wipe off the stain of injustice that has happened to you.'

'But when have I ever thought of it as a stain?'

'But how can I shut my eyes to its darkness? Every time I close my eyes, the darkness only spreads. Won't you listen to even this small thing I ask of you?'

Tightening her embrace, Teeja murmured, 'If I hadn't listened, where would we have found this happiness?'

'But why do you think this is the limit of happiness?'

'Because it *is* the limit, that's why I think it is the limit.'

'No, no, the limit is still a long way off.'

'That is nothing but an illusion. But after all this, if you still feel that the ambit of our happiness lies further ahead, then go on, ask for the boon yourself.'

Beeja freed herself of the embrace. Chiding Teeja sweetly, she said, 'You still have not comprehended this fully, have you? Teeja, my sins will be washed away only if you ask for the boon!'

'But I don't wish to be a man in any birth. You were brought up as a man. If you desire to be turned into one, I won't object to it. Let us see, then, if this dessert of domesticity can be any sweeter.'

Nothing could change Teeja's mind. So, it was Beeja who had to give in. And with this, there rose an itch in her fingers to twirl the ends of a moustache. There would now be a true man in the garb of a man!

As soon as they returned to their palace, they found the chief of ghosts standing in the doorway. Beeja could not wait another instant. She left Teeja behind, and rushing to where he stood, asked unflinchingly, 'The boon you gave our friend's husband – will it not work for me too?'

'Why would it not?' he replied loudly, so that Teeja could also hear what he had to say. 'I was hesitating to pose the question to you myself. It will be as you wish. Where do I lack in the boons I can give!'

A shroud of shyness crept over Teeja's face. With her face lowered, she asked, 'What is the rush? Let us enjoy the rapture of this life one last time!'

Smiling, the chief said, 'If you are so fond of this life, then I can keep a way back to it. If Beeja gets tired of being a man, then she can become a woman again as soon as she so wishes!'

Beeja, lost in dreams of becoming a man, shot back, 'This boon has come to hand after much difficulty. Why would I desire such a thing?'

'That is entirely up to you,' the chief replied instantly.

At that hour, stars were beginning to appear in the evening sky. As soon as Teeja saw them, she said, 'But this night is mine. I won't let you catch even a wink of sleep!'

Beeja would not be left behind. 'I will keep you up all night every night afterwards! Think it through again.'

'Once tonight passes, I won't think at all.'

Beeja heard Teeja's words clearly, but did not quite fathom what they meant. Teeja was very impatient that night. By the time Beeja took off her kaanchli, Teeja had already undressed. Pulling Beeja by her arm, she said, 'How come you have so much patience tonight? You are always in such a rush!'

And then the pink kurja birds began to flutter their wings and embrace without resting the entire night! While Teeja kept hoping that this night would never end, Beeja yearned for the first light of day to burst forth. But irrespective of what the two thought, the night was to end when it was supposed to. And so it did. And the soft light of the rising sun felt very sharp to Teeja's eyes.

And there, with the light of the sun, Beeja felt a spasm run through her body. Even as she watched, her chest became flat. Her cheeks and the skin above her lips became itchy and began to sprout hair. Even as she scratched herself, she looked at her waist. Truly, she had become a fully grown man! Her body was covered with soft, black, curly hair. When she looked at herself in the mirror, she even felt frightened of her moustache – bushy and twisted at the tips. But what use was it to be scared of oneself? The honour of pointy moustaches lay in scaring others!

When he spotted a turban, angrakhi and dhoti hanging from a hook, Beeja darted towards them. He had worn the clothes of men for years with his own hands. So, in no time, he tied the dhoti around his waist and put on the angrakhi to cover his upper body. Then he tied the handsome turban around his head, the cloth of the turban gloriously trailing down to his knees. He looked around with pride.

Teeja was nowhere to be seen, though. She should have waited here for this moment, Beeja thought. He began wandering the palace, calling out to Teeja at the top of his voice. Suddenly, he heard her voice: 'I'm taking a bath. Don't you come inside!'

What was this shyness all of a sudden today? As soon as he heard this, he rushed towards the bathing chamber. He parted the curtain of rubies and entered it. Bending double in shame, Teeja said, 'Please turn the other way. I will wear my clothes and come out.'

Surprised, the husband asked, 'I never saw you be so shy before.'

'Things were different before,' came his wife's response.

'But the two of us are one!' the husband said. 'At least see my new look? This moustache! This turban!'

'The turban was there earlier too,' said Teeja.

The husband got impatient and said, 'Why don't you come out quickly?'

Just then, Teeja emerged in full splendour. She gazed at her husband from top to bottom. What an enchanting form! What luscious whiskers! What a taut body! And that shiny, black, curly hair was another sight altogether!

Teeja spat to ward away the evil eye, then added, 'Come, I will tie a black thread around your wrist.'

Teeja's beauty took on a different allure for the husband today. Such mesmerizing eyes, such intoxicating youth! A thrill began leaping through every pore of his body.

As Teeja's fingers touched his wrist, he could barely restrain himself. A bolt of lightning ran through him. Catching hold of her arms, he said, 'Tonight, I will make you pay all that you owe me!'

Teeja continued to listen in silence, her head bowed low. Ram knows from where such words had started to come to her husband. He teased his bride some more. 'Tonight, even in the darkness, I will light up the chamber so brightly, you will never forget it.'

Teeja chided her husband, 'Enough, be quiet now! You became a man later, but you seem to have learnt these precious incantations before!'

'It feels like the sun will never set today.'

'It will set very soon, be patient! You did not sleep much last night. Have your rotis and lie down for a while in the chamber. I will go around the village for a while and return.'

'You slept as much as I did. But what's this strange thing today? You will leave me behind and go off on your own?'

'Yes, I will go without you! You have no shame at all. But I have not lost my senses, have I? Can one ignore the norms of the world?'

'Oh, now I think I must show you the norms of the world,' the smiling husband said.

Saying this, he picked Teeja up in his arms. She tried to break free but could not. He set her down on the bed of roses and lay on top of her.

For an instant, darkness spread in front of their eyes, and on the very next, the chamber lit up. Teeja felt as if the entire universe was contained in her body! For a while afterwards, both husband and wife almost lost consciousness.

Then, with his eyes closed, the husband said, 'We struggled for so many days in vain.'

'Why in vain?' asked Teeja, as she turned on her side. 'The ecstasy of that love isn't one that can be forgotten even after dying.'

At night, the same sequence of events repeated itself. And in the midst of it, the glimmer of a new thought began to radiate in the husband's mind. That the man was mightier than the woman. How could feeble women match the strength of men? The man was all-powerful!

That very night, Teeja conceived her man's child in her womb. Afterwards, both fell into a deep slumber, from which the husband awoke three hours following daybreak. The chamber was illuminated by the rays of the sun. And beholding that glow, the misbelief that it is the strength and heat of a man that takes the shape of the sun that rises in the sky, took hold of him. The woman is merely his shadow, he thought. Earlier, both lovers were mistresses of the palace. Both were equal, in terms of their say in matters and the possessions they owned. The husband would rest easy only once the new position was clarified, lest Teeja believed that the earlier arrangement could continue.

Surprisingly, this morning, Teeja showed no signs of getting up. Shouting her name repeatedly, the husband shook her. Rubbing her eyes, Teeja asked, 'Why did you wake me? I was fast asleep.'

The wife's question hurt the husband's ears. He replied dryly, 'You can sleep to your heart's content whenever you want to. But I want a response to a question right away: Who is the master of the Ekthambiyo Mahal? You or me?'

Teeja did not quite comprehend the question. She was unable to offer an answer and continued to sit in silence. Impatient, the husband repeated the question. And this time, looking at his pointed moustache, Teeja replied, 'What is there to think about? This palace belongs to both of us in equal measure!'

'I never asked about what we own jointly and what we don't, did I?' said the husband. 'Answer me clearly. Who is the master of all this wealth?'

'The chief of the ghosts!' replied Teeja softly.

Hearing his wife's response, the husband was stunned at first. But the very next instant, he gathered himself and asked, 'Why do you give these convoluted answers? Give me a straightforward reply. After being handed over to us, who does this belong to? Whose is this immeasurable wealth? Yours or mine?'

Teeja now realized what was happening. How did this transformation come about overnight? Beeja had never sought answers to such questions. Everything was undone as soon as she became a man. But if Teeja hesitated now, the matter would get out of hand. She said, 'We are equal owners of this wealth. If you have any further doubts, we can ask the chief of ghosts for a clarification.'

It was as if the blood in the husband's veins had frozen. Agitated, he said, 'What is this about the chief of ghosts you keep saying, huh? He listens only to you. Why would he listen to me? And if he has to side with me, what will be left for him? Not even in my dreams had I imagined such slyness from you!'

'Now you know it.'

The man with the pointed whiskers felt enraged. He began blabbering angrily, 'But I am no less powerful than that boyfriend of yours! I will form a new kingdom! I will amass endless treasure, I will command an army made of horses and elephants and infantry and chariots, I will build a mighty fort with mortar made of lead! Three hundred and forty queens like you will wait on me in the royal chambers—'

'Now what is this quarrel we have started without even rinsing our mouths?' Teeja broke in.

Saying this, she turned away and rose from the bed of roses. Without saying or hearing anything further, she left the chamber. She felt as if its walls were closing in on her. What disaster had befallen them in the space of one night! This was the same loathsome path chalked out by their ancestors. To proceed on it would be to sully oneself with the same filth. Just as darkness spreads everywhere as soon as the sun sets, Beeja's pure heart was filled with darkness no sooner than she assumed the form of a man.

Even after having bathed in the pond of nectar, Teeja felt no peace. Once eclipsed, the sun and the moon too could do nothing. If she stayed here with her husband, it would only result in arguments. Maybe she should go to the friend's marital home and check on her. Why wait for her message? Perhaps, if she left the palace for a few days, the disagreement would be resolved.

She put on a set of plain clothes, and was just about to close the palace door behind her, when her furious husband caught the edge of her veil and asked, 'Where are you going off after burning my heart?'

'If I tell you the truth,' Teeja replied gently, 'you won't believe me. So it's not worth responding.'

'Oh, I will extract worth all right! But you can go nowhere without asking me!'

In a matter of just a day, what was this unbridgeable chasm that had opened up between the two? Teeja tried to placate him, 'You are not thinking straight today. I will go to your friend's in-laws' and ask after her. In about twenty days or so, your head will clear. After that, as soon as I hear from you, I too will come back.'

'Why do you feed me this nonsense? You are conspiring with the gang of ghosts to finish me off. I know only too well the ways of bitches like you! Go back into the chamber quietly, otherwise...'

'Otherwise what?' asked Teeja, smiling.

Seeing the smile on his wife's lips made him lose his mind completely. Leaving the edge of her veil, he caught Teeja by the hair. One pull, and Teeja fell where she stood. Then, dragging her by the hair, her husband yelled, 'I am not made of such soft stuff that I'll care for the whims of my woman!'

Still holding her by the hair, he hauled her and pushed her on to the bed in the chamber. Teeja grit her teeth and shut her eyes tight. She did not even let out even a whimper thereafter. To shed tears in front of a husband who had forsaken his all morals would be a matter of immense shame. She felt suffocated, and in a while, she fainted.

Abandoning the unconscious Teeja, the husband left the Ekthambiyo Mahal. Bolting it from the outside, he began wandering the forest like a madman. He soon reached the mountain where the two girls had clambered up that day. He found it covered with rocks, one piled on another, bare and unsightly. As if all of nature was grieving someone's death.

As he climbed to the top, the spectacle their eyes and souls had beheld that day, began to float in front of his eyes. After a while, when the scene would not disappear even after he had closed his eyes, he opened hem again. Where was that pouring rain? The lullaby of the clouds? Where, that untainted embrace? And where oh where was that boundless trance of love? Every pore of his body craved to turn into Beeja again. And with that desire, he transformed. Again those smooth cheeks, the two lotuses inside the angrakhi, eager for Teeja's loving touch.

Beeja darted down the hill, unbolted the palace, and rushed to the chamber where Teeja lay. Panting, she began to shake Teeja awake. 'Teeja, Teeja,' she said, 'I have left behind the form of a man. Open your eyes and look at your Beeja!'

After being shaken repeatedly, Teeja regained consciousness. And as she opened her eyes, she saw Beeja hovering over her! The same love dripping from her eyes, that same soft body, the same colour of vermilion … The two lovers locked themselves in an embrace and remained entwined, never to part. And it was a miracle from the chief of ghosts that ensured that even that which had been conceived in Teeja's womb from that foul part of a man was destroyed.

Twelve miles this way and twelve miles that, for twenty-four miles around, not even the shadow of a man would dare to approach! Only I received word from Teeja and entered the palace, witnessed the marvel with my own eyes, and wrote this story exactly as she narrated it to me. Had I tampered with even a single letter against her wishes, would the chief of ghosts have spared me?

Hollow Pride

THE BIG DIFFERENCE BETWEEN MAN and animals is
marriage. Humans are married with great pomp and
splendour. But what of animals? They think of neither day
nor night, neither shame nor honour, and have no qualms
about doing shameful things in plain sight. What remains
out of view is another matter. But where there are eyes
that notice, man does not wander down morally suspect
paths. Hence, walls, pillars, doors, balconies and screens,
rooms and chambers. The honour of man is paramount.
Marriage of even children in the womb. Marriage of even
babies suckling at their mothers' breasts. Marriage of even
innocent boys and girls. Marriage of even the old. As many
marriages as the heart desires! Without marriage where can
salvation be found!

Of old times, this old tale. A big night of big regale!
There was once a man who was immensely fond of marriage.
He would prepare his heart for marriage whenever he felt

like it. Ram knows which fool invented that saying that, 'come sixty, one's brains flee swiftly'. But this man's brains continued to shine bright even at three less than seventy. If he did not have brains, why would he want to get married?

With twice the eagerness befitting young men, he dressed up as the beendraja.[81] Decked up in a turban and ornaments. He then mounted a horse and reached the toran to the clamorous beats of dhols.

After the toran was tied, a young man from the bride's side requested, with folded hands, that the guests older than the beendraja please return to their camp. But those younger than him were free to stay on for the pheras. What purdah from them?[82]

In the wedding procession was a mischievous nai. Chuckling, he said, 'There is no one older than the beendraja in this procession. Everyone is younger! Think carefully before you ask!'

Then the request that had to be made was made. But the beendraja felt as if his heart had been branded with a flaming iron. What a taunt that rascal nai had made at the spur of the moment! The nai had grown up eating the grain of the beendraja's house – had it been paid for by

---

81 Beendraja: Groom.

82 Phera: The wedding pheras – circumambulations around the holy fire – usually take place in the bride's home, and older men, particularly those not from the family, are not allowed to be present during the ritual.

the nai's father? Even in that biting cold, every pore of the beendraja's body became soaked in sweat.

Unfastening some of his angrakha strings, he asked for a pot of cool water. Those who heard him were surprised. To make sure if what they'd heard was indeed right, a woman standing close by asked again, 'A pot of water! How can you be thirsty? Even the mention of water makes my heart shiver!'

The beendraja bragged, 'If it was the hour for a bath, I would have bathed too. It is bad enough that my daily routine was disrupted today. But my throat feels parched. Now quickly, get me some water to drink!'

A pot of water arrived without further delay, as per the beendraja's command. He raised the pot and gulped all the water down.

And as soon as he did so, the very air in the courtyard became abuzz with chatter: The beendraja surely left all young lads far behind! How could one gulp down so much water without hotness of the blood!

'What? Did the beendraja send for water himself?'

'Not only did he send for it, he gulped all of it down in one go!'

'What can time and years do, then? Youth lies in the heart.'

When this gossip, buzzing in the breeze, fell on the beendraja's ears, there was no end to his delight. As he sat for the pheras, he sent for a pot of cold water once again. And in no time, he emptied the pot once again.

'O Mother, never before have I seen or heard of such a beendraja! Even looking at water chills the heart, and this beendraja has gulped down a potful of water in a single breath – twice! Didn't even let the stream of water so much as quiver!'

Handing the pot to his sister-in-law, the beendraja demanded again in an arrogant voice, 'One more pot!'

'Is he a groom or a thunderbolt?'

'Has Agan Devta entered his tummy?'

'The great fortune of our sister to have found such a strong beendraja!'

The beendraja's heart still stung from the nai's taunt. But, at least now, he had regained some respect. As soon as another pot appeared, he grabbed it and began drinking. This time, the water felt cold. But it still wasn't cold enough to make him forget that nai's jibe! He hurriedly gulped down every last drop. The chill spread to every pore of his body. It felt as though the blood in his veins had turned into ice. His teeth began to chatter.

A woman, lifting her veil to glance at the beendraja with one eye, said as she gazed at his face, 'May God not make me lie. Had I a daughter of marriageable age, I would have married her off to him happily. Fulfilment only comes from the body's heat. In fact, I think—'

Extending his hand towards that very woman, the beendraja said, 'Another pot!' He thought to himself that, inside a man, there should be fire fiercer than even the sun!

But now he was stuck. When the pot of water arrived, the beendraja emptied it somehow, his teeth still chattering.

The chorus of the women's whispers changed. They began spitting to ward off the evil eye. This is how gold acquires its sheen, they said. They never knew their sister would have such good fortune. In such bitter cold, it was hard to even swallow one's spit, but as they watched, the beendraja had gulped down pot after pot of water. If a young man could drink even a palmful of water in this cold, then they would know what they were made of. Truly, old things were a class apart!

During the hathleva, when the bride and groom held hands during the pheras, the soft touch of his betrothed made the beendraja's courage flare up even more. He loudly ordered a woman standing beside him: 'One more pot!'

Who could disobey the beendraja's command? Here the command was placed, and there the pot appeared. But this time round, as he drank the water, his hands began to tremble. As if every pore of his body was covered with melting snow. Moreover, the water in this fifth pot was especially cold. He could only finish half of it before he collapsed on the ground. The water in the pot spilled on his head. The murmur of the women knew no bounds. No one could make out the writhing beendraja's broken words.

Even so, it was our sister's great fortune that, despite being such an old beendraja, he had gulped down five pots of water!

The Dove and the King

ONCE, THERE WAS A DOVE. While looking for grain one day, she stumbled upon a small shell. She felt as if the wealth of the god Kuber had fallen into her lap. She grabbed the shell and began to fly, until she came to rest by the Raja's palace. The Raja was taking stock of the diamonds and pearls in his coffers.

The dove came to perch by the jewels and began to sing:

'I am the richest, the richest is me!

I will lend to the Raja, he will borrow from me!'

The Raja grew angry and wrested the shell away from the dove. She then began singing:

'The starving Raja snatched my shell from me!

The hungry Raja snatched my shell from me!'

In a quandary over how to react, the Raja returned the shell to the dove. She took the shell and began to fly. And as she flew, she now sang:

'The trembling Raja gave me back my shell!

The frightened Raja gave me back my shell!'

The Creed of Crows

Selfishness is Sai, selfishness is all!
Selfishness in the big, selfishness in the small!
Who's a sister, what brother?
What kinship? Mother? Father?
Who's a friend, what relation?
Self-interest is the only connection!
Religion and rituals, only one gist –
It's one's own grain and one's own fist!
The six philosophies,[83] they're all a lie –
Just empty beads and empty prayers!
False love, fake fondness –
A deep trench and an endless abyss.
Songs for God, teachings and hymns –

---

83 The six principal Hindu philosophies: Samkhya, Yoga, Nyaya, Vaisheshika, Mimamsa and Vedanta.

Arrows laced with deadly poisons!
A barren path, a barren cult!
Handsome garbs and beguiling monks!

So MAY THE SHAPELESS, FORMLESS One, fulfil the selfish
desires of one and all, that in the desert, once there was
such a severe drought which continued for three years
in a row, that even the wealthy were getting blisters on
their feet trying to find one morsel to eat. And what can
one say about the poor animals! There was neither fodder
nor water anywhere. So they collapsed where they were.
Leaving aside the vultures and crows, the mute creatures
themselves did not know when life departed from their
fallen piles of bones.

Countless crows, raucously cawing, began to peck at
them with relish, but not a single animal even shook its
tail. After all, one needs strength to do that. So bountiful
was the mercy of the Giver on the black crows, that such
a feast had not come to pass since the Earth came to be.
Even after they were full, simply pecking at the flesh was
no small delight.

At night, the crows had grown used to resting around
the carcasses. And as soon as it was daybreak, they would
fly and begin pecking and cawing. Soon, the stench would
cause the very air to rot. For men, it was hard to even
breathe. But for the vultures and crows, their births had
become meaningful!

One day, a blissfully contented kagla[84] said to his wife, 'I have heard a lot about Mansarovar, but haven't seen it yet. If you say so, we can go sightseeing there! These bodies won't finish even if we were to peck at them for years.'

'As you please,' said the kagli. 'My heart aches at the thought of leaving this heavenly land, but if I don't do as you say, it will ruin this birth of mine!'

The kagla started to dance the ghoomar gleefully and said, 'Let us go then! Crows are descendants of the sun – the stars are aligned right whenever they choose to fly, and it is dawn when they arrive!'

Even an ant reaches its destination eventually if it moves. These were crows – owners of wings that could fly without pause. The kagla and kagli rested only on the third dawn, once they had reached right up to the shores of Mansarovar.

In the lap of the Himalayas, brimmed water as clear as crystal. One could see the lakebed right through the water. Trees of many different kinds were fanning the mountains in veneration. A variety of flowers were waving and swaying in worship. Vivid creepers were touching the feet of the mountains. A bevy of white swans was chanting prayers to them. Invaluable pearls lay scattered here and there as offerings.

But the eyes of the crows from the desert were not pleased with this spectacle. Those dunes, that barren land, and that rotting carrion was another sight altogether. Those

---

84 Kagla: Male crow. Kagli: Female crow.

slumped animals, those bleeding bodies, those entangled intestines! Here, these poor swans seemed to be pecking at pebbles. They did not take to the horrid scenery of Mansarovar. So much they had heard about this place – all rubbish! A yearning for the land of their birth began to rise in their hearts. When have crows pecked at pebbles? But as they were about to take flight, the swans surrounded them. The chief of the flock greeted them and said, 'It is our great fortune that guests such as you have arrived here. If you go away without giving us the chance to serve you, how poorly it will reflect on us!'

The kagla cawed and said, 'But you will not be able to serve us. No one in our land pecks at pebbles!'

The swans were astounded. From which world had these nobilities come? Who did not like pecking at pearls? The chief spoke again with humility, 'Please look one more time carefully. These are not pebbles! To this day, we have never had any other grain except for pearls and rubies! Your Highness may eat whatever you please – rubies, pearls, emeralds, sapphires…!'

The kagli twisted her mouth into a grimace and said, 'Go burn those pebbles somewhere else! And this fit-to-set-on-fire whiteness blinds me! Where in this world is rain to be found other than in black clouds? Let's please leave, so the agony in my heart may go away too!'

The chief of swans gestured, and all the swans flew away save his wife. Then he began to look at the black colour of the crows closely and said, 'For years we believed that there isn't a home as beautiful as ours anywhere else in the world. But today our illusion has been shattered. To which world do you swans belong?'

The kagli cawed, 'We are swans from the desert world! The sights of that world are not to be found even in one's dreams. Your birth will be complete if you came over once and saw it for yourself.'

The swan couple whistled softly together, 'If your blessings are with us, we will surely see that land one day.'

When the chief and his wife made up their minds to leave with the crows, all the swans in the clan insisted that they would go with them. The chief said, 'The two of us will see that land first and return. Wait until then. After we come back, I won't stop anyone.'

The swans gave in. But at the time of their departure, none could stop their tears. As soon as they fell to the earth, the teardrops assumed the form of pearls and began to shimmer!

The crows sat on the swans and returned to the desert rather quickly. Even before they landed, the stench began to overpower the swans' senses. What sort of place was this desert world! Not a tree in sight. In all four directions, just brown dunes and more dunes. Stacks of corpses littered everywhere, and vultures and crows pecking at them! At every step, intestines lying tangled and strewn like coils of thread. These despicable crows had played a nasty trick on them!

'What are you thinking so hard about?' said the kagla. 'Gobble up as many corpses as you want! There is no one to stop you while I am around!'

The swan couple was finding it hard to even breathe. Even laying one's eyes upon such a sight had to be a sin! The chief's wife said, 'This desert world suits only you crows! I could not survive here for even a day!'

That said, the swans began to fly back. Ram knows what signal that scoundrel crow gave out, that a number of crows began flapping their wings and flying after them. But for how long could those crows follow the swans? They tired and returned on their own. Not all birds are as intelligent as crows, are they? What did those poor swans know about the sumptuousness of corpses?

To escape from the crows was in their hands, but it wasn't in their hands to reach all the way home! This is what happens when you fall into the trap of crows! The storm and the rain surrounded them from all sides. Amidst the crackle of lightning, it started to pour. Gusts of cold wind began to bear down on them. The swans' drenched feathers made it hard for them to descend. After getting tossed around, they somehow managed to alight on a jaal tree. Each and every feather of theirs was trembling.

There was a large hollow in that tree. Shivering, when both the swans entered the hollow, they felt somewhat warm. But they also found something else there: some ten–twenty rats who were squeaking after getting soaked in the downpour. The swan couple felt pity for them. How could one bear to see another in pain! Both took turns to alleviate the distress the rats shivering in the cold felt. As soon as the rodents were wrapped in the swans' feathers, they warmed up.

The swans had done good by the rats, and for this, they were sure to be punished! When have rats changed their ways, pray? As soon as they warmed up, they started gnawing at the swans' feathers and did not stop all night!

At dawn, the chief swan said affectionately, 'We will leave now. You stay well. We tried to help as much as we could…'

The chief's wife blessed the rats and emerged from the hole with her husband. But how come their bodies felt so light? They turned around and looked. There lay two separate heaps of feathers! Both of them stared at each other, tears streaming down from their eyes. What an awful thing to happen! It was better to die than shed one's feathers. But pining for death does not melt death's heart. One deserved such punishment for trusting crows and being kind to rats!

But who can fathom the fickleness of chance? Not even the sun can peek beyond its curtain. The morose swan couple was sitting on the road with crestfallen faces when the son of a wealthy seth happened to pass them on his way back home from distant lands. On the upcoming teras was his wedding. While he had learnt the art of business quite well while still young, he was still somewhat silly and eccentric. He would make gestures with his hands and talk to himself. A golden stick in his hand. A flask of water slung over his shoulder. Wheatish complexion. Well built.

Lost in his thoughts, he passed the swan couple without noticing them. Hungry and thirsty for two days now, the swan-wife beseeched, 'Traveller, why hurry past like this? At least listen to the ordeals of us unfortunate swans.'

He started upon hearing her words and looked back. Smiling, he came closer to them and said, 'I did not even notice you. It's great that you are swans – but where are your feathers?'

The chief swan narrated the tale of their woes with a choked throat to the traveller. He said, 'If you have water in the flask, then give us some to drink. Our throats are parched!'

Then, the seth's son made both the birds drink fistfuls of water, one at a time. He stroked their unsightly bodies affectionately. Suddenly, the churma in the box he was carrying came to mind, and he put some of that sweet mush on his palm and offered it to them. The swan shook his long neck and said, 'We eat no grain other than pearls and rubies!'

The whimsical young man laughed and said, 'That's no problem at all! I have many pearls and rubies. I will keep a record of those against your names! When I visit Mansarovar, you can pay me back.'

Having drunk water, the swans felt refreshed. The wife said, 'Good you spoke of repayment. If we are able to reach

Mansarovar, we will not be able to repay your debt even if we gave you urns full of pearls. But how do we get there?'

The seth's son got impatient and said, 'Aren't you silly! I am the only son of a rich seth. After my wedding, I will have you sent off to Mansarovar in a carriage. Just come with me.'

These were innocent swans. They had believed even crows, then why would they not believe his words?

That seth's son fed the birds pearls and made them sit on his shoulder. Then, in his carefree way, muttering to himself, he set off for his village.

When he reached home, the seth created a lot of fuss about the swans, but finally, he had to bend to the wishes of his son. Every now and then, the son began to explain to his father that the pearls these birds were fed would never go to waste. That the father did not quite know the new ways of doing business.

After the wedding, the beendni began to look after the swans. She was full of good qualities, intelligent and good-natured. She was extraordinarily beautiful and fair. She would stroke the birds with her mehndi-dyed hands, feed them pearls and rubies, shower them with love as if they were born from her womb. Those hands cast such a magic that the feathers began to grow back on the swans in no time. Soft as satin and smooth! She would make them sleep with her at night. The touch of her kisses and the warmth of her caresses made the swans grow twice as large. Every day, she would make them bathe with her, holding them close to her chest. Even stones would find it hard to resist sprouting feathers at her touch, and these were living swans! Their feathers began to gleam like the white rays of the sun. And as she did on her own hands, the beendni drew with mehndi on the swans' feathers too. Then, the birds soared up in the sky twice or thrice, and returned to her lap.

At the hour of departure, the eyes of the swan couple welled up. The beendni too wept no end. But it was a matter of great surprise that, as soon as they mixed with the beendni's, the swans' tears became pearls!

Seeing this confluence of tears, the seth's son said, smiling, 'Enough! Do stop now. These poor swans are finally ready to fly back home. Do not jinx it by crying so much!'

The seth and his wife were also present there. The seth told off his son: 'Foolish boy! When has crying been known to bring bad luck upon someone? Don't you see the miracle of these pearls? What can be a better omen than this? Let them cry as much as they want. Their hearts will feel lighter if they do. Do not stop them until I tell you to.'

In any case, the swan couple had to repay their debt. For three days and three nights they continued to weep tears of parting. In the courtyard of the seth's mansion glimmered four times the number of pearls they had consumed. The silly son's way of conducting business had borne great fruit. Each pearl was worth a lakh and a quarter. What good fortune the beendni's footsteps had brought to the household! God does watch over the innocent. What a remarkable thing the foolish son had done by feeding pearls to those ugly swans! Never again must he be barred from doing anything he pleased.

Then, one more time, the beendni clasped the swans to her bosom, and after that, finally, the swan couple soared into the sky. The breeze from the flapping of their wings brought forth a shower of pearls to the seth's courtyard yet again!

How those dreadful crows had made these poor swans suffer! Every time they would come and sit on the ledge and go caw-caw, the seth's son would shoo them away. One day, the seth got annoyed and said, 'Son, what is this silly thing you do? Feed these crows treats with your hands. If they had not betrayed the swans, how would this wealth have come our way? Use your brains a little bit at least!'

'You use your brains, I can't!' Saying this, that half-mad son got angry and stopped speaking to his father altogether. With great difficulty did the beendni get him out of this ill-humour. Then, when the son would not let it go, the seth employed an attendant whose only job was to drive away crows all day with a stick.

Amidst all this, the cart of the seth's family life kept trundling along peacefully for three years. And then, one day, the seth said to his son, 'If you scrape long enough, in the end even a mountain can be wiped out. Eating off saved wealth in this way – how long can it go on?'

The son lost it. Snapping at his father, he said, 'This habit of meddling in other people's affairs has turned the entire community against us! It would be much more beneficial if you went abroad. You may fret and fume as much as you want, but until my wife bears a child, there is no way I am going anywhere on business!'

'Silly boy! Is conceiving in anyone's hands? All the astrologers have read their charts and come to the conclusion that you are not destined to have any offspring. Those swans must be remembering you every day. At least go to Mansarovar once and meet them.'

This arrow shot by the seth hit its mark. The son began jumping with joy and said, 'Arre! They had completely slipped my mind! The poor things must have withered into skeletons.'

After this, the seth had a large carriage harnessed, and at an auspicious hour, he set the son off for Mansarovar. The beendni gazed at the clouds of dust kicked up by the carriage with sorrowful eyes until her husband was no longer visible.

Rattling and trudging along, the carriage finally reached Mansarovar in the fifth month. As soon as the chief of swans saw him, he flew to his protector like the wind, fanned him with his wings and snuggled in his lap. The chief's wife was playing with her babies, but as soon as she found out about the arrival of the seth's son, she flew to him. She asked after the well-being of the beendni and his parents. When she asked about their child, the seth's son smiled and said, 'The beendni is not expecting yet. And despite that, my father forced me to come meet you.'

'But why should you be forced into this?' asked the chief's wife. 'We would wait for you every dawn. If you had not come for another five–seven months, we would have come over.'

As time passed, the number of swans assembled there only grew. All of them were utterly grateful to the seth's son for looking after their chief couple. Such beautiful and innocent swans these were, their hearts as pure as the water there. Heaps of rubies and pearls lay piled up all around. But it was too embarrassing to talk about filling up his cart.

Every now and then, the chief swan's wife would say that the seth's son should have brought his beendni along. Such a large carriage, and he had come all alone. Really, seeing the extraordinary sight of Mansarovar, the beendni would have been beside herself with joy. He should definitely get her along the next time he travelled here. She pampered the seth's son as much as anyone could. With soft malpuas and kheer, and a preparation of lotus stems tempered with rubies. He could not stop eating.

They were done with supper early one evening, and were sitting around chatting when, on the magical, wish-fulfilling kalubirach tree, a chakvi said, 'Chakva,[85] tell me a story…'

'Someone else's, or mine?'

---

85 Chakvi (female), chakva (male): Chakravak, the ruddy shelduck. In folklore, they mate for life and are devoted to one another. But they must separate at night and reunite at daybreak.

'What's there in telling or hearing one's own stories?' the chakvi replied. 'Your glory lies in telling others' tales!'

The chakva said with relish, 'Lucky for you, I'm a connoisseur of others' tales. I never go wrong in telling them. Listen carefully.'

The chakvi listened intently as the chakva began to tell a story with great flourish: 'The wealthy seth's son is visiting the home of the chief of swans. The young man rescued the swan couple from great suffering. If he had not looked after them, they would have died in great agony. Today, the time is right to pay off his debt.'

Alongside the chakvi, the chief swan couple and the seth's son too began to listen to the story attentively. The chakva continued: 'In this young man's mansion are chests full of treasure, but fate has not given him a child. Very soon, it will be the Imrat Pal – the Nectar Hour. If he unites with his beendni right after midnight, a son will be born to them. The stars will be propitiously aligned. While he's a child, his drool will turn into invaluable pearls, and when he grows up, a ruby worth a lakh and a quarter will come out every time he clears his throat!'

The chief of swans could not contain himself after hearing this. Impatient, he asked the seth's son, 'Did you hear that…?'

'But how will merely hearing that help?' asked the seth's son despondently. 'I cannot reach her by midnight, not even in my dreams.'

The swan said with hope in his voice, 'Whether one can or cannot reach there in their dreams can be ascertained only in a dream. But I can get you to the beendni's chamber before midnight for sure. I trust my flight. Close your eyes and sit on my back. If I don't get you there before you reach there in your dreams, you can chop my feathers off!'

Ram knows why, but that seth's foolish son believed the swan! When the swan's wife, eager to meet the beendni, also wished to accompany them, they both agreed. As soon as he shut his eyes and sat on the swan, they soared into the sky – the swan above and the swan's wife below. They flew faster than the wind, and all three of them landed at the doorway of the beendni's chamber just before midnight. The beendni was lost in her own dream in which she lay entwined in the arms of her man. She awoke with a start, hearing a knock on her door. Startled, she unlocked it, and in front of her stood her husband, smiling in the moonlight! Who knew that the moon of the fourteenth day had such magic! And beside him stood that dear swan couple, flapping their wings.

The four of them entered the bedchamber. The swan told the beendni everything about the chakva and the chakvi in detail, after which the beendni lit a lamp filled with cow's ghee. What shame from innocent birds! The swan couple watched as the man and the woman drowned in the nectar of their entwined bodies! And at the Imrat Pal, the beendni's hopes bore fruit!

If they stayed on, the seth would surely be angry with them. So the three of them left for Mansarovar before daybreak. The beendni's dream had come true. These swans who fulfilled the wishes of her heart – may good befall them, birth after birth.

But are there not people who, despite dwelling in the settlements of humans, are no less than crows? But who would care for their cawing if one's wishes were fulfilled in such a way? Once, when all such respectable crows of the community had gathered, the sound of their cawing ringing out, a clever naayan[86] broke the news that the beendni was expecting. For days the seth had been meddling in the affairs of the community. But he could not take care of the affairs of his own house! He could see the mountain burning but did not see what burned at his feet!

Three or four of the seth's competitors saw their chance to disgrace him and brought the matter to the panchayat. The seth said with confidence that this was all gossip and lies. That the beendni would explain if asked.

The panches retorted that there was nothing to explain – this was right in front of their eyes. Can a pregnant woman's belly remain unnoticed? Women can neither hide secrets, nor a child! In the ninth month, it would have to come out. She should be asked properly whose child it is that she bears!

Hearing this, the seth was furious! Red with rage, he went to the beendni. This cawing had already reached the

---

86   Naayan: The wife of a barber (nai).

beendni's ears. The seth stroked her head and said, 'My dear, you are my daughter-in-law. Do not conceal anything from me. Tell me, what is all this chatter about?'

There was no sin in the beendni's heart. She revealed in detail the whole truth. As soon as he heard what had actually passed, the seth's head was in a whirl! He said, his voice trembling, 'Where are there men who will believe such a thing? They have found prey after days, they will not let it go easily!'

The beendni's heart sank. Would the truth be mauled by lies? She said, 'Even you don't believe what I say...?'

The seth shook his head and said, 'What good would me alone believing it do? People make out of things what they want to.'

The embarrassed seth left no stone unturned to try and explain the events, but not a single panch believed the story. It was not something that intelligent humans could believe! The sarpanch said, 'Seth, your ruthless meddling has ruined many a household! Today, they are all gathered here. They have been lying in wait for just such a day. If you were to listen to me, I'd say you should drag the beendni out of the house! If her face is blackened, the matter won't go further. Otherwise, saving your household's honour is not in our hands.'

The seth pleaded, 'Impose what penalty you will, but do not make me punish the honourable beendni in this way! As soon as she hears this, life will abandon her.'

The panches responded cleverly, by asking if there ever was anyone in this world who was born immortal. Everyone had to die one day. If one's honour remained intact as long as one was alive, that was a big thing! They gave him a warning: 'Either throw the beendni out, or the entire family will be cast out from the community!'

If shoes wore out, new ones could be bought. But how could one not obey the judgement passed by the panchayat? The beendni wailed a lot, she pleaded aplenty, but the seth was unshakeable. He caught her by the hand, dragged her out and left her on a deserted road. Cast out of her marital home, how could she find shelter in her parental home? What was this poison the Imrat Pal had sprouted!

A deserted road. A barren desert. The paths of return – closed. The way forward – unknown. Where could she go?

Wandering by the light of the sun during the day and by the light of the moon during the night she came back to her in-laws'. No sooner did he see her than the seth pushed her out again. He screamed, spittle flying from his mouth, 'Aren't you ashamed to show your blackened face…!'

The beendni sobbed. 'I have not done anything of which I should be ashamed!'

'Then whose child do you bear?'

'It belongs to your son…'

'Your tricks won't work here!' the seth shouted. 'If the roof of this house was so dear to you, you should have kept your heart in check. There is no place here for a whore like you!'

The beendni folded her hands and said, 'You tell me! A lone woman – where am I to go?'

The seth sneered, 'You should have asked your lover this question!'

That said, he slammed the door shut and bolted it. Once, she had entered this mansion through this very door to much celebration and the sound of drums; today, the door had closed on her forever. It was futile protesting now. If she kept her eyes open, she would see the same house yet again. So she turned around and closed her eyes. And set off in the direction her feet took her. Ram knows why, owing to the sin of which birth, the crows had exacted revenge on the beendni through those swans. Who knew how many faces the blackness of the crows would blacken.

She was passing by a kumbhari's house with her eyes shut when the kumbhari called out to her, 'My dear, where are you going with your eyes closed...?'

'I myself do not know,' replied the beendni, her eyes still shut. 'What do I tell you?'

The kumbhari caressed the beendni's cheeks affectionately and said, 'No need to say any more now. You are my daughter, and I am your mother. With one's eyes closed, one can reach nowhere but the doorstep of one's mother!'

The beendni started to cry, so her eyes pried themselves open. In front of her stood an old woman. A mesh of wrinkles on her face. Small beady eyes. Toothless mouth and white hair.

With her eyes closed, the beendni had at least been able to find a shelter. If they had been open, who knows which well she would have jumped into!

It had been three years since the head of the house had passed away. The kumbhari had seven sons, all of them married. The house was teeming with grandchildren, but without a daughter, the home felt rather empty. Now, with the arrival of one, it seemed complete. The kumbhari's happiness knew no bounds. It was as if the revelry of youth had returned, once again, to that shrunken skeleton.

It was a family of kumbhars who farmed the land. Where was the grandeur of the seth's mansion to be found here? Nevertheless, somehow, the days began to pass by. Everyone followed the example of the old woman in taking good care of the beendni. The beendni, too, helped out as much as she could, and started to take on a fair share of the chores. Grinding grain, preparing rotis, feeding the animals, milking them…

The day that dawns must end. And after it ends, the day must break again when it is time. In this way, the beendni was now closing in on her ninth month. The kumbhari was attending to her all the time. Then, one midnight, she started to have contractions. She called out to the old woman and woke her up. The sun's first rays saw the birth of a son.

The kumbhari clanged bronze thaals.[87] And she began jumping and prancing like a child herself!

As the son was massaged, he slobbered – and no sooner had he done so than his drool transformed into an invaluable pearl! This extraordinary incident astonished the kumbhari no end. What was this little white pebble that was glimmering so? Upon being asked, the beendni told her everything, concealing nothing.

When the kumbhari's sons heard of the pearl, they were unable to contain themselves and went running to the sunaar.[88] The sunaar could not take his eyes off the pearl! And to whom are sunaars loyal? They can cut the breasts of even their mothers! As soon as deviousness reared its head in the sunaar's heart, he broke into a smile. He shook his head and said, 'Brothers, why do you fool me? If you had consulted me before concocting this tale, at least you wouldn't have a story so absurd. Tell me the truth, from where did you steal this invaluable pearl? Otherwise, I will take it to the king.'

'What would we get by lying?' said the kumbhari's eldest son. 'If you have had a change of heart, then keep the pearl with you. Or else, come with us and see with your own eyes.'

---

87 A ritual where the birth of a child, usually a son, is announced by clanging bronze thaals (or plates) with wooden rolling pins.

88 Sunaar: Goldsmith.

It was hardly something that could be believed, but despite his misgivings, the sunaar went with the sons. Someone's refusal to accept what is real does not change the truth, does it? Even after he had seen everything with his own eyes, he could scarcely believe the strange sight before him.

With the promise that he would pay a hundred gold mohurs for each pearl, the sunaar left happily. The kumbhari's family was delighted too. But the beendni was entangled in the web of the past. Where was her husband? Her marital home? And where were her parents? Not even in her dreams had she imagined this twist of fate. Even by the light of the sun, one can see no further than the present moment. Had she known better, would she have let her husband leave that night? But greed, and the fear of his parents, had made him hurry back. He had come at midnight and departed while it was still dark.

In this world of humans, everyone is caught up in their own struggles. If one has time left after this, it is then that one thinks of the future. Having seen the remarkable sight of a child's drool turning into a pearl, there was nothing less than a storm in the sunaar's heart. Even after paying a hundred mohurs for each pearl, he would make no small profit. Easy money – and boundless too! In a matter of just one day, he could keep poverty at bay for seven generations. But greed knows no limits. At last, God had heard his prayers. If he could steal the child, not only would the curse of childlessness be lifted, he would have countless glittering pearls as well! The king himself would bow down before him. Who else but Ramji could present one with such great things at the right time?

With God watching over, what cannot be achieved? The sunaar's wife would go to the kumbhari's on the pretext of asking for buttermilk, and stay back and play with the child for an hour or so. One day, she seized the chance! She stole the child and hurried back to her husband. The sunaar had already got the best camel readied and was waiting. On the front seat sat the husband, and on the back seat, the wife with the child in her lap. And then, the camel began to run as fast as the wind on its four legs.

The sunaar stopped the camel only once they reached the Raj Durbar. Seven times he touched the feet of the king who was seated on the throne. Then, with folded hands, he howled, 'O benevolent king, I have come to seek refuge. Help me!'

The Raja consoled the sunaar and asked him the reason for his plight. The sunaar said that he had five children, but an evil witch had devoured all five of them. 'Where could we even go, leaving our home of generations? Wailing and sobbing, we hardened our hearts and somehow bore the pain. But for how many days can a mother's heart be at peace? The wife renounced food and drink, so I was left with no choice but to seek your protection! We do not have the strength to give up this sixth child, too, to the witch. If we are punished for this, we will accept it happily. The witch pursues us and will not leave us be even here!'

Hearing the sunaar's sufferings, the Raja's eyes welled up with tears. Everyone gathered at the Durbar fell silent. The Raja wiped the sunaar's tears with his own hands. He gave his diwan clear instructions that there should be no lapse in arranging for the strictest round-the-clock vigilance. If any unknown woman arrived, then she must be reported to the Durbar first. The inspectors at all four corners of the fortress were given the witch's description. Assured of royal protection, the sunaar was guarded against all danger. Had God ever blessed anyone like this before?

The very next day, the sunaar bought a three-storeyed haveli and began to live in splendour. Every day, he would gift the king a pearl with his own hands. The king revered the sunaar more than even the diwan. There was no end to the power he enjoyed in the Durbar.

And there, the beendni and the kumbhari's family were immersed in endless grief. The beendni cried so much that her tears dried up. If her son's drool did not turn into pearls, would this tragedy have befallen her? The kumbhari's sons cried too. How would this emptiness – the size of a hundred mohurs for each pearl – be filled? All seven brothers searched here and there, but no trace of the sunaar was to be found. The kumbhari took the beendni and set out to look for the sunaar. She would ask whoever she would meet – birds and animals, stones and pebbles, trees and bushes – she would leave no one out. But the sunaar was neither seen nor heard of again! The beendni had been thrown out of her home because of this child. Now she began to wander from home to home looking for him.

Once more, she hardened her heart and went to her in-laws' haveli. The seth's son had returned home from Mansarovar with a carriage full of extraordinary gems. When he found out about the verdict meted out by the panchayat, he flew into a rage. He shouted and screamed no end. He repeatedly said that the story of the events of the Imrat Pal was fully true. Flying on the swan's back, he had indeed visited the beendni's chambers at midnight. Afraid of his father, he had left with an hour of darkness remaining. When even his father didn't believe this strange tale, then where was even the question of the panches believing it? The seth scornfully remarked that the honour of a household could not be saved in this manner. That, before spinning such a yarn, the son should have at least consulted one of the panches.

Then, that half-mad man shot back, 'I will smack such unworthy panches a hundred times with a shoe! I do not need to consult anyone.'

The panches, pulling long faces, left one after the other, muttering among themselves. Then the eccentric son looked at his father and said, 'I have come back after six months, and even before I returned, you threw that poor innocent woman out! Tell me now, who will I go to bed with at night?'

The father was embarrassed to hear such a question from his son's mouth. Turning around, he said, 'What is there to be so upset about in this? I can have you married this evening itself, if you say so! There is no dearth of beendnis for you!'

'When I set off for distant lands again, you might throw her out too! How can I trust you? No, I will not stay with you even if I die. Now, if you take even one pearl from the carriage I have brought back, there will be no one worse than me!'

After this, that half-mad son of the seth would listen to no one. As soon as he got married again, he moved out of his father's house. He built a separate mansion for himself.

The water of one well is bitter, while that of another is sweet. The water of one pond is light, while that of another is heavy. But drinking from either quenches one's thirst. Similarly, so what if the bodily shapes and natures of women are different? The pleasure one derives from them while in bed is the same. If, sometimes, old memories surge to the surface, what of them? Eventually the seth's son's heart became fully rapt in his second wife, when one day, all of a sudden, he spotted his first wife standing at his door. As soon as he recognized her, he came there and said, 'Why have you landed here after wandering around for so long? I am not as foolish as you think I am. You are of no use to me now!'

The beendni could scarcely believe her ears. What were these words she was hearing coming from her husband's mouth? However, she had to at least speak her heart out.

Shocked, she said, 'You continue to blame me despite knowing everything?'

'Why should I not? I am not scared of you! When Father threw you out, it would have been better if you had hit your head against a rock and died! Now this water which has been tasted by everyone does not suit me!'

Extending her hands towards her husband's feet, the beendni said, 'No one has savoured this water but you! The child for whom we went to such lengths, even that child is not with me today. Greed for pearls made the sunaar betray me. But I do not covet your bed! There is enough work in the mansion. There is no dearth of stale scraps in this house that can be given to me in exchange for cleaning, washing, sweeping and scrubbing. The deeds of my last birth are such that in this birth I have been born a woman. It will be hard for me to survive anywhere other than at my husband's.'

Then, the beendni started to weep. But that half-crazy husband's heart would not melt. Forgetting the relationship they had shared in the past, he jeered, 'I will not be deceived by all this drama! If you stay here, you will get jealous of the new beendni. You will quarrel with her. Why, it is bad enough for a woman to stay out for even a day! And God knows where you have been roaming about all these months! You can beg all you want. But there is no way any decent man will trust you. Leave aside the mansion, you cannot even stay in this village!'

Hearing these words from her husband, she did not feel like begging or arguing any more. Wiping away her tears, she departed quietly. It was as if she had been startled awake from her slumber and her dream had been broken. And it was a matter of great astonishment that, when she was insulted and sent away from the mansion a third time, it did not upset her as much as the first time. Sita had been sentenced to exile just once, but this Sita had had to endure the punishment thrice over. That, too, all alone! Her own husband was not by her side in the turmoil.

But she would rest only once she had found the son born from her womb. How could a mother's heart be at peace otherwise? She searched everywhere by the light of the sun. Amid the gleam of the moon and the stars, she sought her son in every home, but there was not a sign of him to be found anywhere. In the end, she wandered and wandered, and reached the Raj Durbar. This was exactly what the sunaar had feared. He recognized her instantly. He went to the Raja and said with folded hands, 'Your Highness, the witch has arrived after all! I lay my son's life at your feet now.'

What was there to fear when one had been given shelter by a king? And the sunaar's daily gift of a pearl to the Raja was no less either. No one even listened to the beendni's entreaties. The executioners were commanded to hang her to death at once.

The crafty diwan even suggested that it would not be enough to deal with such wicked witches by merely hanging them! They ought to be put to death every day to be adequately punished. The courtesan Lakkhu's youth was waning now; she would happily pay one lakh rupees for this whore. The treasury too must be taken care of after all!

The Raja agreed to this arrangement. Lakkhu the courtesan had an eye for beauty. She handed over a lakh and a quarter, no questions asked. Along with praise, the diwan was showered with gifts, and Lakkhu got beauty and youth in exchange for money. Both were delighted.

Does the sun that is on its way down cease to shine? In the same manner, Lakkhu was no less beautiful even though her youth was fading away. But as soon as she lay eyes upon the beendni, she spat and said, 'My pride lies shattered on seeing you. Such beauty can be honoured only by allowing everyone to partake of it. Tying it up to one will only taint it.'

The beendni failed to comprehend the drift of Lakkhu's words at first. But slowly, she came to realize what they meant. Everywhere she had gone, she had received only insults. At least Lakkhu the courtesan valued her highly. Even so, the beendni said with trepidation, 'I will ruin my life on this path of sin! This birth of mine has already been spoilt. The next one too will be wrecked.'

Hearing her say this, Lakkhu wanted to laugh. Women are so innocent! They live in delusion and die in delusion. Somehow, she suppressed her laughter and said, 'What better path is there in this world of men? Even I used to be under this mistaken belief. You will not get it if I try to explain it to you now, so doing that would be futile. Time and hardship are the best teachers. I have ten other women with me. There is no greater Ramayan than the story of their lives! But it takes intelligence to understand that. And until that intelligence develops, I will give you one more chance. A lakh and a quarter rupees have been spent, so be it! Go, meet your family, your parents, your mother's family. Do not keep anything in your heart. Only after doing this will you comprehend what I tell you!'

The beendni hesitated. 'What if I do not come back...?'

Smiling, Lakkhu replied, 'If you don't, that is your wish! You are free. I trade in women's bodies, not in their lives!'

The beendni stared at Lakkhu, dumbstruck. To hear such words coming out of the mouth of a courtesan! It was as though a swollen blister had been slit open with a sharp needle. Tears began streaming down from her eyes. But Lakkhu found the tears of women very annoying. She scowled and said, 'I am sick of seeing these tears. Now, as I get older, I do not have the strength any more. Don't cry. It is these purposeless tears which defeat us! There is no mightier enemy!'

The beendni replied in a choked voice, 'If you listen to my Ramayan once, my heart will feel unburdened—'

Lakkhu interrupted her: 'But what is the need to unburden? My ears have lost their hearing, listening to such Ramayans. I can barely hear anything now. But, if you still wish to, then tell me your story once you return. By then, your mouth and my ears would have grown used to one another. Then you can let out all that is simmering inside you. I know the hearts of all women without even hearing them. Now, go. I gave all my girls this one opportunity. Only three of them killed themselves under the influence of their delusions. The rest, they came back here. Not one betrayed me. What's the need for deception and trickery in the house of a courtesan? There is no dearth of householders and their hypocrisies for that!'

Quite a few things had begun to dawn on the beendni as she listened to Lakkhu. She turned around and said, 'Now I am in two minds, wondering if I should go at all!'

'No, this I will not accept!' replied Lakkhu. 'I do not thrive on the helplessness of others. And I am reminding you yet again – come back only if you wish to. You owe me nothing. I had money, so I paid it. The doors of this house are open for you at any time of the day. Don't you hesitate.'

The beendni's heart felt heavy as she departed. But how could the parents who had given birth to her turn her away? A son can be a bad son; but a parent can never be a bad parent. The umbilical bond cannot be renounced. Her mother had kept her in her womb for nine months, after all! But still, she felt awkward about it. Nevertheless, asking and enquiring along the way, she reached her nanere.[89]

Everyone there knew about her already. Talk travels faster than the wind! If they had suddenly spotted a lion, they might not have been as scared as when the uncles and aunts spotted their niece. It was as if the blood in their veins had dried up in an instant. At first, they pretended

---

89 Nanere: Mother's natal home.

not to recognize her. Then, when she told them who she was, they chastised her and humiliated her. She had not hoped for much, but she had not been prepared for such harsh words either.

As he fondly threw his dog a piece of a sogra to eat, one of her uncles said, 'Blood and kinship are all fine, but one cannot disregard the rules of society. Could you not find a well to jump into on your way here? All problems would have been solved. Why did you go through the trouble of coming here?' The dog excitedly stood up for another piece of sogra, and the uncle chided the animal a few times. 'Dhurre, dhurre!' he said.

For the intelligent, a hint is enough! The beendni left and did not even turn to look at her nanere. But her mother would hug her as soon as she saw her, she was certain. She would caress her head, and kiss her on the forehead and cheeks as before!

But the beendni's hopes were shattered once more. Her mother recognized her at once, but no love poured forth. Creases appeared on her forehead. She frowned and said, 'If my womb had borne a stone instead of you, it would have been better! You serpent! Why have you come here with your blackened face? Even death must be disgusted with you, or you'd have drowned yourself in a puddle somewhere! You have brought shame on the milk I fed you!' Having rebuked her daughter, she began calling out lovingly to the dogs in the lane. And wagging their tales, they came from all directions. Then, she threw them pieces of puris fried in ghee – charitable work done on the dark night of the new moon has special merit.

Hearing such words from her mother's mouth, the beendni forgot how to speak. Instead of a welcome with food and water, such humiliation? She turned to leave as quietly as she had come.

Meanwhile, hearing the mistress of the house yell, the master had left his puja and come outside. Even as he counted his prayer beads, he asked, 'Who were you shouting at? I have told you so many times not to tell off the chhachheris![90] Is chhaachh something so precious? She seemed to belong to the Lakhaara caste…'

The mother held her head and said dryly, 'She was no chhachheri! Good man, can't you even recognize the daughter whom you raised with your own hands? She was your dear daughter … your daughter!'

As soon as he heard mention of his daughter, anger surged inside him. Grinding his teeth in rage, he said, 'But why did that imbecile turn up here! Were you not wearing any shoes? You should have given her at least seven or eight smacks with them! You're such a silly woman!'

The beendni turned around. Smiling, she said, 'Do not let this wish of yours go unfulfilled.'

When her father could not muster up the courage to smack her with a shoe, her mother said, 'Shameless woman!

---

90 Chhachheri: A woman who comes asking for chhaachh, i.e., buttermilk.

You stand and smile at us?' Then she looked at her husband and derided her daughter further, 'If I'd had the strength to strike her right from the start, then we would not have had to see this day! You are the one who spoilt her silly!'

The father was not one to listen to jibes that were untrue. Keeping his prayer beads aside, he said, 'If she did not have the support of her mother, there was no way she could have learnt such ways!'

The mother and father continued to trade barbs, while the beendni quietly left. Now, there was no shelter other than that of death – or of Lakkhu the courtesan. If being born is not in our hands, then why meddle in the workings of death? She could think of no shelter in the whole wide world except one. Without stopping to rest, she went straight back to Lakkhu's doorstep and rapped the knocker on the door.

As she unbolted the door, Lakkhu said, 'I knew you would return soon. I had full faith in your intelligence. Now, my seat will not be left empty. A major apprehension is resolved. None of the other girls here are as bright as you.'

What was this Lakkhu saying? Was it praise or an insult? But the beendni could detect not a trace of mockery in her tone – just completely straightforward words. 'If you knew I would return, then why let me go at all?' she asked.

Closing the door, Lakkhu said, 'It was important for you to go. Not everything can be understood by merely hearing it with one's ears. Now perhaps there is no further need to explain at all. Rest for a bit, then go and bathe. After that, I shall listen to your story as you eat.'

The beendni said not a word. Many a storm was rising up in her mind and heart. However learned a man may be, even if he lives out a thousand births, he cannot understand a woman's life or her mind. Even if all the men in this world gathered together and racked their brains, they would not stand a chance.

After eating her meal, the beendni said, 'Now, whether I speak or not, it is all the same. The storm inside me has died down anyway.'

Lakkhu said, 'No, daughter, that is not true. It may appear to be so. But even though it seems like they are no different, we find each other's stories to be distinct. All the women in this world have the very same fate – to be cheated by men, and then to spend their lives paying for this thuggery! No woman has been saved this destiny. The illusion of family life only obscures this.'

Along with Lakkhu, all ten women were also seated surrounding the beendni. One of them said, 'It is the tradition of this house: when one returns to its doorstep, one has to narrate one's life story. The munim then comes over and notes it all down in a register.'

So, with a deep sigh, the beendni began: 'If my fate had not crossed paths with crows, my Ramayan would read very differently.'

After this, she narrated the story of her life from beginning to end. How the crows had cheated the swans of Mansarovar and brought them to the desert. How the poor swans managed to escape from their trap, and on their way back, how, in the midst of a storm, they took shelter in a hole in a jaal tree. How the rats who were wrapped in their wings had cut through their feathers. How her husband had brought the featherless swans back home, and after arriving at her marital home, how the beendni gave them rubies and pearls to peck on. How being caressed by her mehndi-darkened hands and being held close by her grew their feathers back in no time. After that, how her husband harnessed a large chariot and reached Mansarovar, how warmly the swan and his wife hosted him, and how, listening to the conversation between the chakva and the chakvi, they had all flown back to her chamber. And then, how the panches had made a mockery of justice after she was with child, and how she was banished from her home. How she walked in the dark with her eyes closed. How the kumbhari gave her shelter. And then, how the sunaar stole her son and how she wandered everywhere in search of her child. And following that, all the events that occurred one after the other until she reached Lakkhu's doorstep – she sang her full lament.

But this time, the beendni's eyes did not well up. She had not forgotten that tears annoyed Lakkhu. Tears do not do anything except bestow upon one a false sense of comfort. It was now that she fully understood Lakkhu's irritation.

Hearing the beendni's tale in its entirety, Lakkhu said, 'Daughter, this dharam–karam, wisdom, devotion, non-violence, ritual, tradition and society are all delusions. The only truth is the creed of crows! Ahead of every learned man, saint, avatar, tirthankar and ascetic are the followers of this creed. There is nothing greater than the self. Everything else is a delusion, a deception. The poison of the slyness of crows spreads through society. Even though you carried your husband's child, the panches meted out injustice to you. But if you read the records we maintain here, then you will understand the real ways of men. One woman carries her father's child, another carries her brother's, her uncle's, her brother-in-law's, or her nephew's! It is only the woman who must bear hardship. There is no escaping it anywhere! Nature does not respect the lines of family or caste. When exposed, the man snarls and growls, rushes to bite. You will get to know how tainted the hands of men are, beyond what can be seen by the light of day, only once you are here. The householder's eyes are forbidden from seeing this blackness. The rules of the homes of householders are blasphemous here, and the rules we follow here are blasphemous there. The sullied honour of householders must be forgotten here. If not, needless conflicts will arise. What they do behind closed doors is done in the open here, without fear. Whoever pays enough has the freedom to fulfil his desires! Here, caste, clan, relations between father and son, brother and nephew … none of these matter. Only those who swear by this can bear to continue in this profession. At first, these things are hard to swallow, but later, there will be no problems. It is not easy to forget the messy rules of householders and their society. I, too, realized it quite late. I endured a lot because of my father's deeds! I cried and wailed, but not a soul would believe me. Finally, it was upon entering this trade of the flesh that I saw this deceit for what it was.'

In this way, Lakkhu explained the new Gita, and like Arjun, the beendni listened in silence. Following Lakkhu's words, she swore to the rules of this trade.

The next day, two hours after nightfall, the diwan headed to Lakkhu's brothel. He had desired the beendni as soon as he had first seen her at the Raj Durbar. Today, when he received Lakkhu's missive, he arrived on horseback.

The beendni had lighted lamps of ghee and was sitting lost in thought, bedecked in her finery. By the light of the lamps, her first night with her husband began to glimmer in front of her eyes. That night was one of joy, and this night too was one of joy. But the nature of the sentiment in each case was as far apart as the earth and the sky.

The diwan was completely inebriated. The beendni was not used to the stench of alcohol. The first breath she drew made her head swirl. Her stomach churned. She pleaded with the diwan to return the next day, but he would not agree. She had been bought for the night, after all!

The diwan enjoyed himself immensely, so he tipped her with an invaluable gem-encrusted ring! The beendni had never imagined that a night could be worth so much.

The diwan had come by after darkness had fallen and left an hour or so before dawn. After he had gone, Lakkhu came into the chamber. For a while, the beendni and the courtesan continued to gaze into each other's eyes. If one of them did not speak up, this night would come to a standstill! Finally, Lakkhu parted her lips to say, 'It will feel strange for the first ten nights or so. Nothing after that.'

The beendni replied softly, 'But the stench of alcohol made my stomach churn. If such drunkards could be banned, it would be a relief!'

'That is beyond us. You will get used to this smell as the days go by, but many other odours won't leave you even in your dreams! You must try to stay away from them. Many a highborn man will promise marriage, will put on an act of love. Don't you believe them! This diwan has five wives. Making a pretence of love towards any woman is child's play for him. Tonight, you are invited to Rajaji's! You will be surprised to know that Rajaji has sixteen queens. The desires of these people have no bounds. You too must leave no stone unturned in making a show of love. But never let yourself get soiled in this mud. Make special note of this advice I give you. Hate no one, love no one!'

As soon as darkness fell in the evening, a chariot driven by sixteen horses came to fetch the beendni. Lakkhu had adorned her with diamonds and pearls. The whip was cracked, and in no time at all, the chariot pulled up by the jharokha of the rangmahal. Four female attendants led the beendni to a golden bed even as they fanned her.

In a while, the Raja arrived, drunk and tottering. The female attendants who were walking beside him would hold him every time he wobbled too much. As soon as he sat on the bed, he passed out on the velvet spread. Instantly, two women began to press his hands and legs.

Seeing this spectacle, the beendni forgot all the other nights of her life! Stunned, she stared at the scene unfolding before her eyes.

An hour and a half or so passed like this. Finally, the Raja came to and desired to quell the lust arising within him. His hands started to move everywhere. An attendant near his head and another by his feet. The beendni was almost doubling up in mortification. The Raja's speech slurred, and he spoke in a wavering voice, 'These women are special favourites of mine. What shame from them? They tend to me in this way, night after night!'

The Raja wanted to continue, but he could barely speak. He bent over and threw up all over the beendni. Her face, her unbuttoned kaanchli blouse, her breasts – everything was soaked. Disgusted, she got off the bed. The Raja heaved a couple of times more and then passed out again on the bed. Two female attendants replaced the sheets. Changed his clothes. Cleaned his beard and whiskers thoroughly. But the Raja remained unconscious.

When the beendni spoke of washing her face and changing her clothes, one of the women said in a hushed whisper, 'To be repulsed by Rajaji's vomit is to invite death! It seems Lakkhu has not told you these things yet.'

But is revulsion under one's control? The beendni felt her head would split down the middle. She replied sharply, 'Death does not abide one's invitation. It comes upon one, uninvited and swift! And will spare neither Rajaji nor us!'

Then, even though the women warned her, she washed her face and her kaanchli thoroughly. When the kaanchli had dried somewhat, the beendni gathered the courage to say, 'Rajaji isn't even conscious! What is the point of me waiting in vain? And today, I am not feeling well either. Please have me sent home.'

The female attendants were astonished at her words! One of them said, 'Who knows when Rajaji will wake up! Have you not been taught the ways of waiting on a king?'

What could the beendni say? She kept reminding herself of Lakkhu's advice and continued to stand there, unmoving, like a wooden doll.

The Raja's eyes did not open even when a soft light spread through the rangmahal. An hour passed after sunrise, then an hour and a half more ... Finally, three hours after sunrise, the Raja awoke from his intoxicated sleep. After seeing his two attendants, his eyes fell on the beendni. Yawning, he said, 'Who is this strange woman?'

One of the attendants narrated to the Raja the events of the night past. He remembered nothing, but sat up with a start and reproached them, 'Why did you not wake me up? Lakkhu sent me her choicest fare and you did not bother at all?'

The women begged for forgiveness and then tattled about the beendni's disgust. Ram knows why the fickle Raja felt no anger. As he beckoned to the beendni to come sit beside him, he said, 'It is as though every fibre of her being is exuding beauty!'

Chanting Lakkhu's advice to herself, the beendni came and sat beside the king. As he ran his hand over her face, he ordered the attendants to stand as they would every night, facing each other.

Thereafter, the Raja felt no shame even in front of the sun god! The sun was embarrassed, so it hid its face behind some clouds. But the beendni had to uphold the honour of her profession, as Lakkhu had taught her. And drunk on the power the throne bestowed upon him, the Raja was rendered insensible to the light of day or the darkness of night.

Just like the diwan, the Raja too relished the encounter immensely. Pleased, he gifted the beendni a navlakha necklace[91] that he was wearing! After that, he tried to lure the beendni with the tantalizing offer of making her his chief queen. But there was no way she would agree to that. She explained the rules of her trade. As soon as she

---

91 Navlakha necklace: A necklace worth nine lakh rupees; a common motif in folk tales.

mentioned Lakkhu's name, the Raja understood everything. Nor would she accept the invitation to come to the palace on seven consecutive days. The code of practice in her trade prohibited her from being with the same man two days in a row. Death was acceptable, but she would not break the rules. The Raja was so mesmerized by the beendni's beauty that he ordered the attendants to send for her every other day!

Alighting from the chariot, the beendni rushed to Lakkhu. She hugged her and began weeping inconsolably. Lakkhu patted her head and said, 'Don't cry, my daughter. I understand the pain in your heart without you uttering a word. Passing out after throwing up like this is no new thing for the king. However, this is surely new for you. But nine days from now, all this will seem old. Married women tolerate such retching day after day. Even then, instead of being given jewellery, their heads are thrashed with shoes. Can one even try and account for their misfortune?'

Even as she sobbed, the beendni said, 'What do we have to do with the misfortunes of others? For how long will this sense of illusory contentment give us the strength to endure?'

'Forget about our endurance!' Lakkhu replied sharply. 'These depravities of men are our greatest riches! What is a mere navlakha necklace against it? Don't you get unsettled by vomit. Treasure it like infinite wealth.'

In this way, seventeen years passed with the beendni treasuring such experiences. And fortunately, her youth and beauty did not wane much. Age imparted a special glow to her face. There was talk of her beauty everywhere, on everyone's lips!

The sunaar's son was no fool either. Talk of this beauty fell on his ears too. He was a handsome young man. Telling his father that he would be travelling, he landed up at Lakkhu's door. A woman promptly welcomed him in.

The son followed her and reached Lakkhu. Instead of haggling later with this stranger, the woman told him up front about the price to be paid. To which, the son just smiled and said, 'Why worry about rates! Those who cross this doorstep check their pockets before doing so. But I cough up a ruby every time I clear my throat! And each ruby is worth a lakh and a quarter! It does not hurt me to clear my throat either.'

As soon as she heard this, Lakkhu's head began to spin. She asked him a few more questions and realized who he was.

Bedecked in her finery, the beendni was regarding her beauty in the mirror by the light of the lamps.

Today, Lakkhu's tutelage would undergo a trial by fire! Lakkhu climbed up the stairs to the beendni's chamber slowly. Gazing at her beautiful face, she said, 'Daughter, today the honour of this house is in your hands! Do not be shaken by your relation to this man. Invaluable rubies will fall into your hands every time he clears his throat!'

The beendni turned around and rose straight up like a snake! Her gaze was lost in the maze of Lakkhu's wrinkled face.

Where was the time to think so deeply? Lakkhu prodded her impatiently, 'Should I send him to your chamber?'

The beendni said, as if she was mumbling in a dream, 'Yes, without a doubt! No kinship means anything to me any more! When will such an auspicious night come my way again?'

VIJAYDAN DETHA (1926–2013) is one of the most prolific and celebrated voices in India, and is undoubtedly the most important writer of Rajasthani prose in the twentieth century. He spent decades of his life collecting folk stories from in and around his village Borunda and retelling them. His work received national and international acclaim – he was awarded the Padma Shri, the Rajasthan Ratna Award and the Sahitya Akademi Award among various others. Detha's timeless classics have been adapted into major plays and movies, some notable names being *Duvidha*, *Charandas Chor* and *Paheli*.

VISHES KOTHARI has a keen interest in the oral, musical and literary traditions of Rajasthan. His first book of translations of Vijaydan Detha's stories, titled *Timeless Tales from Marwar*, was published by Penguin Random House in 2020. He has led the creation of the digital archive of Rajasthani literature and oral traditions, Anjas. He is also a Founding Trustee of the Rajasthani Bhasha Academy.

30 Years *of*

 HarperCollins *Publishers* India

At HarperCollins, we believe in telling the best stories and finding the widest possible readership for our books in every format possible. We started publishing 30 years ago; a great deal has changed since then, but what has remained constant is the passion with which our authors write their books, the love with which readers receive them, and the sheer joy and excitement that we as publishers feel in being a part of the publishing process.

Over the years, we've had the pleasure of publishing some of the finest writing from the subcontinent and around the world, and some of the biggest bestsellers in India's publishing history. Our books and authors have won a phenomenal range of awards, and we ourselves have been named Publisher of the Year the greatest number of times. But nothing has meant more to us than the fact that millions of people have read the books we published, and somewhere, a book of ours might have made a difference.

As we step into our fourth decade, we go back to that one word – a word which has been a driving force for us all these years.

Read.

Harper
Collins

HARPER
PERENNIAL

HARPER
BUSINESS

HARPER
BLACK

हार्पर
हिन्दी

HarperCollins
Children'sBooks

HARPER
DESIGN

HARPER
VANTAGE

Harper
Sport